"The book's language evokes its Edwardian era. Conversation is genteel and the prose is dignified without being pretentious. This formality is refreshing and draws the reader into the story more deeply . . . The author presents most of her characters in just a few words but manages to make these brief depictions comprehensive. By the end of the book, all of them seem like people the reader knows quite well. Given the large number of characters involved in the story, this is an amazing accomplishment."

—*Mystery Scene*

"The author draws as much from *Fawlty Towers* as she does from Agatha Christie, crafting a charming . . . cozy delicately flavored with period details of pre–World War I rural England." —*Publishers Weekly*

"A charming cozy . . . entertaining." —*Midwest Book Review*

"Charming . . . Its straightforward writing and tight plotting are reminiscent of Agatha Christie's books . . . *Slay Bells* is the fourteenth in Kate Kingsbury's Pennyfoot Hotel Mysteries—having thirteen more of these delicious stories will give new readers something to cheer about."

—*Cozy Library*

"A return visit to the Pennyfoot Hotel brings a great mystery for the holiday season . . . Cecily Sinclair Baxter is a delightful heroine . . . The secondary characters add great texture and richness to the setting. This book has it all: a great mystery, wonderful characters, and a charming setting."

—*Romantic Times*

Praise for the Pennyfoot Hotel and Manor House mysteries of Kate Kingsbury

"You'll enjoy your visit to the Pennyfoot Hotel."

—Hamilton Crane, author of *Bonjour, Miss Seeton*

continued . . .

Manor House Mysteries by Kate Kingsbury

A BICYCLE BUILT FOR MURDER
DEATH IS IN THE AIR
FOR WHOM DEATH TOLLS
DIG DEEP FOR MURDER
PAINT BY MURDER
BERRIED ALIVE
FIRE WHEN READY
WEDDING ROWS
AN UNMENTIONABLE MURDER

Pennyfoot Hotel Mysteries by Kate Kingsbury

ROOM WITH A CLUE
DO NOT DISTURB
SERVICE FOR TWO
EAT, DRINK, AND BE BURIED
CHECK-OUT TIME
GROUNDS FOR MURDER
PAY THE PIPER
CHIVALRY IS DEAD
RING FOR TOMB SERVICE
DEATH WITH RESERVATIONS
DYING ROOM ONLY
MAID TO MURDER

Holiday Pennyfoot Hotel Mysteries by Kate Kingsbury

NO CLUE AT THE INN
SLAY BELLS
SHROUDS OF HOLLY

SLAY BELLS

KATE KINGSBURY

BERKLEY PRIME CRIME, NEW YORK

THE BERKLEY PUBLISHING GROUP
Published by the Penguin Group
Penguin Group (USA) Inc.
375 Hudson Street, New York, New York 10014, USA
Penguin Group (Canada), 90 Eglinton Avenue East, Suite 700, Toronto, Ontario M4P 2Y3, Canada
(a division of Pearson Penguin Canada Inc.)
Penguin Books Ltd., 80 Strand, London WC2R 0RL, England
Penguin Group Ireland, 25 St. Stephen's Green, Dublin 2, Ireland (a division of Penguin Books Ltd.)
Penguin Group (Australia), 250 Camberwell Road, Camberwell, Victoria 3124, Australia
(a division of Pearson Australia Group Pty. Ltd.)
Penguin Books India Pvt. Ltd., 11 Community Centre, Panchsheel Park, New Delhi—110 017, India
Penguin Group (NZ), 67 Apollo Drive, Rosedale, North Shore 0632, Auckland, New Zealand
(a division of Pearson New Zealand Ltd.)
Penguin Books (South Africa) (Pty.) Ltd., 24 Sturdee Avenue, Rosebank, Johannesburg 2196,
South Africa

Penguin Books Ltd., Registered Offices: 80 Strand, London WC2R 0RL, England

This is a work of fiction. Names, characters, places, and incidents either are the product of the author's imagination or are used fictitiously, and any resemblance to actual persons, living or dead, business establishments, events, or locales is entirely coincidental. The publisher does not have any control over and does not assume any responsibility for author or third-party websites or their content.

SLAY BELLS

A Berkley Prime Crime Book / published by arrangement with the author

PRINTING HISTORY
Berkley Prime Crime trade edition / November 2006
Berkley Prime Crime mass-market edition / November 2007

Copyright © 2006 by Doreen Roberts Hight.
Cover art by Dan Craig.
Cover design by Judith Murello.

ISBN: 978-0-425-21840-2

BERKLEY® PRIME CRIME
Berkley Prime Crime Books are published by The Berkley Publishing Group,
a division of Penguin Group (USA) Inc.,
375 Hudson Street, New York, New York 10014.
The name BERKLEY PRIME CRIME and the BERKLEY PRIME CRIME design
are trademarks belonging to Penguin Group (USA) Inc.

PRINTED IN THE UNITED STATES OF AMERICA

10 9 8 7 6 5 4 3 2 1

This book is dedicated to Bill, whose love, support,
and encouragement inspire and uphold me.
What would life be without you?

ACKNOWLEDGMENTS

As always, I couldn't have created this book without the help and support of others.

My deepest thanks go to my editor, Sandra Harding, whose comments and suggestions help keep me on the right path, and whose constant support and encouragement brightens my day.

My thanks also to Jennifer Hoffman for her diligent critiques and sharp eye, to Ann Wraight for all the helpful research, and to Jeremy Palmer for lending me his name.

Thanks to Judy Murello and the brilliant art department for some truly great covers, and to all who worked to make this book the best it could be.

Last, and by no means least, my thanks to my ever-patient, always understanding husband. I am, indeed, blessed.

CHAPTER

🌸 1 🌸

Phoebe Carter-Holmes Fortescue hovered in front of the fireplace in the hotel library and wrung her hands in despair. "I can't imagine what could have happened to him," she declared. "I specifically told him to be here at precisely two o'clock."

Cecily Sinclair Baxter glanced at the ornate clock perched on the mantelpiece. "I'm sure Mr. Porter will be here soon," she murmured, being sure of no such thing. "After all, he knows the children are waiting for him to appear. What good is a Christmas party without a Father Christmas?"

A loud screech erupted from the corner of the room where a group of children played in front of the glistening Christmas tree. Frowning, Phoebe lifted her hands to straighten

1

her hat. "I really can't have all this upset right now. What with the fuss and bother over the Christmas season, and all this talk about imminent war in France, it's so terribly disturbing. I have a nasty feeling that 1914 is going to be a dismal year."

"Let us sincerely hope not. I'd hate to see England drawn into a war, but if it is, we should at least be safe in our little corner of the southeast coast." Cecily glanced across the room as more shrieks bounced off the walls. "Oh, dear, I'm afraid the children are getting restless."

"I do wish that man would get here. All this worrying is taxing my mind. Why do these events always have to be so complicated?"

From across the room a woman's voice rose above the clatter. "Simply because the woman in charge makes them so."

"Really, Madeline!" Phoebe's plaintive voice rose in a whine above the boisterous chatter of the children. "Must you find fault with everything I attempt? Surely a little tolerance isn't too much to ask? After all, it is the season to be jolly. Or perhaps, as usual, you find yourself above such frivolity?"

Cecily glanced with apprehension at the object of Phoebe's disapproval. Madeline Pengrath stood in the midst of the clamoring children, one hand grasping the shoulder of a red-faced boy while she held a struggling girl at arm's length.

The slim woman's pink muslin frock swirled around her slippered feet in her attempt to keep the quarreling youngsters apart. A dark spot of color dotted each smooth cheek beneath the heavy black tresses that swung about her face.

Her voice, usually as low and melodic as a rippling brook, sounded like a growl when she scowled at Phoebe. "If your dratted Father Christmas had arrived on schedule, these children would have happy, smiling faces instead of doing their best to kill each other—ouch!"

This last appeared to be a reaction to a vicious kick in the shin from the furious boy.

"Oh, for heaven's sake." Phoebe marched across the floor, lifted her gloved hand and cuffed the boy behind the ear. "There. Now behave, you ungrateful little hooligan."

The boy yelled, while the little girl laughed, only to let out a bellow of indignation when Phoebe batted her, too.

"Phoebe!" Madeline encircled a child in each arm. "You are a fine one to bleat about tolerance. If you want the children to behave I suggest you produce the guest of honor in the next five minutes. That's if you'd rather not have a full-scale rebellion with which to contend."

"I certainly would produce the man if I could." Phoebe held out her arms to Cecily in appeal. "I have no idea where he could be."

Deciding it was time to take charge of the situation, Cecily loudly clapped her hands. "Children! Gather around the tree and soon we will hand out the presents."

Squeals of excitement answered her, and the young revelers rushed to secure the perfect spot in front of the sparkling Christmas tree.

Madeline really had achieved miracles this year, Cecily thought as she helped settle the little ones down. The library was her favorite room in the Pennyfoot Hotel, and had recently undergone a renovation after being gutted by a fire just a year ago.

Madeline had swathed the spacious fireplace with bountiful garlands of feathery cedar and pine. The heavenly fragrance permeated the entire room. Huge red velvet ribbons edged with gold thread added a splash of color and were complemented by pinecones painted silver.

Similar garlands hung from the light oak paneling, which had replaced the dark mahogany, much to Cecily's delight. The new walls brightened the room considerably.

She particularly liked the colored-glass baubles, ribbons, and gilded walnuts that dangled in the branches of the sturdy pine tree. The tiny white candles, however, set in their copper saucers, gave her chills.

In previous years, the candles on the tree had been lit on Christmas Eve for a ceremony of carol singing. However, last year Cecily had come close to losing her life when the candles had set the tree alight. Now, as long as she remained the manager of the Pennyfoot, future carols would be sung without the benefit of flickering candles, thank you very much.

Having accepted Madeline's generous offer to keep the youngsters occupied with a fairy tale, Cecily retreated to the fireplace. Phoebe joined her, and immediately attempted to peer up the wide chimney. The maneuver required a good deal of bending, accompanied by painful grunting as she struggled against the confines of her corset.

"I wouldn't get too close," Cecily advised. "You're likely to get soot in your eye when Father Christmas arrives."

"I thought you had the chimney swept yesterday."

"I did, but I never know if those chimney sweeps are as thorough as one expects."

Phoebe straightened, and brushed an imaginary speck from her immaculate dove gray suit. The jacket, trimmed with white fur, fitted her to perfection, as did the gored skirt that skimmed her pearl-buttoned high shoes. Even in her less fortunate days Phoebe had managed to look like a fashion plate, but since she'd married Colonel Frederick Fortescue her wardrobe had become quite impressive.

"I'm sorely disappointed," she murmured. "I was quite looking forward to seeing Father Christmas appear out of the chimney. Quite a spectacular entrance, if I do say so myself." She sent a malevolent glance in Madeline's direction. "Some people just don't realize how much creative talent and fortitude is required to plan such an event as this."

"I have to admit, I've been concerned that you may have been overly ambitious this time." Cecily smiled at her friend to alleviate the sting in her words.

Even so, the wide brim of Phoebe's hat, weighed down by an abundance of white tulle and an assortment of ribbon roses, trembled with her resentment. "And what, pray, do you mean by that remark?"

"Only that it must have been difficult to persuade someone to actually descend the chimney. He must be a slim fellow to make such a hazardous journey."

"As a matter of fact, he is. Which is how the whole idea came about. My original applicant was a much stouter man, and would never have managed the task. When he fell ill, however, I was forced to find a hasty replacement. I was fortunate to find Mr. Porter, who was willing to oblige at very short notice. Since he was far less corpulent, the idea of using the chimney presented itself. I had to offer the man a larger stipend than I'd anticipated, but once I named a generous figure, he was more than willing to accommodate me."

"I imagine he was," Cecily murmured. "I have to wonder, however, how the children will receive a scrawny Father Christmas."

"I've taken pains to remedy that, of course." Phoebe gestured at the fireplace with an elegant wave of her hand. "I had one of the footmen hide a large pillow on the ledge inside the chimney, above the fireplace well, together with the sack of toys."

Cecily glanced at Madeline who, judging from the frantic manipulation of her eyebrows, had neared the end of her story. Once more the children were growing restless, constantly glancing in the direction of the fireplace.

"We shall have to retrieve the toys," Cecily said in a hushed tone, "and hand them out ourselves. We cannot wait any longer. The children are impatient, and soon the parents will be arriving to take their little ones home."

Obviously put out by the setback, Phoebe clicked her tongue. "Yes, well, I never have been enthusiastic about entertaining the village children. Admirable of you to offer such generosity, of course, but one never knows what kind of people one is entertaining when inviting peasants into one's home."

Well used to her friend's unfortunate comments, Cecily bit her tongue. Phoebe's first marriage had been to an aristocrat. Sadly, her husband's family had never accepted her, and upon his death had cast out the grieving widow and her son to fend for themselves.

Having become accustomed to the respect and comfort afforded by her marriage, Phoebe had found it particularly hard to adjust, and had formed a bitter animosity toward the lesser fortunate with whom she had been forced to associate.

Her marriage to the Colonel proved to be a mixed blessing. While providing his wife with a standard of living more in keeping with the luxurious life she had once known, Colonel Fortescue's faculties had been severely damaged during the Boer War, leaving him somewhat demented and unpredictable.

Phoebe had accepted his limitations in return for the comfort and security he could offer her. With their marriage she had risen above her miserable existence once more, but she'd never forgotten her dismal life among the poor, and despised any reminder of it.

"I do hope you didn't pay the fellow in advance," Cecily said, wincing as the clock on the mantelpiece chimed the hour. "It's safe to say he has had second thoughts about navigating the chimney."

"Drat. No, of course I didn't pay him. In fact, if I see him again I shall give him a very large piece of my mind. How dare he disappoint the children!"

Cecily hid a smile. If anyone was disappointed it was most certainly Phoebe, who hated to have one of her grand gestures demolished. The sad truth was that the vast majority of her plans ended in disaster. Phoebe, however, never lost her conviction that the very next idea was her most brilliant and would undoubtedly be applauded as an unmitigated success.

Cecily still waited for that particular miracle to occur. "I shall ring for Samuel," she said, and hurried over to the bell pull rope hanging by the door.

Within a few minutes, during which the children's voices had risen again to an ear-splitting crescendo, Samuel entered the library. His pleasant face contorted with pain as shrill shrieks erupted from around the tree.

"You rang, m'm?" The young man sent an agonized glance toward the squabbling children. "Want me to get them out of here?"

Cecily hurried to set him straight. "No, Samuel. I want you to retrieve a large sack of toys that is hidden on the ledge in the fireplace."

Samuel's eyebrows twitched—the only sign of his surprise. Having been with the Pennyfoot staff since he was a young boy, with the exception of a year or two spent in London, Samuel was accustomed to encountering all sorts of odd situations. Over the years he'd worked as a footman and a stable manager, and was now in charge of not only the horses and carriages, but also the motor cars, which had become more prevalent each year.

Samuel could also be relied upon to take on any task, no matter how peculiar, without question or hesitation. He had come in very useful indeed during Cecily's numerous skirmishes with various despicable villains who seemed bent on disrupting her duties at the renowned seaside hotel.

"In the chimney, m'm?" Samuel inquired, darting a look at Phoebe.

"Of course in the chimney," Phoebe said sharply. "Where else would Father Christmas leave the toys?"

In her irritation she had forgotten to keep her voice low. Upon hearing her words, the children rushed for the fireplace, tumbling over each other in their excitement.

Phoebe uttered a startled shriek and fled to the window, where she stood with a hand pressed to her heart. Madeline grabbed at the nearest child, managing to snatch a handful of hair to halt the little girl's progress. The child immediately screamed and burst into tears, and Madeline hugged the sobbing girl to console her.

Spreading his arms wide, Samuel headed off the main pack and yelled above the racket. "No one gets toys unless they're sitting on the floor!"

Every child promptly dropped to the carpet, and silence settled over the room.

Realizing she'd been holding her breath, Cecily puffed out her cheeks in a sigh. "Thank you, Samuel." Turning to the eager faces of the children, she added, "Christmas Eve is just a few days away, and Father Christmas is extremely busy getting his sleigh ready. I'm afraid he won't have the time to visit us today."

A chorus of dismay rose from the small group. Before things could get out of hand again, Cecily raised her voice. "His elves, however, have dropped off some toys for you all, and if you are really quiet, perhaps we can ask Samuel to get them out of the chimney for us."

The groans turned to cheers and loud applause. Samuel nodded, and with a wary expression, stepped over to the fireplace. Reaching Cecily, he whispered, "You're sure them elves left toys in there, m'm?"

Cecily smiled. "Quite sure, Samuel." Even so, once more she held her breath as the young manager stepped into the fireplace and reached up inside the chimney. Unlike Samuel, Phoebe was not always reliable.

To Cecily's relief, a large sack came swinging down in Samuel's hand, and loud shrieks of joy greeted the sight of toys sticking out of the top.

Madeline stepped in to help Samuel hand out the gifts while Phoebe sank onto the gold brocade Queen Anne chair, one hand at her brow. "Thank goodness that's over," she muttered. "All this confusion is most tiring." She peered hopefully up at Cecily from beneath the brim of her hat. "I really shall need something to stimulate my heart before I can return home to dear Frederick."

"I'll have Samuel bring you a glass of sherry," Cecily promised, "just as soon as he's finished handing out presents to the children."

A few minutes later, with peace restored and the small guests happily occupied with the new treasures, Cecily gave Samuel permission to leave.

He surprised her by asking that she accompany him to the door. Anxiously she followed him, hoping his request had nothing to do with bad news. The past year had been remarkably uneventful for a change.

If she were hard pressed, Cecily would be forced to admit she missed the excitement, but the fact remained that the absence of dastardly deeds in the hotel boded well for the Pennyfoot's reputation. She had spent far too many years worrying that the local constabulary would close down the establishment.

Her apprehension seemed well founded when Samuel turned an anxious face toward her. "I don't want to concern you, m'm, but Mr. Baxter wasn't on his train when I met it tonight."

A stab of anxiety caught her under the ribs. "He wasn't? I dare say something in the office kept him long enough to miss the train." She glanced at the clock. "The next one should be due in about two hours. I'm sure he'll be on that one."

"Yes, m'm." Samuel touched his forehead. "I'll be there to pick him up."

"Thank you, Samuel." Cecily closed the door behind him, her face creased in a frown. It wasn't like her husband to be late without ringing her. Moreover, she'd rung his office earlier to ask him to run an errand for her, and his assistant had informed her that Baxter was already on his way home.

She knew better than to have a fit just because he'd missed the train. Even so, she was aware that the niggling worry would not go away until he'd safely arrived.

* * *

Below stairs in the kitchen, Mrs. Chubb winced as a saucepan lid crashed to the red tile floor. Michel was in one of his moods again. The volatile chef rarely went a day without at least one outburst of temper, and sure enough, this day had been no exception.

Mrs. Chubb toyed with the idea of offering him a drop of his special brandy. After all, it was supposed to be for medicinal purposes, and when Michel flew into one of his tantrums, there was always the danger he'd do some harm to himself with one of his kitchen knives.

Only one problem: once Michel got a taste of the fiery spirits, he didn't know when to stop. An inebriated chef was worse than a bad-tempered one, especially in Michel's case. The pots and pans would be joyfully crashing all over the place, and the chef's fake French accent would disappear under a barrage of foul jokes.

Mrs. Chubb shuddered. She'd rather deal with the sober Michel, temper and all.

In an effort to mollify the irritable man, she tried a bit of conversation. "It'll be hard for Gertie this year, having to face Christmas without her husband. Such a sad thing, losing her Ross last winter like that. I thought she'd never get over it."

"Gertie is young," Michel said, stooping to pick up the lid he'd just dropped. His tall white hat fell sideways and he shoved it back with an impatient hand. "She will find ze new man soon, *non?*"

Mrs. Chubb shook her head. "I don't know. Not many

men are willing to take on a woman with little ones. Her twins are a handful, that's for sure."

"Ah, but Gertie, she is a good woman. A wise man will know that and . . . how you say . . . snatch her up!" Michel snapped his fingers and sent a knife spinning across the table. Muttering curses under his breath, he made a grab for it, missed, then let out a string of oaths as it clattered to the floor.

Mrs. Chubb was still reeling from the shock of Michel describing Gertie as a good woman. The chef and her chief housemaid had been at loggerheads with each other ever since Gertie had arrived at the Pennyfoot years ago.

At fourteen Gertie had been brash, defiant, and at times unmanageable. Every other word that came out of her mouth was a curse, and as housekeeper it had been Mrs. Chubb's job to train the unruly child in the manners befitting a member of her staff. She had been tempted, many times, to give up on Gertie.

Two marriages, rambunctious twins, and the recent loss of her husband had mellowed the tempestuous housemaid a little, but the defiance still glimmered beneath the surface, just waiting to be released once more.

In spite of her dedication to protocol, Mrs. Chubb rather looked forward to that day. Gertie wasn't the Gertie she knew without a little fire under her cap.

"Well," she said, "I hope you're right. Gertie needs a man to take care of her and those little ones."

"Per'aps one of ze new waiters Mrs. Baxter hired?" Michel slapped a frying pan on the stove. "One of them might be willing to put a smile on Gertie's face, *oui*?"

"Reggie and Lawrence?" Mrs. Chubb shook her head. "No, they're much too flighty to take care of a wife and family. They spend half their time chasing the housemaids up and down the stairs. Now that nice Mr. Jeremy Westhaven in room twelve. He'd be a good catch, all right. Comes from a good family, that he does. I can tell just by looking at him. Nice looking chap he is, too."

Michel let out a caustic bellow of disbelief. "How can you think such a man would be interested in a common housemaid? *Mon Dieu!* Are you crazy?"

Mrs. Chubb dug her fists into her hips and glared at the chef. "I seem to remember young Lord Withersgill taking an interest in our Daisy."

Michel snorted and shook the frying pan. The delicious aroma of fried onions made Mrs. Chubb's stomach rumble with hunger. "Gertie is not Daisy," he muttered.

"Daisy was a housemaid, just like Gertie, before she became nanny to Gertie's twins. She—" Mrs. Chubb turned her head as a young woman burst through the door of the kitchen.

Gertie's cap hung over one ear, and hanks of her dark hair fell across her face. "I knew it!" she declared, as she slumped down on the nearest kitchen chair. "I knew it was too bleeding good to be true."

Mrs. Chubb cringed. Life might have mellowed Gertie, but it had failed to curb her wayward tongue. "What's too good to be true?"

"We'd gone almost a year without anything really bad happening at the Pennyfoot." Gertie swept back the loose strands of her hair and straightened her cap. "After my Ross

14

died it got real quiet around here and I thought we was over all the bad things happening."

"What are you talking about?" Mrs. Chubb folded her arms. "And sit up straight, for goodness sake, Gertie. Try to at least look like a lady."

Gertie scowled. "What for? I'm a bloody housemaid, not a blinking lah-de-da lady's companion."

Michel started to laugh, then turned it into a hail of cursing.

Both Mrs. Chubb and Gertie stared at him.

"What's up with him?" Gertie said, as Michel started shoving pots around, sending lids crashing once more to the floor.

"My knife!" Michel howled. "Someone has stolen my best knife. It has disappeared!"

"Nonsense." Mrs. Chubb puffed out her breath, annoyed with both him and her disheveled housemaid. "You've probably dropped it on the floor, like you've dropped a hundred other things this afternoon."

Michel glared at her as if she were responsible for the missing knife. "I never use it unless I am slicing the beef. It is my special knife. Look, it is not here."

"Crikey, Michel." Gertie jumped to her feet. "Here you are moaning about a lost knife when that poor bugger's lying dead out there."

Mrs. Chubb felt as if a hand had grabbed her throat. "What did you say? What poor bugger—I mean—person? Who's lying dead?" Her heart started pounding. "It's not anyone we know, is it? Gertie, please tell me it's not someone from the Pennyfoot who died?"

Gertie turned her face toward her, and Mrs. Chubb felt quite faint. She could tell from Gertie's expression that her worst fears were about to be realized. Holding her breath, she waited for the dreaded axe to fall.

CHAPTER

2

Gertie sat there looking as if she wanted to cry. "It's Roland," she said, her voice trembling. "You know, that new footman what Madam hired a month ago. Fell off the bleeding roof, he did. He's as dead as a bloody doornail." She plopped back onto her chair and slapped a hand over her mouth, muffling her next words. "I was the one what found him, wasn't I. Made me sick, it did."

"Oh, my goodness gracious." Mrs. Chubb rushed over to her and patted her shoulder. "There, there, duck. Never mind." She looked at Michel who, after a brief, shocked moment of silence, had resumed hunting for his knife. "Get her some brandy," she ordered. "She's had a nasty shock, poor thing."

"I'm the one who needs brandy," Michel muttered. "My

best knife. It is gone. *Allé! Pouf!*" He snapped his fingers in the air.

"You'll be gone, too, if you don't stop whining about that silly knife." The housekeeper glared at him and shook her fist. "Now get that brandy this minute!"

Michel sent her a black look, then shuffled off to the pantry, muttering under his breath.

Mrs. Chubb turned her attention back to Gertie. She could feel the girl's shoulder quivering beneath her hand and it worried her. Gertie was the strongest person she knew, man or woman. The sturdy housemaid had seen death before, more than she should, yet this one seemed to have shaken her up more than usual.

"I didn't know you were that well acquainted with the young man," she said, as Michel sauntered back with the half-filled bottle of brandy.

She took it from him, suspecting that the sly devil had already swallowed a gulp or two while hidden behind the pantry door.

"I didn't." Gertie sniffed. "It's just that being Christmas and all, I dunno . . . makes it all seem so much worse somehow."

Mrs. Chubb had an idea it was more likely Gertie was missing Ross this Christmas, and that was what had really got her so upset. Gertie would never admit that, though. She'd announced back in September that for the sake of her twins, she wasn't going to spend a whole year mourning her late husband. The children would always miss their father, but they all had to learn to go on without him.

Brave words from a brave woman, but Mrs. Chubb knew it wouldn't be that easy for Gertie to forget her Ross. In spite of the vast difference in their ages, she had been devoted to the kindly Scotsman.

"So, how did it happen?" The housekeeper reached for a snifter from the cupboard and held it out to Michel. "Must have slipped on the snow up there, I suppose. Wonder what he was doing on the roof in the first place?"

"Samuel says Roland was up there helping Father Christmas come down the chimney."

Michel stopped pouring the golden liquid. "That Samuel, he must have been at my brandy. Father Christmas does not come to the houses until Christmas Eve, and I never heard before that he asks for help."

Gertie took the glass from Mrs. Chubb and gave Michel a pitying look. "Not *that* Father Christmas, silly. I'm talking about the flipping Father Christmas what Madam hired for the kiddies' party, that's what."

Instead of the outburst Mrs. Chubb expected, Michel merely shrugged and went back to hunting for his precious knife. "I'm sorry for the poor lad," she said, watching her housemaid drain the spirits. "What a tragedy for his poor family."

Gertie choked, handed the glass to Mrs. Chubb and wiped her mouth with her sleeve. "I'm just glad me twins weren't with me. He weren't a pretty sight, I can tell you, with his head all twisted to one side and his eyes staring at nothing." She shuddered.

"Someone will have to tell Madam." Mrs. Chubb sent a worried glance at the clock. "It's almost time to start serving the evening meal. Pansy is supposed to be here by now. Where is that girl?"

"Samuel said he'd tell Madam." Gertie got to her feet. "I'll go and find Pansy. She's probably still laying the tables in the dining room."

Mrs. Chubb shook her head. "That girl. Slower than a one-legged tortoise, she is."

"She hasn't been here that long." Gertie tugged her white apron until it settled more comfortably at her waist. She looked down at the toes of her oxfords peeking out beneath the hem of her black frock. "Me flipping shoes are grubby," she muttered. "I'd better clean them before I start serving."

"That you had, my girl. And be quick about it." Mrs. Chubb shook her head and went back to the table, where a pile of lightly starched serviettes waited to be folded. "Madam's not going to like this at all," she murmured, to no one in particular. "Looks like the Pennyfoot curse is still with us after all."

Pansy paused at the top of the stairs to catch her breath. After climbing up three flights dragging the carpet sweeper behind her, her chest heaved with the effort to breathe.

Making sure no one was around to see her, she sank onto the top step. If only she were built like Gertie, whose arms were twice as strong as hers. Maybe then she wouldn't get so tired.

It had taken her more than half an hour to sweep the

dining room and lay the tables, and now she had to put the carpet sweeper away and get back downstairs in time to start serving the evening meal. Sometimes, by the time she got to bed at night, she barely had the strength to undress.

Giving in to the urge to sit a moment longer, she clasped her arms around her knees and rested her chin on them. Just a few seconds, that's all she needed, and she'd be as right as rain.

Weariness made her eyelids heavy and she closed her eyes, her ears alert for any sound of footsteps. She must have nodded off, as a faint noise jerked her awake. She frowned, tilting her head to one side to listen more closely. There it was again. It sounded like . . . bells. Little tinkling bells, like the wind chimes hanging behind the kitchen door.

Climbing to her feet, she propped the carpet sweeper against the banister and peered down the hallway. The gas lamps shed a faint glow across the flowery patterned carpet, but shadows obscured the far end of the passage. She could see nothing that looked like bells.

In fact, the sound had ceased. She listened again to make sure, but all she could hear was the faint hum of people talking far below in the lobby.

Deciding she had to have been dreaming, she turned her back on the hallway and reached for the carpet sweeper. She found it easier to push the thing than pull it, so she dragged it around in front of her and started down toward the broom closet.

As she lifted her head, she heard the bells again. Only

this time, something moved in the passage. Something very large and brightly colored, with a big round white face and frizzy ginger hair.

The man paused, and in the flickering gaslight she saw the wide red curve of his mouth. A clown? Now she really must be dreaming. She shut her eyes tight and pinched her arm. The pain made her wince.

No, she was awake all right. Carefully she opened her eyes. The clown had disappeared.

She spun around, just to make sure. Her eyes had been closed for only a second or two. He would have had to go right past her to get to the rooms at the other end of the hallway or go down the stairs. *Where had he gone?*

Unable to believe he'd actually vanished, she took a few steps forward. Nothing. It was as if he'd never been there. Yet she'd seen him.

Her heart started pounding and her hands shook. It was a ghost, that's what. She'd just seen a ghost. Fear made her teeth chatter. Without bothering to put the carpet sweeper away, she flew for the stairs and dashed down them two at a time.

Cecily stared at Samuel's pale face in dismay. "Roland? Dead? How on earth did it happen?"

Samuel shook his head. "Don't know, m'm. He were just lying there, all twisted up. I reckon he must have slipped off the roof."

Cecily sat down hard on the settee. Thank goodness everyone had left the library, she thought, as she struggled to make sense of what she'd just heard. This news would surely have cast a pall over the gaiety. "Where is he? You didn't leave him lying out there, did you?"

"No, m'm. One of the lads helped me get him into the stables. I thought it best to leave him there until the doc gets here."

"Very good. Has anyone rung Dr. Prestwick?"

"Not yet, m'm. I can ask Mrs. Chubb to ring him, if you like?"

"No, that's all right. I'll ring him myself. Oh, dear Lord." Cecily did her best to sort out her thoughts. "We shall have to let Roland's parents know, of course. I'll have Baxter send them a letter. No, I suppose he should go in person. What a terrible thing to hear right before Christmas."

"Yes, m'm." Samuel cleared his throat. "Speaking of Mr. Baxter, m'm, I have to get the horses ready to fetch him from the train station."

"Yes, of course." Cecily gave him a tired smile. "Don't let me keep you, Samuel. Hurry and bring Mr. Baxter home. He'll be very upset at the news, I'm sure."

"Yes, m'm. I'm sure he will."

The door closed behind her stable manager, and Cecily briefly closed her eyes. Roland was so young. What a tragedy. With a sigh she rose and crossed the room to the door. The only telephone in the hotel was situated at the reception desk. She would just have to hope that no late arrivals would be waiting there while she talked to Kevin Prestwick.

Thinking about the doctor on her way to the lobby, it occurred to her that Madeline hadn't mentioned him lately. Her good friend and Dr. Prestwick had been keeping company for about a year now, and any day Cecily expected Madeline to announce their betrothal.

Although neither of them professed to be in any hurry to tie the knot, Cecily knew quite well how fond they were of each other. Since they were both far beyond the age one might be expected to venture into wedded bliss, Cecily could see absolutely no point in postponing the happy event.

Madeline, with her vast knowledge of herbal remedies, was often at odds with her beloved doctor, who used a more scientific approach to his profession. Otherwise they seemed to get along splendidly, though Cecily did wonder how the practical, steeped-in-logic physician dealt with Madeline's strange powers that enabled her to see and hear things hidden to the normal human being.

She reached the lobby just in time to find Philip, her new desk clerk, engaged in a heated discussion with a gentleman whose harsh voice echoed down the hallway.

"You'll find me a room on the first floor, you sniveling little weasel, or I'll have your guts for garters!"

Philip's thin face was paper white as he stared at the angry guest. "I can assure you, sir, if I had a room to spare on the first floor—"

Cecily hurried toward the pair, almost tripping over her skirt in her haste. "What is the trouble here?" She smiled at the irate face of the guest. "Perhaps I can help?"

She cringed when the man swept a disdainful stare from her head down to her toes. "Who are you?"

Shackles rising, Cecily jutted out her chin. "Mrs. Cecily Sinclair Baxter, the manager of this establishment. And you are?"

Her icy voice appeared to have little effect on the man's unfortunate attitude. "Desmond Atkins. My wife and I are unhappy with the room we're in. We want to move to another room." He jabbed a vicious thumb at poor Philip. "And now this imbecile refuses to honor our request."

Cecily, who was rather fond of Philip, felt an intense dislike toward the belligerent lout. The man's square face, set on a bulky body, overpowered her desk clerk, whose frail shoulders and bony features appeared to wither up even more in the face of such abuse.

She turned to the nervous clerk and said gently, "Philip, would you please ask the telephone operator to connect me to Dr. Prestwick's office. Tell him I need to talk to him as soon as possible."

"Yes, m'm." Philip nodded so hard his teeth rattled. "Right away, m'm." A fringe of gray hair slid down over his forehead and he thrust it back into place with his thumb. Stumbling a little, he fled to the end of the desk and picked up the earpiece of the phone.

Cecily waited until the loud cranking of the handle had ceased before turning back to Desmond Atkins. "Now, Mr. Atkins, let me take a look." She moved behind the desk and stared down at the open pages of the register. "I see you have been assigned a room on the second floor."

"Quite. Quite. When I made the reservation I specifically

requested a room on the first floor. One flight of stairs is quite enough to climb. When we arrived three days ago my wife was escorted to our room, while I went out to the stables to make sure those fools were taking proper care of my motor car. By the time I came back my wife was settled in the room and begged me not to make a fuss."

"I see. I assume you now want to move down to the first floor, then?"

"I most certainly do. Those stairs are abominable." He sent a disparaging glance across the lobby. "I can't imagine why a place this size doesn't have a lift, or at least some rooms on the ground floor. Not everyone can climb up and down all those stairs, you know."

Ignoring that, Cecily ran her thumb down the list of guests. "I see the Rochester-Harlands have not yet arrived. I'm sure they won't mind exchanging rooms with you and your wife. I'll have your luggage moved to room eleven, which I'm sure you'll find more to your liking."

"Is it on the first floor?" Mr. Atkins had a bulbous nose that glowed like embers of a dying fire. No doubt attributed to a fondness for spirits, Cecily thought, as she made the corrections in the ledger. The man was obviously suffering from the aftereffects of imbibing. Which would account for his assumption that she, as well as poor Philip, were complete ignoramuses.

"Isn't that what you're requesting?" she asked sweetly. "A room on the first floor?"

Atkins coughed and grunted something she couldn't catch. She reached for the bell and shook it harder than usual. By the time she'd directed the footman who answered her summons to transfer the Atkins's luggage to the new room, the despicable man had stomped off—with a pronounced limp that tempered her judgment of him. No wonder the man preferred a room on the first floor. Though that hardly excused his rudeness.

Philip hovered anxiously at her elbow. "I have Dr. Prestwick on the line," he stuttered. "He says he's rather busy."

"Thank you, Philip." Cecily moved to the end of the desk and picked up the earpiece. Pressing it to her ear, she leaned in to speak into the mouthpiece. "Hello? Kevin?"

The doctor's mellow tones answered her. "Cecily! How good to speak to you. It has been far too long."

"Yes, it has." Cecily glanced at the front door and hoped no guests would arrive until she had completed her conversation. "I do not have good news, I'm afraid."

"You're not ill, are you?"

The concern in his voice soothed her frayed nerves. "I'm as healthy as a horse. It's one of our footmen. It appears he must have slipped off the roof. I'd sent him up there to help Father Christmas, who failed to arrive anyway, so it was all a terrible waste. Poor Roland needn't have been up there at all, and now . . ." Her voice shook, and she paused for a moment. "I feel responsible for his death," she added, when she was sure she could speak without a tremor.

"Now, now, you know better than that. It was an accident, that's all. You were not at all to blame." Kevin's voice changed to his brisk professional tone. "I'll be there just as soon as I can."

"Thank you, Kevin." Again she hesitated. "I suppose we shall have to inform P.C. Northcott?"

"I'm sorry, Cecily. You know I should do so in a case like this."

"Yes, I suppose I do. One can always live in hope, however. I do hate to have a police constable on the premises when the guests are supposed to be enjoying the festivities. It's tragic enough to lose a young man like that, without having Sam Northcott poking around with his interminable questions and total lack of sensitivity."

"Well, it sounds straightforward enough. I'm sure he will conduct his business and be off in no time."

"When it comes to Sam," Cecily said with a sigh, "one can never be sure of anything."

She hooked the earpiece onto its handle and turned to Philip. "If you have any more trouble with Mr. Atkins, please refer him to me or to Mr. Baxter."

"Yes, m'm." Philip nodded in obvious relief. "I'll certainly do that."

Mentioning Baxter's name brought back the pang of anxiety. She glanced at the tall grandfather clock that stood in the corner of the foyer. It would be at least half an hour before Samuel would be back, hopefully in the company of her husband. More than likely, he and the doctor would arrive together.

That brought a grimace to her face as she made her way to the kitchen. Baxter disliked Kevin, mostly because,

Cecily suspected, the doctor had pursued her before Baxter had declared his intentions. Her husband had been jealous of Kevin, and was still sensitive about any of her encounters with the handsome doctor.

She could only pray that the Christmas spirit would prevail and the two men would be, at the very least, civil to one another.

The kitchen appeared to be in its usual state of mealtime chaos when Cecily pushed the swing door open. She paused for a moment to inhale the heavenly aroma of fried onions and bacon before stepping inside.

Across the spacious room Michel shouted orders, amidst a good deal of banging and crashing about, while maids scurried back and forth in an effort to obey him.

Mrs. Chubb stood at the sink, waving a large wooden spoon at Pansy, the new housemaid, who seemed to be in tears. Gertie staggered toward the door with a huge tray loaded with steaming bowls of soup and Cecily sidestepped out of her way.

"Evening, m'm!" Gertie sang out as she shouldered her way through the door.

Cecily watched her unsteady progress down the hallway. Thank the Lord, Gertie had the sturdy build of a carthorse, and a hide just as thick. Cecily couldn't imagine the Pennyfoot without her chief housemaid.

She stepped back, startled, as Pansy darted past her, mumbling a greeting as she flew out the door. The new maid's dainty form reminded Cecily of a ballerina, and presented quite a contrast to the strapping Gertie.

Having caught sight of her, Mrs. Chubb hurried over. "Sorry, madam. Didn't see you standing there. Things are in a bit of a turmoil, what with the shocking news about Roland and all the new visitors arriving for Christmas."

"Quite, which is why I won't keep you." Cecily glanced at the subdued maids. "I imagine the news has upset quite a few of the staff."

"That it has, m'm. Nice boy, he was, that Roland. Terrible for his parents. Specially at this time of year."

"Michel seems a little put out."

"Can't find his favorite knife, m'm. You'd think the entire meal depended on it. Silly man, he's got plenty others. I just don't know what all the fuss is about, I really don't."

"Well, you know how temperamental he can be. If it can't be found we shall have to order him another one."

"Yes, m'm. I'll see to it."

After one last lingering inspection of the busy kitchen, Cecily left. The truth was, she felt out of sorts. Distressed about Roland's death, irritated by the exchange with Mr. Atkins, and more than a little concerned about the late hour of Baxter's return, she preferred not to be alone just then.

The library was still empty when she returned to it, however, and she reached for a book from the crammed shelves. There was nothing left for her to do but wait—something to which she did not take kindly. Settling herself down on her favorite gold velvet armchair, she began to read.

*   *   *

Dodging around the tables in the dining room, Gertie reached the side of the gentleman waiting patiently for his soup. She felt sorry for him, being alone so close to Christmas. Placing the bone china bowl in front of him, she gave him an encouraging smile. "Will that be all, sir?"

He had nice eyes, the sort of blue that made her think of Deep Willow Pond in summertime. He looked up, his steady gaze making her tummy do funny things. "Thank you, yes," he said, in a soft voice.

"I'll be right back with your steak and kidney pie."

"Thank you." He nodded, and picked up his spoon.

Gertie didn't generally care for the toffs, but this one seemed nice. He had a kind face, but he didn't smile all that much. Probably because he was lonely. She wondered if a lady friend planned to join him for Christmas. That would be nice for him. A gent like that should have a lady by his side to keep him company.

The gentleman paused, the spoon halfway to his mouth.

Realizing she'd been staring a little too long, Gertie said quickly, "I was just waiting to see if the soup tastes all right, sir."

His mouth twitched. "The soup is quite excellent, thank you."

"Yes, sir." Feeling like a fool, she backed away, right into the path of Pansy, who crashed into her and stepped painfully on her toe.

Fortunately Pansy had only empty bowls in her arms. She clutched them to her chest, smearing the front of her lace-trimmed apron with bright red tomato soup.

"Oh, bugger it," Gertie muttered, then slapped a hand over her mouth as a primped-up lady seated nearby gasped in shock and glared at her.

Out of the corner of her eye, Gertie caught a glimpse of the gentleman she'd just served. He looked quite handsome when he smiled, she thought, warmed by the notion that she'd been the one to crack his indifference.

The next instant a loud wail from Pansy snatched her attention. "Look what you've gone and done!"

Hastily, Gertie grabbed some of the bowls and hustled Pansy out of the room. "Look, I'm sorry, but you can't make a fuss in the dining room with all the visitors there. Chubby will box your bloody ears for upsetting them."

Pansy sniffed, and ran the back of her hand under her nose. "Chubby?"

"Mrs. Chubb." Gertie puffed out her breath. "And don't let on you heard me call her by that name. She bleeding hates it, she does."

Pansy's mouth stretched into a smile. "I won't say nothing, honest I won't."

"Good. Now let's get back to the kitchen, before we're both in the old battle-axe's bad book." She followed the tiny girl down the hallway, wondering how on earth anyone managed to have a waist that small without breaking in half.

A light tap on the door disturbed Cecily's immersion in the wild adventures of Toad of Toad Hall. She put down the book and looked up, expecting to see Samuel's cheery face. Instead, the tall, fair-haired man who entered wore a somber expression that worried her.

Kevin Prestwick was a dedicated doctor and a great favorite among the ladies of Badgers End. One could count on a lengthy stay in his crowded waiting room, where a preponderance of women tittered amongst themselves before being ushered into the handsome doctor's office.

For several years he had been considered the most eligible bachelor in town, and although several ladies had been known to set their cap at him, he had managed to resist them for the most part.

Cecily had been an exception, and while flattered, she'd had no desire to return his attachment, and eventually he had turned his attention to Madeline, who was a far better match for him, in Cecily's opinion.

He smiled now as he crossed the floor toward her, one hand held out to greet her. "Cecily! You look absolutely stunning, as always."

Kevin could always be counted on to say just the right thing. She rose, and allowed him to take her hand in a warm grasp. "Why, thank you, kind sir. You're looking very debonair yourself, if I may say so."

Kevin raised her hand, bowed his head, and pressed his lips to her fingers. Straightening, he looked deep into her eyes and murmured, "It is always most gratifying to be complimented by a beautiful woman."

Her fingers still grasped in his, Cecily felt a tiny flutter of pleasure. Angry with herself for succumbing to such flattery, she was about to pull her hand free when another deep voice spoke from the doorway.

"And it is always most annoying to find my wife being solicited by a gentleman who should know better."

"Baxter!" Cecily snatched her hand from Kevin's. Her husband was home at last, and judging by the scowl on his face, he was none too pleased with her.

CHAPTER

3

Gertie's usual method of entering the kitchen with a pile of dirty dishes was to stretch out a foot and give the door a hefty kick. This sometimes backfired on her when someone happened to be standing on the other side. To prevent slamming an unfortunate victim in the face, Gertie resorted to yelling a warning as she barged down the hallway.

"Coming through!" The noise in the kitchen this particular evening must have been louder than usual, since the door banged into a solid object and sprung back to smack her knee.

"Bloody hell," she muttered, shouldering the door open again. This time it opened all the way, and she charged into the room, to find Reggie, one of the new waiters, holding his nose, his eyes streaming with tears.

At least, she thought it was Reggie. He looked a lot like Lawrence, his younger brother, who was also waiting tables. They both had thin faces, big brown eyes, dark hair, and droopy mustaches. Only Reggie smiled a lot more than his brother. Except he wasn't smiling now. In fact, he looked as if he was about to clobber her one.

"Sorry, luv!" Gertie grinned at him, hoping his sense of humor would rise to the occasion. "I yelled, but you must not have heard me." She hurried past him, over to the sink. Shoving aside the maid, whose arms were half buried in the hot soapy suds, she dumped in the pile of dishes. The maid uttered a shriek as water splashed her face.

"Cripes," Gertie muttered, and backed away from the girl's murderous glare.

"Is it your intention to maim every member of the staff, or are you simply picking on people you don't like?"

Spinning around, Gertie found Reggie almost nose to nose with her. No, it wasn't Reggie, she realized a second later. He still stood by the door, mopping his eyes with a large white handkerchief.

"Bugger off, Lawrence," she snapped. "I didn't mean to hit Reggie. It's his own bleeding fault for standing too close to the door. Anyhow, aren't you both supposed to be in the dining room?"

Lawrence folded his arms. "So who died and made you bloody king?"

"Lawrence!" Mrs. Chubb's voice rose above the clatter of dishes. "Get back into the dining room and take your brother with you."

Gertie flinched at the malevolent gleam in the waiter's eyes. "Yes, Mrs. Chubb," he muttered through clenched teeth. "Right away, Mrs. Chubb."

Gertie watched him spin on his heel and head for the door. Reaching it, he grabbed Reggie's arm, then just before he disappeared, he raised his spread fingers in a rude gesture and thumbed his nose. Lucky for him Mrs. Chubb didn't see him. Gertie wished the housekeeper had noticed him. She'd have given him what for, all right.

Rolling her eyes, Gertie was about to follow the waiters out the door when something caught her eye. She stared up at the ceiling, her eyes widening in disbelief.

"What on earth are you gawking at, girl?" Mrs. Chubb thundered. "Don't I have enough to do keeping those lazy louts of waiters moving without having to watch you, too? What's the matter with you then?"

For answer, Gertie jabbed a finger at the ceiling.

Michel, having heard the exchange, followed her pointing finger. His howl of outrage made Gertie jump.

"What on earth . . ." Mrs. Chubb's voice trailed off as she stared at the ceiling, one hand clutching her throat. "Mercy me," she murmured.

"My knife!" Michel started jumping up and down, snatching at the carving knife that had somehow got half its blade buried in the ceiling. Realizing he couldn't reach it, the chef leapt onto the table, sending a pile of bone china saucers crashing to the floor.

The noise brought Gertie's hands to her ears. "Flipping heck. I'm off to the dining room where it's bleeding quiet."

She flew out the door, narrowly missing Pansy, who was on her way back with more dirty dishes. "Don't go in there," she warned the anxious girl. "It's bloody bedlam."

She didn't wait to see what Pansy did next, but fled down the hallway, Michel's shrieks still ringing in her ears.

"Baxter! I've been so worried about you." Cecily hurried toward her husband, praying he wouldn't cause a scene. "Where have you been to keep you so late?"

Baxter looked over her head at Kevin. "Good evening, Prestwick."

The doctor bowed his head in response. "Baxter. Pleasure to see you again."

Cecily could tell by Baxter's face that he did not return the sentiment. "Baxter, darling," she said hurriedly. "I assume you've heard the dreadful news. Poor Roland. I feel so awful. It was all my fault for sending the boy up on the roof. I should have known better. Now the poor boy is dead and we shall have to convey the sad news to his parents, and it's such a dreadful time to lose someone, I really don't know how—"

"Hush, Cecily." Baxter's cold gaze softened as he looked down at his wife. "You must not blame yourself. It was an accident. I'm quite sure that Roland's parents will not blame you for what happened."

"Exactly what I said." Kevin beamed at her. "You see, you are fretting about nothing."

"I would hardly consider the death of a young boy of such little consequence," Baxter said, his displeasure quite clear on his face.

Cecily felt a twinge of apprehension. Normally she would consider her husband extremely handsome. She found his rugged face and strong jaw especially appealing, and when in a good mood, his gray eyes sparkled in a way that could make her heart sing.

Right at that moment, however, those eyes looked more like a stormy sea, with deep creases furrowing his brow. The lines failed to disappear, even though Kevin sounded quite charming with his reply.

"Of course not, dear boy. I fully understand the distress this death has caused everybody, and I couldn't be more saddened. I must go at once to the stables, where I understand the body lies, and conduct my examination before the constable arrives to complicate matters."

This less-than-flattering comment about P.C. Northcott helped to smooth out the angry lines on Baxter's face. If there was one man her husband disliked more than Kevin Prestwick, that man was Sam Northcott.

It had taken Cecily years to discover the reason why. It seemed that Baxter and the constable had once been rivals for the same young lady. Sam Northcott had won her fair hand, and Baxter had never forgiven him for stealing the object of his affection right from under his proud nose.

"I think that's a very good idea," she murmured, slipping her hand through her husband's arm. "I hope you will return and inform us of the results?"

"Of course." Nodding at Baxter, Kevin crossed the room to the door. "I'll do my best to be discreet. I wouldn't want to upset your guests."

"Don't worry," Baxter said. "Northcott can be relied upon to achieve that all by himself."

He waited until the door closed behind the doctor before turning to his wife. "I'm so sorry, my dear. I was delayed at the office, and left too late to catch the train. I was forced to wait until the next one. I do wish the railways would run an extra train at night. I know I'm not the only man to travel on it back and forth to work. Makes things so difficult when I have to work late."

Cecily frowned. She'd rung him several minutes before he normally left the office, and had been told he'd already departed and was on his way home. Either his assistant had been mistaken, or Baxter was not telling her the truth. She couldn't imagine that he would deliberately lie to her. Nevertheless, a niggling anxiety would not let the matter rest.

"Baxter—" she began, but before she could complete the question a sharp tap on the door interrupted her.

Baxter clicked his tongue and strode across the room to answer it.

Cecily heard a shy female voice and guessed it belonged to one of the maids.

Baxter's scowl conveyed his displeasure when he returned to her side. "That blithering idiot is on his way here," he said, his voice thick with disgust.

Knowing he referred to P.C. Northcott, Cecily hid a smile. "You don't have to stay. I can tell him what he wants to know. We really should notify the boy's parents. Would you mind doing that for me? You always know so much better than I what to say in these circumstances."

"I'll do my best, though nothing I can say will lessen their grief."

"I trust you to be gentle with them. Tell them we'll have the body removed to the morgue. They can claim the body from there."

"Very well."

"Thank you, darling. After that why don't you retire to our boudoir, and make yourself comfortable. I'll join you just as soon as I can get rid of him."

Baxter narrowed his gaze. "What about that Prestwick fellow? Is he coming back?"

"He may, but I'm sure he won't stay long." She patted her husband's arm as his scowl deepened. "Don't worry, Bax darling, you must know that no one could ever take your place in my heart."

He grunted something under his breath, but she could tell he was somewhat appeased by her comment. He lifted her hand and brushed his lips across her fingers. "I could hardly blame the fellow for trying." He reached the door and turned back to look at her. "Don't be long."

"I won't." She watched the door close behind his back, her smile fading. She'd chosen a bad time to attempt to question him about his misleading her, if that was truly what he'd done. She was, however, fully determined to do just that once she was alone with him in the boudoir.

Another sharp tap on the door prevented her from dwelling on the situation. At her command to enter, a gleaming bald head popped around the door.

"It's only me, Mrs. Sinclair. Police Constable Northcott at your service. The maid said it were h'all right."

"Mrs. Baxter," Cecily said, with a hint of impatience. Heaven knew how many times she'd corrected the silly man. He still insisted on calling her by her previous married name. "Come in, Sam."

"H'oh, yes. I keep forgetting you married what's his name." Northcott shuffled in, his helmet tucked underneath his arm. "Well, m'm. This here's a pretty kettle of fish, all right. Nasty business, this."

"Yes." Cecily heaved a sigh as she seated herself and waved the constable to a chair. "It is indeed."

"Is the doctor here yet?" The constable balanced his helmet rather precariously on his knee and dug into his chest pocket for his notebook.

"Dr. Prestwick is in the stables, examining the body."

Northcott stared at her. "How'd he get in the stables, m'm? It were my understanding that the young man fell down from the roof."

"I had him carried there. I didn't want the guests falling over him."

"Ah." He dragged a pencil out of his pocket and licked the end of it. "Well, that explains it then." He wrote something down in the notebook, his pencil moving slowly over the page. "And what was he doing up there on the roof then?"

Cecily explained about Father Christmas. "I believe Phoebe said his name is Mr. Porter. In any case, he failed to keep the appointment."

"H'ah, yes. Sid Porter." Northcott slowly nodded his head. "Well, there you are then. The man's a boozer, m'm, ain't he."

Just then yet another tap on the door heralded the return of Dr. Prestwick, and saved her from needing to answer.

He gave the constable a brief nod before addressing Cecily. "Broken neck, I'm afraid. You were right, Cecily. Looks like he slipped and fell from the roof. He died instantly."

She took a moment to compose herself. Roland hadn't been working at the Pennyfoot for very long, and she didn't know the boy well. Even so, she had lost one of her staff, and the tragic death of one so young at a time when most people were celebrating was particularly distressing. Her heart ached for his family.

"There's something else." The doctor held out his hand and opened his fingers.

Cecily stared at the scrap of white fur. "Where did that come from?"

"It was clutched in the boy's hand. Look." He held the piece up to show her. "There's a tiny fragment of red velvet attached to it here, see?"

Cecily caught her breath. "Father Christmas's suit?"

"I'd stake my practice on it."

"Then Mr. Porter must have kept the appointment after all. I wonder what could have happened to him."

"Well, that settles it. Now I shall be off." Northcott finished scribbling in his notebook, snapped it shut, and tucked it, together with the pencil, into his pocket.

Kevin raised his eyebrows. "Finished with your report already?"

"Open and shut, isn't it." Northcott rose to his feet, his helmet securely tucked under his arm once more. "The way I see it, I'd say Porter has a belly full of beer before he arrives.

Climbs up on the roof, gets into the old fisticuffs, as Sid is want to do when he's sozzled, and *bang*!" He slapped his hand on the back of the armchair. "The boy slips off the roof. Sid sees what he did, gets in a big panic, and has to beat a hasty retreat, as it were."

The doctor's look of amazement would have been amusing if Cecily hadn't been so distressed. "Oh, dear," she said. "I do hope you're wrong."

Kevin shook his head. "Wonderful story, Northcott. Can't imagine how you conjured up that one."

Northcott frowned. "I've been trained to h'ascertain certain events," he said, with more than a hint of resentment. "That's the way I see it, and that's the way I shall report it to the inspector."

At the mention of Inspector Cranshaw, Cecily suppressed a shiver. She'd had more than one confrontation with the formidable policeman and had no wish to repeat the ordeal.

"If that's the case," Kevin said briskly, "I trust you will pursue the matter with Mr. Porter. If he is responsible for that boy's death he must be held accountable."

"No doubt it were an accident." Northcott bowed his head at Cecily and shuffled over to the door. "Nevertheless, it were wrong of him to just take off like that. Indeed it were."

"Then you'll see the man answers for his transgression?" Kevin persisted.

"I shall follow the proper procedures, just as soon as Christmas is over." Northcott paused to look at Cecily. "Me and the missus will be going up north to visit her family. So I'll 'ave to take care of business when I get back. Meanwhile, I'll leave Dr. Prestwick to get the body to the morgue." He bowed again. "Goodnight to you, Mrs. Sinclair, and may I take this h'opportunity to wish you and yours a very 'appy Christmas, indeed."

"Baxter," Cecily murmured, but the constable was already out of earshot as the door closed behind him with a snap. Kevin stared at it for a moment or two then exploded in wrath. "That fool is a disgrace to the constabulary. He's so eager to begin his Christmas holiday he'll make up anything to satisfy the inspector."

"He could be right," Cecily said mildly. "It could well have happened that way."

Kevin frowned at her. "Shame on you, Cecily. You, of all people should insist on finding out the truth. Isn't that what has driven you all these years? Isn't that why you risk bodily harm in your pursuit of justice?"

She sighed. "You're quite right, Kevin. I'm afraid I momentarily put the comfort and enjoyment of my guests above my good sense. I just hate the thought of an investigation spoiling Christmas for so many people."

"Of course you do." He moved closer and reached for her hand. "Perhaps that won't be necessary. I shall contact the inspector myself and inform him of the details. He will most likely want to question Mr. Porter, but that may well settle the matter. Let us hope so."

"Indeed." She rose, allowing him to raise her hand to his lips. "You will let me know what the inspector has to say?"

"Of course." He walked to the door and she trailed unhappily after him. "Try not to let this dampen your spirits, Cecily. You know you would never forgive yourself should you allow a scoundrel to escape a just punishment."

"If it's deserving."

"Quite." He smiled at her. "Happy Christmas, my dear."

"Happy Christmas, Kevin. Will you be spending it with Madeline?"

"I hope so." He shook his head. "One never knows what to expect from that lady."

"Isn't that what makes her so fascinating?"

"Always the matchmaker." He smiled at her. "Though I do have to admit, Madeline is one of the most fascinating ladies I have ever met."

He touched his forehead in farewell, and she closed the door behind him, unable to dispel the feeling of gloom. Once more disaster had struck the Pennyfoot at Christmastime.

Shivering, she rubbed her hands together. The room felt uncommonly cold without a fire roaring in the fireplace. She reached for the bell pull and gave it a tug.

Samuel appeared within a few minutes, giving her time to replace *The Wind in the Willows* on the shelf.

"We must light this fire," she told him. "Some of the guests may want to enjoy a late-night brandy before retiring. The chill in this room will certainly chase them away."

"Right away, m'm." Samuel knelt in front of the yawning fireplace and reached for the matches. Striking one, he held it to the crumpled newspaper beneath the kindling. Within seconds flames snatched greedily at the dry wood.

Cecily watched him as he opened the large wooden box beside the hearth and took out several lumps of coal with the brass tongs. Placing each one carefully among the burning sticks, he leaned closer and blew on the flames to heighten them.

Much as Cecily disliked the cold, the sight of flames still gave her chills. After her near brush with death a year earlier, she had a healthy respect for the grave danger a fire could represent.

Samuel sat back on his heels, his cheeks glowing from his exertion. "Looks like it caught, m'm. Shouldn't be too long—" His words ended in a cough, as thick, black smoke billowed out of the fireplace and enveloped his head.

Cecily yelped in dismay. "Samuel! For heaven's sake, what's the matter with it?"

"I don't know, m'm." Samuel backed away, still coughing. "I made sure the damper was open before I lit it. It shouldn't be smoking."

"I had it cleaned yesterday." A thought struck her and she grasped Samuel's arm. "Good Lord, I forgot the pillow. It must still be up there on the ledge."

Nodding, Samuel grabbed the tongs and started pulling the smoldering coal off the kindling. Some of it fell onto the hearth and Cecily backed away with a sharp cry.

"It's all right, m'm," Samuel assured her. "I won't let it off the hearth. It'll just burn out."

Appalled at the smoke still pouring into the room, Cecily groaned. "This room has just been redecorated. The smoke will ruin it again."

Busy beating the flames with the tongs, Samuel coughed harder. "I'll have it out in a tick, m'm. It didn't have time to really get going."

To her utter relief, he was right. Gradually the smoke thinned out, then disappeared altogether, leaving behind a black, charred mess on the hearth and an acrid smell in the room.

Hurrying over to the windows, Cecily examined the heavy damask curtains. "Thank goodness, there doesn't seem to be any real damage." She shook the curtain. "We'll have to thoroughly air the room, of course, before we can let our guests in here again. Please tell Mrs. Chubb to see to it right away, will you, Samuel?"

Still with her back to the fireplace, she heard an odd sound, as if someone were in pain. Spinning around, she stared at Samuel.

He stood facing her, his hair ruffled, his forehead smudged with soot. In one hand he held the tongs, the other grasped a markedly scorched pillow.

"Oh, thank goodness," Cecily began, then paused when she saw the expression on her stable manager's face. His eyes seemed fixed, as if he were looking at something she couldn't see.

"Samuel? Are you not feeling well?" Her heart racing, she started forward, then paused, as Samuel said in a high-pitched voice quite unlike his own, "I got the pillow."

"Yes," she said uncertainly, "I can see that you did."

"That's not all that's up there."

"Oh?" Her voice rose to a squeak, and she cleared her throat. "What are you talking about?"

"There's a boot up there, m'm."

"A boot?"

"Yes, m'm."

The conversation was beginning to take on an air of farce. Feeling rather stupid now, Cecily said carefully, "Then I suggest you get it down, Samuel."

"I tried, m'm, but it won't come down." Samuel seemed to be having trouble swallowing. "Someone's still wearing it."

CHAPTER
✽ 4 ✽

"How the devil did that get up there?" Mrs. Chubb stared in amazement as Michel finally grasped the carving knife and dislodged it from the ceiling.

"You ask me?" Michel jumped to the floor. "Sacre bleu! How the 'ell do I know how it got there? Someone must have thrown it up . . . so." He jabbed his closed fist up at the ceiling.

"Oh my goodness." Mrs. Chubb clutched her throat. "It's a jolly good job it didn't fall down on one of us. Could have killed us, it could."

"It is I who shall kill whoever did this." Michel ran his long fingers up the blade. "It is ruined. Look at that." He thrust the knife at Mrs. Chubb, who jumped back in alarm.

"Can't you sharpen it?"

"Of course I can sharpen it. But half ze edge is gone, *non?*"

"Well then, we'll have to ask Madam for a new one."

"It is not a new one I want. It is the head of whoever did this." Michel started prancing around, brandishing the knife like a sword.

Two of the maids, who had been silently watching his performance, squealed and rushed from the kitchen.

Mrs. Chubb clicked her tongue. "Now see what you've gone and done. Frightened the tweenies, you have."

"It does not take much to frighten those nincompoops." Michel stopped prancing and gazed mournfully at his knife. "I would like to get my hands on ze bastard who did this. I will show him what it feels like to be pinned to the ceiling by a knife."

Mrs. Chubb was about to answer when the door swung open and Gertie tumbled in. Her cap had slipped sideways again and strands of hair hung over her eyes, which were wide open and staring.

"It's happened again!" The pile of soiled serviettes she carried slipped through her arms and fell to the floor. Paying no attention to them, she flapped a hand at Mrs. Chubb. "It's bleeding happened again!"

"What's happened?" Still unsettled by Michel's wayward knife in the ceiling incident, Mrs. Chubb's question was no more than a whisper.

"You was right about a curse. It's struck again."

Mrs. Chubb had trouble finding any voice at all. "Not somebody else dead?"

Gertie looked at Michel, who still brandished the knife

aloft as he stared back at her. "What the flipping heck is he doing?"

"Never mind him. Tell me what's happened. Who is it this time?"

"It's Father Christmas. Got himself stuck in the chimney, didn't he."

Mrs. Chubb sagged in relief. "Gertie! That's not funny. I thought you was serious. Gave me quite a turn, you did."

Michel burst out laughing. "That's a good one," he said between chuckles. "Father Christmas stuck in the chimney. Zat I would like to see."

Gertie sat down on the nearest chair and thrust out her feet. "Well go on up to the library then, if you don't believe me. It's that Sid Porter bloke, what Phoebe hired to play Father Christmas. Mind you, all you can see is his feet, but he's stuck up there all right and he ain't bloody moving, neither."

Mrs. Chubb felt quite faint. "You telling us he's dead?"

"They don't know for sure, but Samuel lit a fire under him and he didn't squeal or nothing, so he's probably not feeling too chipper."

Mrs. Chubb patted her ample bosom. "Oh, Lord. It's happening again."

"That's what I said." Gertie shook her head. "Two in one day. Getting bleeding scary, it is."

"Did you see these feet?" Michel demanded.

"Nope, I didn't. But Samuel did. He told me all about it. He gave the poor bugger a tug, but he couldn't move him. He's gone after Dr. Prestwick to bring him back."

"Does Madam know?"

"Yeah, she was there when Samuel lit the fire. That's how they knew something was stuck up the chimney. Samuel said with all the smoke the library smells like bad eggs. He said to tell you that Madam wants the room aired out."

"Well, in that case, my girl, it looks like you've got yourself a job."

Gertie groaned and got to her feet. "How did I know you were going to say that? I suppose I'd better get to it." She stepped over the pile of linen and walked slowly to the door, then paused, looking back over her shoulder at Mrs. Chubb. "I'm not looking forward to cleaning that room, I can tell you. Being in there with a Father Christmas what might be dead in the chimney."

Mrs. Chubb glared at Michel when he uttered what sounded suspiciously like a smothered laugh. "There's a lot of strange things going on around here," she said darkly. "I'd think twice before I laughed about it if I was you."

"If I do not laugh, then I cry instead." He slotted the knife back into its stand.

Sighing, she bent to pick up the serviettes. "This is not a good start to the Christmas season. I just hope and pray the guests don't hear about this. We can't afford to have them walking out of here and going to that new hotel across Putney Downs. Madam's already worried about them taking away all our business."

Michel snorted. "The Pennyfoot Hotel will never lose any business to that monstrosity. It is too ugly, too big, too modern. It has none of the charm of the Pennyfoot." He threw back his head and raised his voice. "And it does not 'ave the greatest, most creative French chef in the world!"

He punctuated his words by beating his chest with both hands.

Mrs. Chubb turned away. "French chef, my ass," she muttered, though she was careful to keep her voice too low for Michel to hear. Two disasters in one night was quite enough.

"Is he dead?" Cecily looked anxiously at Kevin Prestwick as he reached up inside the fireplace.

"Can't say for certain." The doctor straightened, stepped off the hearth, and brushed his hands together. "But if we don't get him out soon he surely will be."

"Oh, Lord." Cecily glanced at the door. "I sent one of the maids to tell Baxter to join me here. I can't imagine what's keeping him."

As if in answer to her words, the door opened and her husband strolled in. He'd changed into a burgundy smoking jacket and wore a faint smile, which quickly vanished as he came to an abrupt halt. "Good Lord! What the devil is that smell? Is something burning?"

"Not anymore. Samuel put it out." Cecily was about to explain, but just then Baxter caught sight of Kevin. His face changed, and his clipped words seemed to cut across the room.

"I had assumed you'd left long ago."

"I did," Kevin said, keeping his tone reasonable. "I came back."

"May I ask for what reason?"

Kevin nodded at Cecily. "Perhaps your wife should tell you."

Baxter crossed the room to stand next to her. "You're not ill?"

"Of course not." She gave him a worried smile. "But I'm afraid our Father Christmas might well be."

Baxter looked mystified. "I beg your pardon?"

"His name is Sid Porter." Cecily gestured at the fireplace. "He's stuck up there. We can't get him down."

Baxter's eyes widened in disbelief. With a suspicious glance at Kevin, he stepped onto the hearth and peered up the chimney. "Good Lord. What's he doing up there?"

"Phoebe hired him to play Father Christmas."

Baxter grunted. "Well that explains a lot. How long has he been up there?" He cupped his hands to his mouth and his voice echoed up the chimney. "I say, old chap, are you all right?"

"I don't think he's going to answer you," Kevin said helpfully.

"He must have been there since early this afternoon," Cecily said. "We had no idea he was in the chimney until Samuel lit a fire and it smoked."

"So that's what that abominable smell is." Baxter pulled back from the chimney and addressed Kevin. "Has he said anything?"

Kevin shook his head. "I'm pretty sure he's dead. He's cold to the touch." He looked hopefully at Baxter. "I could use some help getting him out."

To Cecily's relief, Baxter stepped forward. "I'll give you a hand."

She watched anxiously as the two men tugged and pulled, grunting and puffing with the effort. When it became apparent that nothing they did was going to dislodge the man, they both stepped back.

Baxter looked rather red in the face when he muttered, "Now what?"

"I'd like to feel for a pulse." The doctor peered up the chimney once more. Reaching up, he muttered, "If . . . I . . . can . . . just . . . pull . . . damn!" This last word erupted in a shout as he fell back and sat down quite hard. In his hand he held a black, scuffed boot. "I beg your pardon, Cecily," he said, scrambling to his feet. "At least now I can feel his ankle pulse."

She held her breath as he pushed his hand into the chimney one more time.

"As I thought." He shook his head. "No pulse, I'm afraid. It appears we have another dead body to deal with."

"Oh, my." Cecily stared at him in dismay. "What do you think happened?"

"Hard to say. I'm assuming Roland was supposed to lower Porter on a rope. Is that right?"

"I imagine so. Phoebe took care of all the arrangements. All I know is that Roland was to help Mr. Porter down the chimney."

"It would seem to me that Roland must have slipped while holding the rope. He let go, fell off the roof, and Porter descended a great deal faster than he'd intended. Most likely broke his neck in the fall. I'll know more once we get him out of there."

"A double tragedy," Cecily murmured. "Could anything be worse for our Christmas season?"

Baxter quickly crossed to her side. "Let me handle this, Cecily. You go up to the boudoir."

"No." She took a deep breath. "We must send for Sam Northcott again. We have to get that poor man out of there somehow."

Baxter exchanged glances with Kevin. "I'm afraid it's going to require more than we can handle on our own. We shall have to wait until tomorrow, and hire the services of someone with equipment to pull his body out from up on the roof."

"Drat." Cecily spun away from the two men and paced across the carpet. "There's no point in calling the constable back here until we get him out."

"Quite." Baxter paused, then added to Kevin, "I suggest you go home, old chap. I'll make arrangements in the morning to remove the body from the chimney, and I'll let you know when that's been accomplished."

Cecily managed to hold her smile in place until Kevin had left, then collapsed against her husband's broad chest. "This could ruin our business. Now that they've built that new hotel across the downs, people have somewhere else to go if they decide to leave. I hear the Bayview is charging far less than we are for their rooms."

Baxter folded his arms around her shoulders. "You worry too much, my dear. The Pennyfoot has always had a loyal clientele and will continue to do so. After all, since we are a country club, we can offer gambling rooms, which the Bayview cannot. It's one of the reasons so many of our customers return each year."

"I hope you're right." Cecily took a moment to enjoy the comfort of her husband's arms, then drew back. "You haven't eaten your dinner yet. I shall order something brought up to our sitting room, where you can enjoy a meal in peace. We'll worry about this tomorrow." She sent a nervous glance at the fireplace. "Though I must confess, it makes me uneasy to think of that wretched man imprisoned in such a cold, dark place all night."

"Don't worry, dearest." Baxter led his wife to the door. "I rather doubt he'll notice."

Breakfast was Gertie's least favorite meal to serve in the dining room. Unlike the other two meals, which were served one course at a time, the breakfast items were served all at once. Steaming bowls of porridge had to be placed before each guest, and while they devoured them, the maids brought to the table an array of smoked haddock, bacon, sausage, poached eggs, salmon roe, fried tomatoes, mushrooms, fried potatoes, and thick, greasy slices of fried bread.

It was a rush to get everything on the table before the last scrap of porridge had been swallowed, and invariably Gertie was kept hopping from table to table to make sure the maids did just that.

This morning seemed particularly chaotic, with maids bumping into each other and food spilling onto the floor. Everyone was jittery now that the news of the deaths had spread among the staff, and Gertie was no exception. Reggie and Lawrence seemed determined to upset her. Normally she would have told them both to sod off, but what with the deaths on her mind and having to watch the maids she just couldn't find the gumption to yell at them.

If it hadn't been for that nice Jeremy Westhaven, her

favorite toff, she'd have been really miserable. The young gentleman's attentions helped to make her forget her troubles.

She'd made sure to be the one to wait on him, and had given him extra helpings of everything. It was worth the nagging she'd got from Mrs. Chubb when the gentleman winked at her.

"That was an excellent breakfast," he said, with a smile that warmed her all the way through.

Her cheeks growing hot, she leaned over to gather up the empty dishes. "Thank you, sir," she murmured, cheerfully accepting the credit for having cooked it all.

With the ease of long practice, she stacked the dishes on her arm and stepped back. At the same moment, she felt a violent nudge in the small of her back, sending her forward again. The dishes shot from her arm across the table and landed with a crash on the other side.

The noise was deafening enough to silence everyone in the room. Except for the smarmy voice that spoke in her ear.

"So sorry. I didn't mean to hit you. Then again, it's your own fault for stepping in front of me."

Furious, Gertie forgot everything Mrs. Chubb had drummed into her about being a lady in front of the guests. She turned on Lawrence, spitting curses at him while he just stood there with a sickly grin on his face.

"And you can bloody well help me pick up the pieces," she finished, after she'd used up her entire repertoire of swear words. "And I'm going to tell Mrs. Chubb it was all your fault, so she'll dock your wages for the damage. So there!"

Lawrence's smile vanished, to be replaced by an evil glare. "Pick up the pieces yourself, you bloated shrew."

"Here, I say." Jeremy leapt to his feet, one hand darting to gather the waiter's shirt at his throat. "Apologize this instant, you miserable cad, or I'll make you pay."

Lawrence's eyes seemed to bulge in his head. "Let go of me, sir," he muttered. "You're making a scene."

Jeremy leaned closer, until his face was inches from the startled waiter's. "Apologize," he said softly, "or I'll snap your scrawny neck."

Gertie gazed in awe as Lawrence turned purple, muttered a fierce, "Sorry," and slunk away.

Fighting the urge to throw her arms around the handsome gent's neck, she dropped a curtsey instead. "Thank you, sir. I'm much obliged, I'm sure."

Jeremy sat down again. "No one should speak to a lady in that disgusting manner." He glanced down at the pieces of shattered china. "What a mess. Do you need any help with all that?"

"Oh, I couldn't possibly trouble you, sir." She rushed around the table and dropped to her knees. Lifting her apron she began piling the jagged pieces into it.

"Oh, do be careful." He leaned so close to her she could swear she felt his hot breath on her neck. "You might cut yourself."

She was going to cut herself, Gertie thought frantically, if he didn't stop hovering over her like that. "It's quite all right, sir. Really. I can manage."

To her huge relief, Pansy appeared at her side, offering her help. Gertie scrambled to her feet, directed Pansy to pick up the rest of the shattered china and fled for the kitchen.

Even Mrs. Chubb's ruthless scolding couldn't banish the glow she felt when she remembered Jeremy West-haven's smiling face. He was a charmer, all right. In fact, she thought about him so much that afternoon a twinge of guilt prompted her to whisper to the heavens, "Don't worry, Ross, love. He'd never pay attention to the likes of me."

Having eaten an early breakfast with Baxter in their sitting room, Cecily was anxious to get Sid Porter removed from the chimney as soon as possible. Reluctant to allow guests to share a room with a dead body, Baxter had locked the door the night before. There were bound to be complaints, and Cecily hoped to avoid having to explain to everyone why they couldn't use the library.

It wasn't until the workmen had arrived and had been dispatched to the roof that she remembered Doris was due to arrive that morning.

The once shy and nervous maid was now an accomplished vocalist, and had actually sung in front of King George V at the very first Royal Command Performance. Cecily was so proud of the young lady's achievement, and couldn't wait to tell her so. It was a shame there had to be such turmoil going on, but Cecily hoped fervently that the body would be safely removed and off the premises by the time Doris arrived.

Unfortunately, she came in on the early train, and Samuel was dispatched to fetch her from the station. Meanwhile,

Baxter had stationed himself by the fireplace in the library in case his assistance was needed, while Cecily dashed in and out as her duties allowed in order to keep abreast of events.

She was on her way back to the kitchen when Doris arrived in the foyer, resplendent in a mauve gown that absolutely shrieked Paris. The brim of her white hat, tastefully decorated with violets and tiny white roses, almost hid her delicate features, though nothing could obscure the sparkle in her eyes when she caught sight of Cecily.

"It's so good to be back here, m'm!" she cried out as she swept across the floor, attracting the attention of a group of new arrivals at the desk.

Cecily grasped both gloved hands and held them tight. "Doris, for heaven's sake. You are a celebrity now. Call me Cecily."

"Oh, I couldn't, m'm." Doris shook her head, making the curls on her forehead dance. "You'll always be Madam to me." She turned as another woman approached. "Oh, there you are. Come here and meet Madam. I mean Mrs. Baxter." She turned back to Cecily. "This is Elise Boulanger. She's a singer, too. We met at the Command Performance and we're appearing at the Strand together next month. At least, it used to be the Strand. They've changed the name to the Whitney Theater now."

Cecily smiled at the woman who towered over her ex-maid. Doris was pretty, but this woman had the kind of grace and beauty that could turn the heads of royalty. Her champagne lace-trimmed gown was exquisite and clung to her rounded figure. Her flame red hair framed a peaches-and-cream complexion, and her green eyes twinkled with amusement as she bowed her head. *"Enchanté,"* she murmured.

Doris laughed. "She's not really French," she said, giving the woman a nudge with her elbow. "She just likes to pretend. I told her she and Michel should get along really well." Both women erupted into peals of laughter.

"I'm sure he'll be captivated," Cecily said, joining in their mirth.

"How nice that some people are enjoying so much merriment," Baxter said from behind her.

At the sound of his dry tone, Cecily swung around. His meaningful stare reminded her of the tragedy unfolding in the library. Feeling guilty, she said quickly, "I've been greeting Doris. She has brought a friend with her. May I present Miss Elise Boulanger. My husband, Hugh Baxter. He—" She stopped short, startled by her husband's expression. He looked as if he'd just stepped off a very high cliff.

Elise's tinkling laugh rang out. "Ah, Mr. Baxter! You look surprised. Did you not tell me to visit your charming hotel one day?"

"Well . . . er . . . yes, I did. . . ." Baxter ran a finger around the inside of his stiff white collar as if it were choking him. "I didn't think . . . I mean . . . I didn't know . . ."

Cecily stared at him. Rarely had she seen her husband at a loss for words. "I wasn't aware you were acquainted with Miss Boulanger," she said pleasantly.

Baxter gave her a hunted look. "Er . . . yes. We . . . ah . . . met in London. I had no idea . . ."

"I persuaded her to come down with me for Christmas," Doris put in. She linked arms with her friend and looked up at Cecily. "We bumped into Mr. Baxter last night, just as we were leaving the theater after rehearsal. We talked about the Pennyfoot and after Mr. Baxter left Elise said she'd like to see it so I talked her into coming down with me. She can share my room, if that's all right?"

"Quite all right," Cecily murmured, her gaze still intent on her husband.

Baxter appeared to be having trouble meeting her eyes. In fact, he seemed quite agitated. He grew even more so when she said sweetly, "I wasn't aware that the Strand Theater was on your way to the station."

"It isn't." He avoided her gaze, staring instead at Doris and apparently attempting to signal a message to her with his eyes.

Beginning to feel disquieted by his behavior, Cecily gestured toward the desk. "Philip will see that your luggage is taken up to your room," she said to Doris. "I have to ask you both to sign the register, since this is a licensed club."

"Yes. Of course, m'm." Doris gave Elise's arm a little tug. "We'll get ourselves settled in, won't we Elise."

"But of course." Elise gave Baxter a wicked little smile that brought fresh color to his already burning cheeks. "I will see you later, *oui?*"

"*Oui,*" Baxter echoed, then cleared his throat. "I mean . . . perhaps." He sent Cecily a desperate glance that did nothing to settle her mind. "I must return to the library." Without waiting for her reply he spun around and hastened down the hallway.

Cecily gazed after him, questions burning in her mind. Why would her husband tell her he had to work late at the office, when he'd obviously left early for a destination that would take him at least a mile or two out of his way? And why hadn't he mentioned he'd met Doris and the delectable Miss Boulanger?

CHAPTER
❈ 5 ❈

Cecily was about to follow Baxter to the library when she heard a familiar voice call out her name. Turning, she saw Phoebe hurrying toward her, followed by a stout gentleman with a full face of white whiskers.

Cecily forced a smile as they approached. Much as she adored Phoebe, the colonel could be quite difficult at times. Mindful of the drama unfolding on the roof, she hoped her friend's husband would be anxious to visit his usual seat at the bar. Colonel Fortescue never missed an opportunity to enjoy a snifter of brandy, no matter the time of day.

"I say, old girl!" Fortescue bellowed, well before he reached her. "Jolly good to see you again, what? What?"

"Indeed, Colonel." Cecily looked meaningfully at Phoebe. "What brings you here at such an hour?"

"Oh, didn't Madeline tell you?" Phoebe's girlish laughter bubbled out. "Madeline asked us to help her decorate the ballroom. We just couldn't resist, could we, precious?" She slipped a white-gloved hand into the crook of the colonel's elbow. "Frederick has very graciously consented to help."

"I have?" The colonel looked confused—a fairly constant condition in his case. "Good Lord! What the devil did I say I'd do?"

"Just help me put up a few decorations, my love." Phoebe snuggled up to him. "I need a pair of broad shoulders."

"You do?" Fortescue stared at his wife in amazement. "What on earth for? Your shoulders are perfectly presentable the way they are."

Phoebe sighed, while Cecily hid a grin. "Not *my* shoulders, precious. I'm talking about your shoulders."

"Oh, I see." For a moment the colonel's face cleared. "Well, why didn't you say so." He turned to Cecily. "Reminds me of the time I was in India, old bean. Had to carry my lackey on my shoulders across the river—"

Knowing the colonel's capacity for stretching out a story to the point of delirium, Cecily rather rudely interrupted. "Ah, Colonel, I'm sure your story is fascinating but—"

"Just a little chap, he was." The colonel twirled the waxed end of his mustache. "Couldn't let the poor little bugger drown, now, could I."

"Frederick," Phoebe cried, covering her mouth with her gloved fingers. "Such language in front of ladies."

"What?" Fortescue focused his perpetually bloodshot eyes on his wife. "Who's using foul language in front of my wife? I'll thrash the blighter."

"You are, dearest." Phoebe turned to Cecily. "Please forgive him. He's not quite himself this morning."

Cecily couldn't remember a time when the colonel was ever himself. "Quite all right," she assured her friend. "But I'm afraid I can't—"

"Dropped him. Right there in the middle of the raging current."

Both women stared at Fortescue.

"Frederick!" Phoebe sounded shocked. "Don't tell me the poor man drowned."

"Drowned?" Fortescue blinked, his eyelashes flapping up and down in rapid motion. "No, no, of course the blighter didn't drown. I took hold of his hair and hung on like grim death. There we were, the enemy bearing down on us from the hills, our equipment floating down the river—"

"The bar is already open, I believe," Cecily said in desperation.

"Don't tell him that. If he hears the slightest mention of the bar I'll never get him to the ballroom."

Phoebe's urgent whisper must have penetrated. Fortescue stopped talking and peered at his wife. "Ballroom? There's a bar in the ballroom?"

"I don't know," Phoebe said sweetly. She took his arm. "Let us go and see, shall we?" She smiled at Cecily. "We'll catch up with you later."

Not if she could prevent it, Cecily thought, as she watched the two of them march down the hallway with Phoebe trying valiantly to keep in step with her husband's long military stride.

The last she heard of them was Fortescue's voice floating

back to her. "Bald as a blasted badger by the time I got him to the other side."

Cecily rolled her eyes at the ceiling. A quick glance assured her that Doris and Miss Boulanger were on their way up the stairs to their room. Now, at last, she could go back to the library. High time she had a word with her own husband and found out exactly what he didn't want her to know.

Just then the Westminster chimes rang out from the grandfather clock in the corner. Eleven of them. Crossing the lobby, Cecily hoped that the workmen had completed their grisly task. She wouldn't rest easy until this whole ghastly business was over.

Just before she reached the hallway she paused, her attention caught by an empty space in the corner of the lobby. Normally a very large aspidistra sat there, its wide, dark green leaves brushing the walls. For some strange reason, it had disappeared.

Frowning, Cecily entered the hallway. She would have to ask Mrs. Chubb about the plant. It would be such a shame if it had died, though it had seemed perfectly healthy the last time she'd seen it.

She forgot about the aspidistra the moment she opened the door of the library. Baxter stood in front of the fireplace, talking to Kevin Prestwick. She hadn't seen the doctor come in, and obviously her husband hadn't bothered to let her know Kevin had arrived.

It wasn't Baxter's negligence that upset her just then, however. It had more to do with the expression on both the men's faces. She knew at once they had news for her, and that it would be something she'd rather not hear.

* * *

"*Gorn?* Whaddayou mean it's gorn?" Gertie shook her head at Pansy, who seemed to be having trouble spitting out words.

"It were there this morning. I dusted it meself. Then it vanished." Pansy's voice trembled. "Just like that."

"Go on." Gertie snorted with derision. "Plants don't just disappear. It's not like someone just bleeding walked off with it, now is it? I mean, the bloody thing must weigh a ton. Who the 'eck could lift it, leave alone carry it off? Who would want it, anyway? It's just a blinking plant."

"The g-g-ghost took it."

Gertie could actually hear the maid's teeth chattering. She felt a chill between her shoulder blades and tried not to shudder. "What ghost? What are you bleeding talking about, Pansy?"

"I seen it." Pansy leaned forward, her voice no louder than a whisper. Which was just as well, seeing as how they were standing outside the ballroom doors with their arms full of balloons. The last thing Gertie wanted was for Madeline to hear them talking about ghosts.

Madeline gave her the creeps, especially when she started talking about spirits and seeing things nobody else could see. Everyone in Badgers End knew Madeline had strange powers. It weren't for nothing that the blokes came by her house to buy her potions. Said it made them more frisky in bed.

Not that the potions worried Gertie, as much as the trances. She'd seen Madeline when she was in a trance. Scared the bloody hell out of her, it did. The last thing Gertie wanted was for Madeline to hear them talking about ghosts and go into a blinking trance.

"You've seen what," she said, hoping her stern tone would chase away the eerie feeling she had looking at Pansy's frightened face. "Shadows, that's what you seen. Nothing but shadows."

"No, I seen it as large as life. I heard it first, like the sound of tinkling bells, it were. Then I saw him. It were . . ." she leaned even closer. "It were him."

"Him who?" Gertie grabbed the string of an escaping balloon.

"Him what's stuck in the chimney. Sid Porter. It were a clown I saw, with paint on his face and a colored silk costume with little bells for buttons. I know it was Sid. My boyfriend knows him and he told me Sid used to dress up like that when he was a clown."

"Don't be daft." Gertie could feel her heart beginning to thump really hard in her chest.

"I seen him, I tell you. Sid Porter is dead, and his ghost is running around moving things. Ghosts do that, you know, when they can't pass on. They give signals so people will know they're still around."

Normally Gertie would have laughed her head off at such a wild story. Except she'd seen a ghost once herself. More than once. Right there on the balcony of the ballroom. So she knew such things really existed.

Mind you, she'd never admitted as much to anyone and Pansy didn't have to know that, neither. "Go on," she said, managing a scornful laugh, even it was a bit high-pitched. "So what things has he been moving around, then?"

"Well, there's the aspidistra, and then Michel's knife. Who else would want to throw a knife up into the ceiling?"

Until that moment, Gertie had been convinced the knife in the ceiling was someone having a joke with him. She'd even thought Michel might have put it there, just to cause a stir. Michel liked to cause stirs, especially if he wasn't getting enough attention. But now, what with the plant and all, it all seemed very strange and frightening.

The thought that another ghost could be roaming the Pennyfoot so unnerved her she let go of the strings, and balloons floated to the floor and rolled away from her.

Taking her fright out on the hapless Pansy, she yelled, "Now look what you've made me do!" She darted after them, and her foot kicked a couple so that they floated away from her.

Cursing, she bent double and grabbed at the strings. Then, all of a sudden, she saw a pair of black shoes. At first she thought Baxter stood in front of her, and she braced herself for his scathing comments.

Then she straightened, and nearly let go of the strings again when she saw Jeremy Westhaven staring at her with a most peculiar look on his face.

Thinking what an utter twerp she must seem, she stammered, "Good morning, sir. I beg your pardon. The balloons sort of got away from me. I'll have them cleaned up in a minute."

She half expected him to offer his assistance, as he'd done earlier in the dining room. Instead, he backed away from her muttering, "Balloons. Hate the things." Then he spun on his heel and stalked off.

Disappointed, she stared after him. Well, he'd certainly changed his mood since breakfast. Someone must have upset him. Maybe he'd had a quarrel with his lady friend and she wasn't coming down for Christmas after all. If so, Gertie was happy about that. Very happy.

Smiling at the thought, she dragged the balloons back to the ballroom. Pansy hadn't bothered to wait for her. She'd gone inside and started helping Madeline hang paper chains over the balconies. Phoebe and her dotty husband were there, too, arguing about something.

Just for a moment, Gertie remembered the ghost of the Scots piper she'd seen a few years earlier. Then, with a shake of her head, she put it out of her mind. She had far greater things to worry about than an imaginary clown ghost.

Her mind going back to Jeremy Westhaven, she began tying balloons onto the pillars that surrounded the ballroom. Maybe she could sneak in there on Christmas Eve. That's when they held the Grand Ball.

Maybe Jeremy would be there alone. She could just happen to bump into him. He'd take her in his arms and they'd start dancing around the floor. Around and around, floating in each other's arms. Humming her favorite waltz, she forgot everything except her wonderful daydream.

"What is it?" Cecily entered the library and crossed to her husband's side. "What's happened now?"

"They've managed to remove Porter from the chimney," Baxter said, his face still wearing that grim expression that worried her so.

Cecily looked at Kevin. "He was dead, I suppose."

"Quite." Kevin glanced at Baxter.

"What aren't you telling me?" Cecily turned to her husband again. "Baxter, I shall find out eventually, so you might as well tell me now."

For a moment a flicker of apprehension crossed his face, as if he realized she'd referred to more than the unfortunate death of Mr. Porter. "I'm sorry, Cecily," he said quietly, "but it appears Sid Porter was stabbed."

"If I'd taken off his other boot last night," Kevin said, "I'd have seen the blood. The boot he's wearing is covered with blood."

Cecily's stomach took a nasty turn. "*Stabbed?* Are you sure?"

"Quite sure," Kevin said, sounding far too cheerful. "Twice in the stomach and once in the side. Whoever did this had a nasty temper."

"I've sent for Northcott," Baxter said. "He'll be here shortly. With a great deal of reluctance, I might add. We're interfering with his holiday plans."

Kevin uttered a snort of disgust. "For all the good he'll do with or without his holiday plans."

"So this entire situation is not an accident after all." Cecily looked at Baxter. "Things did get worse after all."

Baxter placed his warm hand on her shoulder. "I'm sorry, my dear. I know how much this upsets you. Let us hope we can get this all cleared up before news of it spreads."

"I don't see how we can." Cecily gave him a look of pure misery. "Where is Mr. Porter's body now?"

"In the stables, along with Roland. Northcott is coming with the carriage to pick them up and take them down to the morgue."

"I wonder how many people saw you remove Mr. Porter from the roof."

"Not too many, I hope." Baxter glanced at Kevin. "We made sure they lowered him behind the building, out of sight in the rose garden."

"It only takes one person to start off a grapevine," she reminded him.

Just then an urgent rapping on the door turned their heads. Without waiting for an invitation, Phoebe rushed into the room. The pink ostrich feathers on her hat waved and danced with her agitation.

"Cecily! Is it true? Did you find my Father Christmas dead on the roof?"

"Not exactly—" Cecily began, but Phoebe was far too distressed to heed her words.

"I can't believe it! What happened to him? I do hope he didn't have a heart attack. I should never have suggested he go down the chimney. I told him it would be dangerous, but he assured me that for the sum I'd offered him he was more than willing to take the risk. Now I feel responsible. Oh, dear, oh, dear." She found a chair and plopped herself onto it. "Please don't tell me that poor footman's death is a result of all this. I shall never forgive myself. Never, never, never!" With that she promptly burst into tears.

Cecily hurried over to her. "Phoebe, dear, don't upset yourself so. None of this was your fault. We don't know exactly what happened yet, but I can assure you, Mr. Porter did not die from a heart attack."

Phoebe had buried her face in a dainty lace-trimmed handkerchief, but her sobbing gradually ceased. "Then how," she inquired, her voice shaking with emotion, "exactly did Mr. Porter die?"

Cecily looked at Kevin for help and he quickly came forward. "We have yet to discover that, Mrs. Fortescue. Perhaps you will allow me to offer you a sedative, to help calm your nerves? A glass of sherry, perhaps?"

Phoebe brightened at once. "Thank you so much, Doctor. I really do feel in need of assistance right now. Would you be so kind as to escort me to the bar? I left my husband there, and I would like to join him."

"Why, of course." Kevin managed a sly wink at Cecily as he took Phoebe's arm and led her to the door.

Had Cecily been less preoccupied, she would have enjoyed the expression of displeasure on her husband's face. "Goodbye, Phoebe," she called out. "We'll meet again soon."

The door closed behind them, and Cecily sank onto the chair her friend had just vacated. "So now we have a murder on our hands," she muttered.

"And we are going to let the constabulary take care of it, are we not?" Baxter said firmly.

Cecily gave him a look of pure innocence. "Well, of course, darling. Why on earth would you think otherwise?"

For an answer, Baxter merely scowled at her.

Fortunately, at that moment, one of the maids appeared to announce the arrival of P.C. Northcott. He barged into the library, looking extremely put out.

"The missus is waiting for me at the train station," he said, dragging his notebook from his pocket. "So I'm going to make this swift. I've taken a look at the body, and I've h'ascertained what happened."

"You have," Baxter said dryly. "My, how dashed clever of you."

Sam eyed him with suspicion. "It weren't hard. What with my training and all."

"Quite." Baxter clasped his hands behind his back and started rocking back and forth on his heels. "Perhaps you'd be so good as to share your remarkable powers of deduction with us poor mortals."

Cecily frowned a warning at her husband. "We'd be most obliged, Sam, if you could enlighten us."

"I'll be happy to, m'm." Sam turned the pages of his notebook and cleared his throat. "It is h'of my professional opinion that during the course of fisticuffs h'up on the roof, Roland, the footman, drew a knife and stabbed Sid Porter, causing him to fall down the chimney to 'is death. Roland then, in a state of panic to avoid detection, moved too fast and lost 'is footing, thereby plunging to his death." He snapped the notebook shut, his face glowing with pride.

Cecily hated to deprive the constable of his moment of triumph, but she could not allow the matter to rest there. "If that's the case, then why did we not find the knife?"

"It must still be up on the roof."

Northcott took a step toward the door, then halted when Baxter said quietly, "There was no knife on the roof. Prestwick questioned the workmen who brought down the body. They saw no sign of a knife anywhere."

"Then he must have hidden it before he fell," Sam declared. "Or it got stuck in the gutter, probably."

"Then we should look for it." Cecily stood. "I shall send someone up there immediately."

"You can do as you please, m'm." Sam reached the door and looked back at her. "Since the perpetrator of this crime is already dead, there is no great rush to pursue this matter. I've given orders for my assistant to transport the bodies to the morgue, and I shall be on my way to Northampton. I'll give my report to the h'inspector as soon as I return. May I wish you all a very 'appy Christmas." He closed the door behind him with a loud snap.

"That man," Baxter said fiercely, "is nothing but an unmitigated fool."

"I quite agree with you." Cecily walked over to the fireplace and stared down at the hearth, which had been cleaned until it sparkled. "Look at the bright side. We won't have to deal with his bungling, or the inspector's disruptions of our Christmas events. Doris has promised to sing in our Christmas variety show, and I'd hate to have that spoiled by Inspector Cranshaw's ruthless investigations."

"He can be something of an ogre at times."

"The man is a monster, nothing less." Cecily smiled at her husband. "Now, who shall we send up to the roof to look for the knife?"

Baxter scowled. "I suggest we leave that to the inspector. Once he reads Northcott's report he'll be here posthaste to investigate."

"Quite, which is why I think we should conduct some of the work for him and shorten the time that he'll be obliged to spend here."

Baxter narrowed his gaze. "Something tells me you are planning to conduct an investigation of your own."

"I merely want to tie up the loose ends, so to speak. After all, if Sam is right, the case is already solved."

"But I strongly suspect that you don't believe Roland killed Porter."

She shrugged. "I didn't know the boy very well, but I find it exceptionally hard to believe he would deliberately murder someone. After all, if it happened the way Sam has surmised, and an argument did break out while the two of them were on the roof, how did it happen that Roland had a knife with him?" She caught her breath. "Oh, my, I need to talk to Kevin again before he leaves."

"I'd say there's a very good chance he'll make sure of that."

Ignoring her husband's irony, Cecily sat down again. "Mrs. Chubb said a knife is missing from the kitchen. A carving knife. If that's the murder weapon, then Roland could certainly have taken it from the kitchen without anyone seeing him."

"So you do think Roland could have stabbed Porter, after all."

She felt a shudder down her spine. "I don't know. It does seem more likely, I suppose, since he was on the roof with Mr. Porter. If he did take the knife with him, however, that means he planned to kill him. They say anyone is capable of murder, but the idea of that nice young man scheming to go after someone to stab him over and over again . . ." She paused.

"What are you thinking now?"

"What if Roland didn't kill Mr. Porter? What if someone

else killed him, and Roland, too?" She looked up at him. "We could very well have a murderer still lurking in the hotel. I think we need to find that knife right away."

"Very well. If that will satisfy your insatiable thirst for meddling in police matters, I will ring for Samuel." He gave the bell rope a rather impatient tug. "But I must warn you, Cecily, I will not tolerate you placing yourself in danger again. I almost lost you the last time. I have no intention of living through that kind of hell again."

"And I have no intention of forcing you to do so." She gave him a reassuring smile, though already her instincts were telling her that she just might have to renege on that pledge. She could only hope her instincts were wrong.

CHAPTER
❊ 6 ❊

"Where have you been?" Michel slapped a large roasting pan down hard on the stove. "I've been waiting and waiting for someone to peel the potatoes, but of course, no one is here to do it. I 'ave to do it myself. *Moi*, Michel, the famous French gourmet chef, peeling potatoes. It is an outrage!"

"All right, keep your bleeding hair on." Gertie picked up a knife and reached for a potato. "Pansy and me have been helping decorate the ballroom. The other maids are still cleaning rooms upstairs, and Gawd knows where those lazy sods Lawrence and Reggie have gone. Wouldn't surprise me if they haven't snuck into the card rooms."

"Lawrence and Reggie, they are waiters." Michel pointed a

wooden spoon at Gertie. "You and Pansy, you are the kitchen staff. I trust you to help me prepare the meals. That is a sacred trust and you do nothing but abuse it."

"Sacred blooming trust." Gertie snorted. "That's a good one. You just like to have someone do your flipping dirty work for you."

"That is a lie—" He broke off with a curse as the door slammed open.

Pansy stood in the doorway, her apron bunched in her hands. Gertie noticed with alarm that the young girl's face had turned as white as bleached muslin. "Someone stabbed him!" she blurted out.

Gertie's stomach seemed to dive right down to her shoes. "Stabbed who?"

"Father Christmas!"

Michel groaned. "Here we go again."

Pansy came into the kitchen, her hands shaking as she twisted her apron around in knots. "I mean Sid Porter, the bloke what was supposed to play Father Christmas. Someone stabbed him before he fell down the chimney. That's what killed him."

"How'd you know that?" Gertie demanded.

"Samuel told me. He's going up on the roof to look for the knife."

"Sacre bleu!" Michel stared at his block of knives on the counter.

Gertie swallowed. She could see in her mind, plain as day, Michel's carving knife buried in the ceiling. She knew he was thinking the same thing she was: Could that knife have been used in a murder? Before she could voice her frightening theory, the door opened again.

This time Mrs. Chubb rushed into the kitchen, her eyes flashing fire. "All right, who did it?" she yelled. "Who put it there? If this is someone's idea of a joke—I can tell you, it's jolly well not funny."

Gertie stared at her, while Pansy collapsed onto a chair as if she'd suddenly had more than she could take.

Michel spoke first. "Per'aps if you tell us what the dickens you happen to be talking about, we can tell you who did what."

"The aspidistra." Mrs. Chubb waved an arm at the door. "Someone moved it."

"Oh, yeah." Gertie glanced at Pansy. "I meant to tell you about that."

Mrs. Chubb turned on her. "What do you know about it, then?"

"I don't know nothing. Pansy noticed it were missing and told me. That's all we know, ain't it, Pansy?"

Pansy answered with a nervous nod of her head.

"Well, I'm going to find out who put it there and when I do, I'll give her or him a hefty piece of mind, I will."

Gertie felt sorry for the culprit, whoever he might be. "Where'd he put it, then?"

The housekeeper gave her a suspicious glare. "How'd you know it was a he?"

"I'd like to see a woman lift the bloody thing. Anyhow, how did someone move it without anyone seeing him?"

"That's what I'd like to know." Mrs. Chubb marched over to

the kitchen table and picked up her rolling pin. "I just popped back to my room to get a clean hanky and there it was."

Intrigued now, Gertie left the sink and moved to the housekeeper's side. "There it was where?"

"Right in the middle of my bed, wasn't it."

Gertie nearly dropped the potato in her hand. "Flipping heck!"

Even Michel seemed caught up in the drama. "In the middle of your bed? How can that be?"

"Search me. All I know is that one of the biggest aspidistras I've ever seen is sitting smack dab in the middle of my bed, and I can't even shift it. It'll take at least two footmen and a hand cart to get it off there and back where it belongs."

For a moment an uneasy silence greeted her words. Then everyone jumped as Pansy let out a loud wail. "It's the ghost!" She covered her mouth with a quivering hand. "I told you it were moving things. It's the clown ghost! I know it is!"

"Don't be daft," Gertie muttered, though she had to admit, things were getting really, really strange around the hotel. What with people getting stabbed, falling down chimneys and off the roof, not to mention things being moved around and ending up in weird places, it looked very much as if the Pennyfoot had landed in deep, dark trouble once again.

Cecily looked up as Kevin tapped on the library door and angled his head around it. "I have to get back to my surgery," he announced. "I have patients waiting."

No doubt, she thought, rather uncharitably. *And mostly women, at that.* "Did you know that Madeline is in the ballroom?" She gave him a faint smile. "I'm quite sure she'd like to see you."

Kevin nodded. "I poked my head in the door. She was busy hanging balloons, so I didn't stop."

Too busy to talk to the handsome doctor? That worried her. "Well, I'm sure she'll have more time to spare for you later today."

"I'll try to take advantage of that." Kevin turned to Baxter. "I'll make sure the bodies are on the way to the morgue before I leave."

"We'd greatly appreciate it." Baxter moved over to Cecily's chair.

"Oh, by the way, Kevin." Cecily ignored the tightening of Baxter's hand on her shoulder. "The stab wounds. Could they have been caused by a carving knife?"

Kevin looked surprised. "A carving knife? Not at all. The knife was far too narrow. More like a letter opener. Why do you ask?"

"Oh, it was just that a carving knife appears to be missing from the kitchen. Though I'm sure it will be found sooner or later."

"Well, I'm reasonably certain it wasn't a carving knife that did the damage, so you can rest assured of that. Anyway, I must depart. I shall see you on Christmas Eve. Madeline has invited me to the variety show." He raised his hand in farewell and disappeared.

"Well, that should put your troubled mind at rest," Baxter said.

"I don't know. They don't seem to be as enamored of each other as they once were."

He made an impatient sound in his throat. "Not Prestwick and Madeline. I'm talking about the carving knife. If it wasn't the murder weapon, it could have been anyone up there with a knife. That means the killer isn't necessarily connected to the Pennyfoot."

"Then why were two people killed on our roof?"

"You're forgetting that the man who was murdered was a drunk hired by Phoebe. No doubt he was connected to all sorts of shady characters, any one of whom might have had reason to do away with him. I suggest you put the entire matter out of your mind until after the New Year, when our esteemed professional will have returned from Northampton and can do his best to pursue the investigation."

"And you, my dear husband, are forgetting that one of our staff has also died, which puts the responsibility to find out how and why squarely on my shoulders."

"I most emphatically disagree. This is a case for the constabulary. I strongly suggest you allow them to follow the proper procedures."

This was an argument that Cecily had been faced with so many times she knew better than to indulge in it now. "By the way," she said, smiling sweetly at her husband, "I've been wondering about something. Why did you neglect to tell me you met Doris and her charming friend last night in London?"

Baxter's expression changed so swiftly her uneasiness grew. "I . . . er . . . it must have slipped my mind." Avoiding her gaze, he stepped over to the fireplace. "Surely you remember I arrived home to the news that a footman had died? It's a small wonder I forgot to mention it."

She could have accepted that, had it not been for the odd look on his face, and the way his gaze shifted away from her. This was not the time to engage him in an argument, however. She needed his cooperation if she were to find out exactly what happened up there on the roof. The questions about his supposedly chance meeting with Doris and Miss Boulanger would have to wait until later.

Having been instructed to make a thorough search of the roof and the areas below, the midday meal had already been served before Samuel returned to find Cecily.

She had been called to the front desk, where she found Philip once more facing the wrath of Desmond Atkins. Apparently the hot-tempered guest had lost his room key, and had loudly demanded that Philip give him another.

Philip had then informed the gentleman that he would have to have another key cut, since the only spare hung with the others in Cecily's office and had to remain there.

"This is ridiculous," Atkins roared, as Cecily tried to reason with the visibly irate man. "My wife and I are locked out of our room. I insist that you give me another key at once. This is supposed to be a reputable hotel, yet it is run by common incompetents who don't have the slightest idea what they are doing."

Highly offended by the despicable man's inference that she was inept, Cecily had trouble holding her own temper.

Turning her back on him, she instructed a passing footman to take the Atkinses up to their room and open the door for them with the spare key from her office.

"After that," she told the young man, "take the key to the village and have a copy of it cut. Then deliver the copy to Mr. Atkins and replace the spare in my office."

All the time she issued the orders, Desmond Atkins stood grumbling and muttering beneath his breath. He didn't even have the decency to thank her as he tramped off after the footman. Deciding she thoroughly disliked the man, Cecily turned her attention back to her flustered desk clerk.

She had barely finished soothing Philip's ruffled feathers when Samuel appeared, beckoning to her from across the lobby.

Hurrying toward him, she clung to the hope that the knife had been found and somehow proved it could belong to no one in the hotel.

Mindful of ever-curious ears, she steered Samuel into her office before asking, "Well, did you find a knife?"

"No, m'm." Samuel seemed worried. "I looked everywhere. All over the roof, and all around the grounds. There weren't no knife anywhere to be seen."

"Drat. Now we'll never know what happened to Michel's carving knife."

Samuel raised his eyebrows. "Oh, it's *that* knife you're looking for? I should have told you. Michel found his knife. It were stuck in the ceiling."

Cecily sank onto her chair behind her desk, while Samuel

still hovered by the door. "In the ceiling? What on earth was it doing there?"

"Nobody knows. Pansy thinks a ghost put it there."

"A ghost?"

"Yes, m'm. Pansy swears she saw the ghost of a clown wandering around the hotel. She says it's Sid's ghost, 'cos he used to be a clown. He moved the aspidistra, too." Samuel's mouth twitched in a grin. "Mrs. Chubb found it in the middle of her bed."

"Good heavens!" Cecily tried to picture the huge plant sitting on Mrs. Chubb's bed and wondered if her housekeeper had been sampling the brandy. "Well, I hope someone has put the plant back where it belongs?"

"Yes, m'm. I got a couple of the lads to move it back. It were quite a struggle for them, too."

"I imagine it was. Though I seriously doubt a ghost could have put it in Mrs. Chubb's room. They can't move things, you know."

Samuel seemed unsure how to take that statement as he eyed her warily. "They can't?"

"No, Samuel, they can't. I rather think someone is playing a practical joke on Mrs. Chubb."

"They went to a lot of trouble, m'm, if that's what it was. That plant is as heavy as a house."

A faint stirring of uneasiness took her by surprise. "Yes, well, I wouldn't worry too much about it. I'm just so relieved Michel found his knife." *And that it wasn't lying up on the roof somewhere,* she added silently. It would seem Baxter could be right about an unknown assailant following Sid

Porter. Though it seemed an odd place to pick a fight with him.

She was about to dismiss Samuel when he held out his hand. "I did find this on the roof, though. It were lying in the gutter."

Cecily peered at his hand. "What is it?"

"I don't know if it means anything or not, but I thought you might want to see it." He laid a small white card on her desk. It had a narrow red ribbon threaded through it.

She picked it up and read the words printed on it. *Happy Christmas! Welcome to the annual Pennyfoot festivities.* She stared at it for several seconds, then said quietly, "Thank you Samuel. I appreciate you going up on the roof."

"Weren't no trouble, m'm. All the snow's melted off it so it weren't slippery or anything."

When she didn't answer, he hesitated, then added, "I'm sorry I didn't find the knife what stabbed that Porter bloke."

She looked up then, and managed a smile. "That's all right, Samuel. No doubt the constable will want to take a look after the New Year. Maybe they'll find something that will help them figure out who killed Mr. Porter."

"Yes, m'm." He started for the door then turned back. "You don't think it were Roland, do you, m'm? I mean, he was a good lad. Really helpful and nice to the guests. I never once seen him lose his temper. Not once. I just can't think of him killing someone, honest I can't."

"Don't worry, Samuel." Cecily laid the card down. "I'm quite sure Roland wasn't responsible for what happened to Mr. Porter."

Samuel gave her a satisfied nod and left the room.

Staring at the card lying so innocently on her desk, Cecily wished she hadn't insisted that Baxter return to his office. Now that she had something urgent they needed to discuss, he was on his way to the city.

Sighing, she tucked the card into the pocket of her skirt. It would just have to wait until he came home again. Though something told her she'd have a great deal of trouble twiddling her thumbs until that moment.

Midafternoons were normally quiet in the Pennyfoot kitchen. After the delicate china dishes had been washed and stacked away in the cupboards, and the dining room tables laid with fresh white tablecloths, sparkling crystal, and heavy silverware, everyone had an hour or so respite before the mad rush to serve the evening meal.

This afternoon, however, Doris had caused quite a stir by bringing Elise Boulanger to meet the kitchen staff. Gertie's amusement knew no bounds as she watched the celebrated singer charm everyone.

Especially when Doris introduced her friend to Michel, who did his best to impress the young woman with his French. Gertie had to laugh at his shocked expression when Elise answered with a torrent of French phrases. Gertie knew he had no idea what any of them meant, and she really enjoyed his attempts to hide it from the vivacious singer.

Even Reggie and Lawrence seemed enamored of the glamorous visitor, though Reggie paid just as much attention to Doris, much to Gertie's delight.

"You've got an admirer," she told Doris later, when she

saw her in the hallway. "That Reggie's face really glowed when he was talking to you."

Doris laughed. "I didn't think anyone would notice me with Elise in the room. She always attracts attention wherever she goes."

Gertie sighed. "It must be exciting, singing on the stage and having lots of admirers lining up to meet you. Who'd have thought when you first came to the Pennyfoot you'd end up a famous singer. Though you always did have a lovely voice for singing."

"Thank you, Gertie." Doris's shy smile lit up her face. "It is exciting, I suppose, but it can be really lonely, too. Sometimes I remember the days I worked here and wish I were back. Life was so much more simple then."

"Go on." Gertie shoved her with her shoulder. "You know you wouldn't change places with any of us. I bet your friend Elise wouldn't want to leave the stage. Was she born in Paris, then?"

Doris looked up and down the dimly lit hallway, then leaned toward Gertie. "She's not really French. Though don't let on I told you. I mentioned it once to Madam and although Elise laughed she told me off afterward."

"I won't say nothing." Gertie glanced over her shoulder. "So where does she come from then?"

"She's a Cockney, born in the East End of London. Her name isn't really Elise Boulanger. It's Elsie Baker. She changed the letters around in her first name, and Boulanger is French for baker."

Gertie chuckled. "Well, don't tell Michel that. He thinks

she's French, and he felt really silly when he didn't understand what she said. She knows a lot more French than he does."

"She's had a lot more practice."

"I think Michel's got a crush on her. I've never heard him stutter like that before."

Doris moved a little closer. "Well, if Michel is hoping to capture Elise's attention, he's bound for a disappointment. She has her eye on someone else in this hotel, and what she wants, she usually gets. Though she may be aiming her sights a little high this time."

Sensing an intriguing scandal, Gertie was all ears. "Go on with you! Who is it then?"

Doris shook her head. "I can't say. She'd be furious if I said anything. Besides, it could cause a lot of trouble if anyone knew about it. I wouldn't want to cause embarrassment for the gentleman. Some people would be shocked if they knew he was interested in a common music hall singer."

Several feet away, Cecily stood back in the shadows, one hand grasping her throat. She hadn't meant to eavesdrop, but in the quiet of the afternoon the women's voices had carried down the hallway. *She has her eye on someone else in this hotel, and what she wants, she usually gets.*

Ridiculous, of course, but she couldn't help remembering Baxter's expression when he'd come face-to-face with Elise Boulanger in the lobby.

He never had explained what he was doing so far out of his way the night he'd met her in London. Nor had he satisfactorily explained why he'd told Cecily he was working late that night, when obviously he'd left earlier than usual to keep the mysterious appointment.

Feeling dispirited, Cecily made her way back to her office. She trusted her husband implicitly, of course. Still, men would be men, and Elise Boulanger was an extremely attractive young woman.

Impatient with her troublesome thoughts, she sat at her desk and withdrew the card from her pocket. She needed something to occupy her thoughts until Baxter returned home and she had at least two hours to kill until her duties once more claimed her time.

Without giving herself a chance to change her mind, she reached for the bell pull. Baxter might well be displeased with her, but if her suspicions were correct then the matter couldn't wait. Her husband would just have to accept that she had no choice but to pursue the issue at the earliest opportunity.

A few minutes later Samuel knocked on her door. "I need you to get a trap ready for me," she told him. "I need to pay a visit to the George and Dragon."

Samuel's face would have been comical if she'd been in a lighter mood. "The George, m'm? In the middle of the afternoon?"

"I find the middle of the afternoon to be most convenient when I need a private conversation with a publican."

He still seemed mystified. "You want to talk to Bernie Milligan?"

Cecily decided she had no choice but to take him into her confidence. "The card you found on the roof this morning." She held it up to him. "It was attached to a room key.

Every room key for our Christmas guests has one attached. It was Madeline's idea, welcoming guests to the Christmas festivities."

Samuel shook his head. "How did it get up there on the roof?"

"That is exactly what I want to know. The only people, besides Philip, of course, who would have these cards in their possession would be guests of this hotel."

Samuel's eyes widened. "You think maybe the killer dropped it?"

"I think it's entirely possible, yes. I can't imagine how else it got up there."

"But then that means . . ."

Cecily finished the sentence for him. "That means the killer is very likely one of our guests. I think it's time we found out a little more about Sid Porter, and just who might want him dead."

Now Samuel looked worried. "Mr. Baxter is not going to like you going off by yourself, m'm. He won't like that at all."

Cecily rose. "Unfortunately, Mr. Baxter isn't here to accompany me. Besides, I won't be by myself, Samuel. I'll have you with me. Mr. Baxter will just have to understand that I had no time to waste."

She could tell by her manager's expression that he wasn't convinced. Nevertheless, she'd made up her mind. She'd just have to deal with her husband later.

CHAPTER
❁ 7 ❁

Gertie had been looking forward to spending some time with her twins that afternoon, so she wasn't too happy when Pansy called out to her as she was crossing the lobby.

Changing direction, she noticed the aspidistra was safely back in its corner, looking none the worse for wear after its adventure.

Pansy had that wild staring look on her face again, and Gertie hoped it wasn't more bad news. "What's the matter now?" she demanded, sounding as irritable as she felt. It had been one problem after another lately.

"Someone took the carpet sweeper," Pansy said, looking over her shoulder as if she expected someone to come up behind her. "It's disappeared."

Gertie didn't know whether to laugh or beat her head

against a wall. "Disappeared. I suppose next you're going to tell me the clown ghost took it."

Pansy twisted her apron in her hands. "I tell you, that Sid Porter is trying to tell us who killed him."

Gertie stared at her, then let out a belly laugh. "So that's why he put the aspidistra in Chubby's bed. She were the one what killed him. What'd she do, beat him over the bloody head with her rolling pin, then stab him with Michel's carving knife?"

Pansy's lips pinched into a thin line. "This ain't funny, Gertie. Someone killed Sid Porter and Samuel says as how it weren't Roland, but someone else in the hotel what did it."

Gertie stopped laughing. "You're getting awful bleeding friendly with Samuel all of a sudden, ain't you? What else did he tell you?"

"Just that he's taking Madam down to the George and Dragon. She wants to talk to Bernie about Sid Porter." Once more she glanced fearfully over her shoulder. "I know some-one that didn't like Sid. I heard them shouting at each other."

Gertie eyed her with suspicion. "Who was he shouting at then?"

"That bloke that just moved to room eleven. Mr. Atkins. He's the miserable one with the red nose."

Gertie shook her head. "Never heard of him."

"Well, anyway, they was arguing something fierce, they was. I thought Sid was going to hit him."

"Wait a minute." Gertie moved closer to her. "How'd you know Sid Porter?"

"I told you. Me boyfriend, Ned. He knows him. He

pointed him out to me outside the George and Dragon. Said as how he was telling everyone he was going to come down the Pennyfoot Hotel chimney. Ned said as how Sid was showing off 'cos he was getting paid a lot of money to do it."

Gertie frowned. "So where was Sid when he was shouting at the bloke in room eleven?"

"On the top floor. Mrs. Fortescue was there with Sid. She's the one what hired him to go down the chimney. I heard them talking about Sid having been up on the roof to see what the chimney was like before saying he'd climb down it. Anyway, Mrs. Fortescue left him and went downstairs when Mr. Atkins came along. Just as well. She'd have gone into a dead faint if she'd heard how they was talking to each other. Terrible language, it were. Not for a lady's ears, I can tell you."

"Where was you when all this was going on, then?"

"I was cleaning a room, weren't I. I could hear them shouting from inside. I peeked out to see who were making all that noise and I saw the bloke with the red nose. I wonder what he was doing up there. Of course, now that he's moved, he's next to that toff you fancy."

Gertie felt her cheeks warming. "I don't know what you're talking about."

"'Course you do. Everyone knows you get the flutters every time you set eyes on Mr. Westhaven."

"I never heard such nonsense!" Gertie had raised her voice, causing a young woman at the desk to glance her way. Lowering it again, she muttered fiercely, "And you'd better find that carpet sweeper before Mrs. Chubb wakes up, or you'll be in hot water. The dining room has to be swept before the guests come down for supper."

"I can't sweep it without a sweeper."

"Then you'd better find your flipping ghost and get it back." Gertie glanced at the grandfather clock. "I've got me twins waiting for me, and I've wasted enough blinking time as it is. That floor had better be bloody swept by the time I get back."

She stalked off, unable to dismiss the creepy feeling that somehow, somewhere, something really odd was going on in the Pennyfoot.

Samuel sat on the driver's seat, his whip in one hand as he urged the horses into a brisk trot. On the creaking leather seat behind him, Cecily wondered if she'd made a mistake, insisting on driving across the downs on such a blustery afternoon.

The thick scarf she'd tied over her hat and under her chin muffled Samuel's words as he flung them back over his shoulder. They were impossible to hear above the loud clatter of horses' hooves on the hard surface of the Esplanade. She leaned forward, heedless of the salty wind blowing hard across the ocean. "What did you say, Samuel?"

Samuel raised his voice so she could hear him more clearly. "I said Mr. Baxter is going to be upset with me for taking you to the pub, m'm. Perhaps it would be better if we don't tell him about this little trip."

"He's bound to find out, sooner or later. Please don't worry about it, Samuel. I'm sure Mr. Baxter will understand when I explain it all to him."

"Yes, m'm." He added something else, but the wind snatched his words away.

She abandoned the conversation and leaned back, determined to forget her worries for a while and enjoy the excursion. In spite of the frosty wind and threatening clouds, she had to admit she felt a sense of relief to be out of the hotel for a while. Too much had been happening, and she needed time to sort everything through in her mind.

The trap rattled and bounced down the high street, past rows of shops with their bay windows full of Christmas wares. For the next few minutes she enjoyed looking at all the displays as they sailed by—the plum puddings with their sprigs of holly in Dolly's tea shop, the geese hanging by their feet in the butcher's shop, the baskets piled high with fruit and nuts in the greengrocers, and, best of all, the boxes of Christmas crackers in the stationer's window.

Cecily smiled, thinking of the fun everyone had pulling the crackers, each person taking an end of the brightly colored paper tubes and tugging until they snapped and split apart, spilling out a trinket and a printed joke.

How she looked forward to sharing all the Christmas traditions with her beloved husband and their friends. If only she didn't have this worry on her mind, she would be sublimely happy right now.

Minutes later the horses' hooves thudded on grass as they swept across the downs. The fresh, clean air from the stormy North Sea filled her lungs and chased the cobwebs away. She began to feel a sense of peace, as she always did when riding across the expansive downs.

The view of the heaving ocean soothed her frayed nerves, and she leaned back with a heightened sense of well-being. It had been some time since she'd visited the George and

Dragon, and she looked forward to it with a little glow of pleasure.

The pub had changed hands once again since she'd taken over the management of the Pennyfoot. The new owner, Bernie Milligan, was a pleasant giant of a man, always ready with a joke and a smile.

It would be considered unseemly for her to call on the publican in the company of her stable manager during opening hours. During the afternoon closing, however, a different light would be put upon her visit, since they would be received in the man's private quarters, rather than as customers of the pub.

That didn't erase the fact that Baxter would probably be outraged at her taking matters into her own hands once more. Something she'd have to deal with when he arrived home. After all, with the constable on his way to Northampton, she had little choice. Then again, she still had issues to discuss with him over his own behavior lately.

All too quickly the red roof of the George and Dragon came into view. Anxious now to have her conversation with Bernie Milligan, she leaned forward in expectation.

Samuel reined in the horses and their steady clip-clop slowed to a clattering stop. The trap jerked, sending her forward, and she put out a gloved hand to steady herself.

Samuel leapt down and offered her his hand. She accepted his help and stepped down onto the cobbled courtyard. Bernie must have heard the trap arrive. He stood in the doorway, an expansive grin stretching his mouth wide.

"Pleasure to see you, Mrs. Baxter. To what do I owe this unexpected visit?"

"I've come for a small glass of your delicious ale and a moment of your time." She lifted her skirts and stepped across a puddle. "I do hope I'm not inconveniencing you?"

"Not at all. Not at all." He nodded at Samuel. "I'll be happy to serve you, though it will have to be in my private parlor. Can't afford to break the licensing laws, now can we."

"That's quite all right, Samuel will accompany me." She stepped through the door into the cozy little room that had been warmed by the glowing coals in the fireplace. The contrast to the nippy air outside brought a tingling to her cheeks.

She chose an armchair close to the fireplace and removed the scarf that held her hat in place. Samuel discreetly seated himself by the door, his cap in his hands. Bernie disappeared and returned a moment or two later with a foaming glass of ale in each hand. He handed one to Samuel and carried the other over to Cecily.

"I assume you've come about the murder," he said, as Cecily took the tankard from him.

She looked up at him in surprise. "You've heard about it already?"

"Yes, m'm. P.C. Northcott stopped in here on his way to the railway station. Just ten minutes before afternoon closing time. Gave him enough time to swallow a pint before going off to meet his missus."

"I see. What exactly did he tell you?"

Bernie looked uncomfortable. "Didn't say too much, m'm. Just that one of your footman stuck a knife in Sid Porter and then fell of the roof and killed himself." Bernie shook his head. "Can't say I'm surprised. That Sid was a rotter all right.

Turn 'is own mother in for a shilling, that he would've." He coughed, then added hurriedly, "Not that I should speak ill of the dead, m'm."

"That's quite all right, Mr. Milligan. Under the circumstances, the more truthful you are about the unfortunate man, the better." She took a sip of the ale, then set it down beside her. "So please, tell me all you know about Mr. Sid Porter."

Bernie sat down opposite her, looking worried. "I don't know that much about him. Liked his beer, he did. Could put them away, all right. Never went out of here without at least three or four pints inside him."

"How did he come to apply for the job of the Pennyfoot's Father Christmas?"

"Oh, well, that one's easy. Mrs. Fortescue asked me to pin a notice up in the bars. Sid were always looking for odd jobs. Never had a real line of work, he didn't. He'd work on the sands mostly in the summer, leading the donkeys for donkey rides, selling balloons, helping the Punch and Judy man, whatever he could do for a shilling. I've even seen him shoveling the streets after the horses. Not my idea of an enjoyable job, I can tell you."

Cecily had to agree. "You say you're not surprised Mr. Porter came to a bad end. Are you telling me the man had enemies?"

Bernie nodded. "Plenty of 'em. I know quite a few blokes Sid did out of a bob or two. He was a shady chap, always on the make, if you get my meaning. Clever with his hands, he was. Boasted he could open any lock. I always reckoned that if one of the blokes he'd robbed didn't get him, the constables would. There was more than one gent come here looking for him."

"Oh, my, he sounds quite the disreputable character."

"That he is, m'm. When I heard he dressed up as a clown to amuse the kiddies, well, it gave me the shivers, it did. Wouldn't want the likes of him hanging around my young-sters, I can tell you. He kept boasting about being a Father Christmas, like it were a joke. Begging your pardon, m'm, but you couldn't have picked a worse bloke for the job."

"So it appears. Unfortunately, however, I didn't have a hand in the hiring for the assignment. Would you know of anyone in particular who might have had reason to hurt Mr. Porter?"

Bernie gave her a sharp look. "You saying that your foot-man wasn't the one what did Sid in?"

Cecily took another sip of her ale before answering. "I'm just trying to find out exactly what happened up on my roof. I would hate the memory of that young boy to be marred by this dreadful crime if he is innocent. His parents deserve to know the truth."

"Yes, indeed, m'm. Couldn't agree more. Well, now, let me think." His forehead creased into a frown. After a few anxious moments, he added, "I can only think of one bloke what might have had it in for Sid enough to finish him off. Ned Barlow."

Samuel made an odd sound and sat up on his chair as if he'd been stung.

Cecily took note, but her attention remained on Bernie's face. "Who is Ned Barlow?"

"One of my customers. Comes in here all the time. At least, he has since he got out of jail. He and Sid got in a right old battle a few nights ago. Something about Sid being the one what turned him in to the bobbies and got him put in the clink."

"I see. Do you happen to know where this Mr. Barlow resides?"

"Can't say as I do, m'm." Bernie's worried frown deepened. "Mrs. Baxter, it's none of my business, but you're a nice lady, and I wouldn't want nothing bad to happen to you. I wouldn't mess around with the likes of Ned Barlow. He's not a nice person, m'm. He could be really dangerous. That's all I'm saying."

"Thank you, Mr. Milligan. I appreciate your concern." She reached for the silk purse tied to her belt. "How much do I owe you for the ale?"

"That's all right, m'm. It's on me." His frown transformed into a smile.

"So kind of you." Cecily rose from the chair and both men shot to their feet. "I'm deeply grateful to you for being so helpful. If you should think of anything else that might help clear up this matter, I hope you will be so kind as to inform me?"

"Of course, m'm. Anything I can do."

He held the door for her and she stepped outside. Spots of cold rain stung her cheeks and she tied the warm scarf once more over her hat. "Thank you again, Mr. Milligan," she said, as Samuel stepped out behind her.

"My pleasure, m'm." The publican touched his forehead with his fingers. "You will be careful, won't you."

"I shall indeed." She smiled at him, then followed Samuel to where the horses waited, impatiently stamping their feet.

They tossed their heads and steam erupted from their nostrils as Cecily climbed back into the trap. With a gracious wave of her hand at Bernie Milligan, she settled back in her seat.

"Back to the hotel, m'm?" Samuel asked cheerily as the horses started back across the downs.

"I don't think so, Samuel." Cecily leaned forward to make sure he could hear her words. "I'd like to visit Ned Barlow. I think you know where he lives?"

Samuel took his time answering her, which confirmed her suspicions. "Me, m'm? Whatever makes you think I know the bloke?"

"I saw your expression when Mr. Milligan mentioned his name. I do hope you're going to be truthful with me, Samuel."

"I might know of him, m'm." He said something else, but once more the wind plucked his words away and she didn't catch them.

"What was that, Samuel?"

"I said, Ned Barlow is keeping company with Pansy, m'm. She happened to mention his name to me, that's all."

Cecily felt a pang of dismay. Surely that sweet child couldn't be attached to a common criminal? "Did she happen to mention where he lived?"

Again Samuel's pause gave her hope. "She might have done, m'm. I'm not really sure."

"I suggest you think hard, Samuel. It's important that I talk to the man."

"I don't think Mr. Baxter would be too happy with me as it is." Even over the thud of horses' hooves and the creaking trap, Cecily could hear his anxiety. "I'm quite sure he wouldn't want me taking you to no dangerous criminal's house, of that I'm quite sure."

"Samuel." Cecily put as much authority in her voice as she could manage. "For whom do you work? Me or Mr. Baxter?"

"You, m'm," came the unhappy answer.

"And how long have you worked for me, Samuel?"

"Close on ten years, m'm, but—"

"Then stop concerning yourself about Mr. Baxter and worry about what I might say if you don't take me to see Mr. Barlow this minute."

"Yes, m'm."

She had to feel sorry for the young man. Samuel had incurred Baxter's wrath more than once for obeying her orders, despite her best efforts to prevent the altercations. Yet he remained loyal, and she knew he would rather die than let her down when she needed him.

She only hoped she wasn't leading him into more trouble. As long as there remained a doubt, however, that Roland was in any way responsible for Sid Porter's death, she felt compelled to seek out the truth.

Anyone who worked for her deserved as much, and if she had to take a risk or two in order to clear the boy's name then so be it. She would just have to trust, as she always did, in luck and judgment to get her through.

Having enjoyed a pleasant hour with her twins, Gertie wore a smile on her face as she walked back to the kitchen. She'd even had time to make sure her cap sat straight on her head, and that she'd tied her apron strings in a neat bow in the middle of her back.

The scent of pine hung thick in the lobby as she walked across the blue Axminster carpet. Madeline had set up another Christmas tree—not as big as the one in the library, but it was pretty all the same with its gilded walnuts and colorful paper chains.

Lillian and James had been bubbling with excitement all afternoon at the thought of what Father Christmas might be bringing them. It wouldn't be as jolly as last year, what with Ross gone and all, but Madam had always been good to the twins, them being her godchildren, and Gertie felt reasonably sure everyone would have a good time, in spite of all the strange things that had been happening lately.

Deep in thought, she failed to see the gentleman in front of her until she'd almost bumped into him. She started back, her heart thumping at the sight of his handsome face. "Mr. Westhaven, sir. You gave me quite a stir."

"I do beg your pardon."

He gave her a little bow, the kind that gentlemen gave to real ladies, and it thoroughly enchanted her. "Oh, it's all right, sir. I should've been looking where I was going."

He smiled at that, and she felt relieved that his bad mood seemed to have disappeared. "I was wondering if I might trouble you to arrange for a bottle of fine wine to be brought to my table this evening."

Some of her pleasure evaporated. Obviously he expected a visitor. The lady friend, perhaps, that he'd been moping about since he'd arrived. "Of course, sir. I'll be happy to bring you a bottle."

"A Beaujolais, I think."

"Yes, sir." She didn't have the faintest idea what he meant, but she didn't intend to let him know that.

"Or perhaps you could recommend something from your fine cellar?"

Taken by surprise, she could only stutter. "What—me—sir? Oh, no, I couldn't. Our guests don't drink that much wine, you see. They drink sherry, or brandy. I'll ask Michel, the chef. He should know a good one to bring you."

His sparkling eyes made her feel quite faint. "I'd be much obliged. Oh, and I apologize for my disposition earlier. I had received some upsetting news. I should not have spoken to you so harshly."

"Not at all, sir. I didn't mind. Really I didn't."

He looked at her for a moment longer, as if he wanted to say something else, then gave her a brief nod and departed quickly for the stairs. Only after he'd disappeared did she notice the bunch of mistletoe hanging right above where he'd been standing. What she wouldn't have given for the chance to take advantage of that. With a rueful sigh, she made her way back to the kitchen.

"Are you sure Mr. Barlow lives up there?" Cecily looked up at the darkened windows of the regal townhouse. "The drapes are fully drawn."

"Per'aps he works nights and sleeps in the daytime." Samuel helped her down from the trap. "Pansy says as how he lives over the ironmonger's shop and Wallace's is the only ironmonger in the high street."

"Very well, if you're sure."

"The only thing I'm sure about, if you don't mind me saying, m'm, is that you shouldn't be here. Mr. Baxter'll have me guts for garters when he hears about this, that he will."

"I do wish you'd stop worrying yourself over what Baxter might say." Cecily lifted her skirts and stepped briskly over to the door. "Let us see if Mr. Barlow is home."

Since she had no occasion to visit an ironmonger, Cecily was not acquainted with Tom Wallace, the owner of the busy little shop.

When Samuel introduced them, however, the little man beamed in recognition. "Yes, yes, of course. The Pennyfoot Hotel. I've seen you many times in the village, Mrs. Baxter. May I say how good it is to have you back in Badgers End."

Cecily thanked him, then asked, "I'd like a word with the gentleman who lives upstairs. Do you happen to know if he's at home?"

The ironmonger's pleasant smile vanished. "Begging your pardon, m'm, but that ain't no gentleman. Been in the clink, he has. I don't like the thought of him hovering right above my head, so to speak, but what can I do? I just lease the shop. I don't have no say what goes on upstairs."

"I quite understand." Cecily did her best to appear sympathetic. "But is Mr. Barlow at home?"

"Far as I know, he is." Tom Wallace nudged his chin up at the ceiling. "Heard him walking about a short while ago and I haven't seen him leave." He pointed at a door in the back of the shop. "Just go on through there and up them stairs. His door is on the first floor, right in front of you."

"Thank you, Mr. Wallace. Come along, Samuel." Cecily marched to the door, followed by her reluctant stable manager.

"I still think we should wait until Mr. Baxter can come with us," Samuel muttered, though his tone implied he'd wasted his breath.

"Mr. Baxter won't be home until much later this evening." Cecily stepped through the door and began climbing the stairs. "I just want to ask Mr. Barlow a question or two. There isn't much that could happen to us with all those people milling about below."

"I wish I could believe that." Samuel tramped up the stairs behind her.

Rather than admit she felt a little uncertain herself, Cecily chose not to answer him. Instead, she climbed the rest of the way in silence. At the top of the stairs she saw a door in dire need of paint. Lifting her hand, she rapped her knuckles against the wooden panel.

Hearing no sound of movement from within, she let out a sigh of frustration. It seemed this would be a wasted visit. Now she would have to return at a later time. Just for good measure, she rapped again, and this time a harsh voice sounded from inside the room.

"Who is it? What do you want?"

"My name is Cecily Baxter," she called out.

Samuel uttered a soft groan.

After a short pause, the voice called out, "From the Pennyfoot?"

"Yes." Remembering something, she added, "I believe you are acquainted with one of my maids, Pansy Watson?"

Another pause, then she heard the sound of a bolt being drawn back. Bracing herself, she waited for Ned Barlow to open the door.

CHAPTER
❁ 8 ❁

"What about Pansy, then?" Ned Barlow's heavy-lidded eyes stared at Cecily through the narrow opening. His head almost touched the top of the door frame. With his drooping mustache and stubbled chin, he managed to convey a sinister air that made her quite uncomfortable.

"This isn't about Pansy, exactly." Cecily beckoned to Samuel to come closer. "I wonder if I could have a word with you, Mr. Barlow?"

"So what's it about, then?"

His harsh tone did nothing to ease Cecily's apprehension. "I'm here to ask about Sid Porter. I believe he was an acquaintance of yours." She glanced at Samuel, who shook his head fiercely at her.

After a long pause, Ned Barlow muttered, "He weren't no friend of mine."

"You are aware, I suppose, that Mr. Porter is dead?"

"I heard he fell down the chimney."

"Yes, well, someone stabbed him with a knife before he fell."

"And what's that supposed to do with me?"

The man's belligerence unnerved her. What on earth was Pansy thinking to associate with such a man? "I simply wondered if you could help me find out what happened. Perhaps you know of someone who might want to hurt Mr. Porter?"

She waited several seconds for his answer, and then the door opened wider.

"If you're thinking I was the one that stabbed him, you're dead wrong." Ned's dark eyes glinted in the glow from the gas lamp above his head. "I never touched him." His gaze switched to Samuel, as if noticing him for the first time, then back to Cecily. "I suppose someone told you about the bust-up I had with him in the pub last week."

"Someone did mention it to me, yes." She watched his face. "I understand Mr. Porter helped put you in prison."

Ned's expression turned nasty. "He got what he deserved, but I didn't kill him. I have to admit, I thought about it, but someone got to him first." He lifted his hand and gingerly touched the tip of his nose as if it pained him to do so. "Can't say as I'm sorry he's a goner. The killer did me one big favor as far as I'm concerned."

Noticing the small round cut on the end of his nose, Cecily wondered if he'd received it during the fight in the bar. At that precise moment, the gas lamp above her spluttered and went out, leaving the hallway in semidarkness. Startled, she looked up, while Samuel's breath hissed out between his teeth.

"It's time we went, m'm," he said, throwing an uneasy glance over his shoulder.

Remembering his talk of ghosts, Cecily felt her spine tingle.

"Dratted lamp. Always going out." Ned Barlow stepped out into the hallway and looked up at it.

His height intimidated her further, and she took a step backward. She almost tripped over Samuel, who stood too close behind her.

"I'll have to take a look at it." Ned's lean face looked even more menacing in the darkened shadows. "If I wait for the landlord we could all be blown to smithereens." He reached up to the base of the lamp and began unscrewing it. "Good job I know about these things. Gas can be tricky to play with. Before I went inside I used to install these gas lamps in buildings. Now no one wants me messing with them."

Her fears began to ease a little. Hoping to learn something useful, Cecily tried to encourage him in conversation. "That must have been quite interesting."

"Yeah." He glanced down at her. "They're coming out with some right fancy lamps nowadays. Like the ones you got in the Pennyfoot Hotel. They didn't have those kind when I was working with them."

"Yes, I do agree. They are most elegant." Out of the corner of her eye Cecily saw Samuel making anxious faces at her. "As I mentioned, Mr. Barlow, I hoped you might know of someone who might have wanted to harm Mr. Porter.

Perhaps someone you overheard in the bar of the George and Dragon?"

Ned Barlow lowered his arms. "I don't know of no one I can put my mind to."

"Mr. Porter never mentioned anyone he might be concerned about?"

The man's penetrating gaze bored into hers. "Mrs. Baxter, take my advice. Leave well enough alone. Let the constables worry about who killed Sid Porter. You'll live longer."

"We have to go, m'm," Samuel said, with a quiet note of desperation.

Reluctantly, Cecily thanked the man and descended the dark stairwell, with Samuel hot on her heels. The daylight had faded as she emerged onto the street. Rain spattered on the backs of the horses and dripped from their flanks.

Fastening her scarf more tightly under her chin, Cecily climbed into the trap. She looked forward to getting back to the hotel and the warmth of her sitting room.

"I'll pull the hood over," Samuel said, starting for the back of the trap.

"Never mind. It's already quite wet in here." Cecily wiped her gloved hand across the seat. "I'm anxious to return to the Pennyfoot and it's not too far now."

"Very well, m'm." Samuel climbed aboard and took up the reins. Within minutes, they had reached the Esplanade and were in sight of the Pennyfoot's white walls.

The cold, damp folds of Cecily's skirts slapped around her ankles as she hurried up the steps of the hotel. Philip's eyes opened wide when he saw her, reminding her that she must look quite a spectacle with her dripping hat and soggy scarf.

She made straight for her suite and pulled off her wet clothes. After dressing again in a warm wool skirt and crisp white blouse, she uncoiled her hair and redressed it.

Satisfied that she at least looked presentable, she dropped her damp clothing into the laundry chute before hurrying down the stairs to her office.

There she rang the bell for a maid, and directed the young girl who answered her to send Pansy to her office. A few minutes later a light tap on the door announced her kitchen maid's presence.

Pansy seemed nervous, and sat on the very edge of her chair, her hands twisting and tugging the folds of her apron.

"First of all," Cecily began, feeling more than a little sorry for the child, "I'd like to hear about the ghost you claim to have seen."

Pansy's bottom lip trembled, but she managed to sound composed when she answered. "It were a clown, m'm. I saw it up on the top floor. Creeping along, it were. Scared me near to death, it did."

"What made you think it was a ghost?"

" 'Cos one minute it were there, and then it weren't. It disappeared right before me eyes."

"I see." Cecily thought for a minute. "Can you remember exactly when you saw this clown?"

"Yes, m'm. It were yesterday, almost dinnertime. It were after the children left the party to go home. I'd just finished sweeping the dining room and laying the tables, and I was taking the carpet sweeper back to the broom closet. I heard the bells first."

"Bells?"

"Yes, m'm. The ghost had little bells down the front of its costume, like buttons, only they were bells. Like the ones they have on horses in their harness, only smaller."

"Did you speak to him?"

"Speak to the ghost? No, m'm, I didn't." Pansy shivered. "I didn't have time to speak to it. I shut me eyes and pinched meself, in case I were dreaming and when I opened me eyes up again, it was gone."

"He made no sound, other than the bells?"

"No, m'm. I know who it is, though."

"You recognized him?"

"Well, sort of. I couldn't tell what it looked like, what with all that paint on its face, but I know it were Sid Porter, what got himself killed yesterday."

Cecily stared at the child. In heaven's name with what sort of people had she been keeping company? "You were acquainted with Mr. Porter?"

"Oh, no, m'm. Not me." Pansy shook her head. "But I know he used to be a clown because me boyfriend told me. And all these things what have been moving around, well, it's the ghost what's doing it. It's Sid Porter, trying to tell us who killed him, I know it is."

Cecily lifted her chin. After the distraction of talking with the unpleasant Ned Barlow, she'd forgotten about the incident with the cumbersome plant. "Ah, yes, I believe Samuel mentioned something about the aspidistra being found in Mrs. Chubb's room."

"It were in her bed, m'm."

"And she has no idea who put it there?"

"I told you, m'm. It were the ghost. Nobody else could have picked it up and put it there. Even if he could have carried it all that way, we would have seen him go past the kitchen."

Cecily had to admit the feat would have been difficult, if not impossible.

"That's not all of it, m'm, neither." Pansy paused, then added in a rush, "There's Michel's knife what was stuck in the ceiling, and now the carpet sweeper's gone and—"

"Carpet sweeper?" Cecily shook her head. "This is ridiculous. There has to be a simple explanation. Have you searched the hotel?"

"Yes, m'm. Me and the other maids looked all over." Pansy seemed as if any minute she would burst into tears. "The last I seen of it, it were on the top floor landing. I left it there when I ran away from the ghost. Now it's gone. I tell you, m'm. It were the ghost what took it."

"Well," Cecily said briskly, "we shall just have to hunt him down and make him cease disrupting everything. We have a hotel to run and Christmas festivities to organize and we simply cannot have a ghost running amok among us."

"No, m'm. I mean, yes, m'm."

Without warning, the door behind Pansy opened, and she shot off her chair with a little shriek.

Baxter appeared in the doorway, looking rather put out. "What on earth?"

"Sorry, sir." Pansy fled past him and out the door, leaving him staring after her.

"Darling!" Cecily rose and hurried over to him, her hands outstretched in welcome. "You're home early. How nice!"

"I couldn't concentrate with this blasted murder hanging over us." Baxter jabbed a thumb over his shoulder. "What's the matter with Pansy?"

"She's been seeing ghosts." In spite of her anxiety, Cecily had to smile at his expression. "Come and sit down and I'll tell you all about it."

He pulled her to him and placed a warm kiss on her cheek. "I'm not going back to the city until after this matter is settled. I don't like the idea of you being here alone with a possible murderer hanging around. You're far too fond of running off somewhere dangerous and getting into trouble."

He waited for her to sit down then pulled a chair up next to her. "Now tell me what all this nonsense is about a ghost."

Cecily sighed. "I don't know if any of this has anything to do with Sid Porter's murder, but I have to admit, I'm baffled by everything that's happened."

Baxter's face turned wary. "I have a feeling this isn't exactly going to lighten my day."

Quickly she repeated everything Pansy had told her. "It's my guess we have an intruder in the hotel. Dressed as a clown for some strange reason."

"Well, I'm happy to hear you don't believe in the ghost theory." Baxter leaned back with a frown. "Am I right in thinking you believe this clown fellow is the person who killed Sid Porter?"

"I think it's entirely possible. Though why he went to all the trouble of moving an aspidistra and stealing a carpet sweeper I can't imagine."

"He must have muscles the size of mountains," Baxter said wryly. "I'd like to know how he moved that plant. It takes three of the maids just to slide it out of the corner."

"Very strange." Cecily thought for a moment. "There's something else I should tell you. Samuel and I went to see Bernie Milligan this afternoon."

She'd braced herself for Baxter's scowl. Even so, she winced when his gray eyes turned icy. "How many times have I told you not to go to the George and Dragon without me? You know how I feel about it. It just isn't fitting for a lady to visit a public house unescorted."

"I was escorted. Samuel came with me."

"A stable manager."

"A very capable stable manager."

"Who deliberately ignores my wishes."

"It wasn't Samuel's fault. I ordered him to take me."

Baxter sighed. "I wish you could understand how much I worry about you and your penchant for plunging into unfortunate situations."

She leaned forward and patted his knee. "I do know, Bax. I appreciate your concern, really I do. You know I would not take any unnecessary risks."

"No, I do not know that. You have done so in the past."

"And learned my lesson."

To her relief, his face smoothed out. "Well, did you learn anything useful from your ill-advised trip?"

"When I asked Mr. Milligan if he knew anyone who might have reason to harm Sid Porter, he mentioned a man by the name of Ned Barlow, a rather nasty fellow who just happens to be keeping company with Pansy."

Baxter raised his eyebrows. "A coincidence?"

"I certainly hope so, for Pansy's sake." Cecily hesitated, then added slowly, "I don't think she should be involved with a man like that. He's been in prison, for one thing, though I don't know what he did. He's a big man with fierce black eyes, and quite menacing."

Baxter wrinkled his brow. "Just how did you make the acquaintance of this man?"

"Samuel and I paid him a visit." She saw his lips tighten and added quickly, "We were perfectly safe. He lives above the ironmonger's shop—"

"Cecily! I absolutely forbid you to pay any more visits to these disreputable reprobates. I am appalled that Samuel allowed this to happen. I shall have a stern word with him at the earliest opportunity."

She lifted her chin. "May I remind you, as I have so often before, that you are in no position to forbid me to do anything. As for Samuel, he followed my orders, as any loyal and competent servant should. And I must insist that you say nothing to him about this."

Ice formed in Baxter's eyes as he answered quietly, "It seems, then, that we are at an impasse. My objections remain. Just keep in mind that your safety is my primary concern."

She melted at once. "I'm so sorry, darling. I know how you hate my little adventures, but you must learn to trust me more. I am quite capable of using caution when necessary."

Baxter tilted his face at the ceiling. "Where have I heard those sentiments before?"

She pulled a wry face. "You worry far too much."

"And you not enough. The price I have to pay, I suppose, for marrying such a willful and disobedient wife."

"You would not have it any other way." She reached for his hand. "Go on. Admit it."

To her relief, his face relaxed in a reluctant smile. "Well, tell me, then, what did this blackguard have to say? I don't suppose he actually admitted to murdering our Father Christmas."

"Of course not. Though he did admit to considering it." She frowned. "I must ask Pansy about him."

"I hardly think it's our place to advise the young lady on her choice of beaus."

"What? Oh, no." She shook her head. "Though I do think I should warn her of the consequences of being seen in public with such an unsavory character. But more than that, there's something else I need to know."

"And that is?"

"Mr. Barlow mentioned our new lamps in the hallway. I don't know how long he was incarcerated, but since they were installed early this year, and Mr. Barlow was released from prison just a few days ago, I wondered how he could have seen them."

"Perhaps Pansy invited him to visit her here."

"That's what I need to ask her."

Baxter's expression changed. "I see what you mean. If he has been in the hotel during the last few days, and if it wasn't at Pansy's invitation . . ."

"Then we need to know the reason for his visit."

"I do hate to keep harping on this subject, but do, please be careful, Cecily. We're dealing with a cold-blooded killer who apparently took a knife up to our roof with the intention of stabbing a man to death. Not the kind of person I care to trust with my wife."

"I will use the utmost caution, darling. I promise."

"Thank you." He rose. "Now, perhaps, we can enjoy an early dinner in our suite for once."

She took his hand and stood with him. "I shall love that. It has been awhile since we've had a leisurely evening. It will be our last, for a time, I'm afraid. The rehearsals for the variety show are being held all day tomorrow since the performance takes place tomorrow night, and the following night the village carolers will be here to entertain us."

"And the night after that is Christmas Eve and the ceremony in the library." Baxter rolled his eyes at the ceiling. "We shall just have to make the most of our evening alone, my dear."

"I heartily agree." She led him to the door. "I'll just have a word with Pansy and then I shall join you upstairs."

He planted a kiss on her lips. "Don't keep me waiting too long, my love."

"I'll be as quick as I can be." She walked with him as far as the stairs, then left him and hurried to the kitchen. Dinner preparations were under way, and maids darted to and fro in response to Mrs. Chubb's sharp orders.

Above the din of clattering dishes, raised voices, and Michel's tuneless singing, Cecily managed to attract Pansy's attention. The young girl scurried over to the door, her face creased with worry.

Shutting out the tantalizing aroma of roasting beef, Cecily closed the door and led Pansy a little way down the hall.

"I understand you are acquainted with a man by the name of Ned Barlow?" she asked without preamble.

Pansy's eyebrows shot up. "Who told you that, m'm? It were Samuel, weren't it. I knew I shouldn't have said nothing to him. He wanted to ask me out, so I told him about Ned." She looked up anxiously into Cecily's face. "Why? Has something happened to him?"

Cecily suppressed the urge to warn the child to stay away from the man. "I just want to know if he's been here to see you, that's all."

"Here? In the hotel? Oh, no, m'm. I wouldn't do that. I wouldn't have him in my room. That's against the rules, it is. I'd never do that."

Aware that the maid was becoming upset, Cecily hastened to reassure her. "It's quite all right, Pansy. I simply thought you might have invited him over to show him the hotel, that's all."

"No, m'm." Pansy shook her head. "I only met Ned a week or so ago when a bunch of us were talking outside the George and Dragon. He walked me home. I've met him twice on the Esplanade, just for a walk and a laugh, but I don't know him well enough to invite him over here."

"I see." Cecily paused, then added, "You are aware that he's just been released from prison?"

Pansy's eyes widened with shock. "Prison, m'm? No, I didn't know that. What he'd do?"

"I really couldn't say. Maybe you should ask him."

Pansy shook her head. "I can't believe it. He seemed so nice and everything. He made me laugh, and he bought me flowers. Nobody's ever bought me flowers before." She gave

Cecily a wistful look. "Are you sure, m'm, that he was in prison?"

Cecily put an arm about the girl's shoulders. "I'm sorry, Pansy. Maybe you should think about accepting Samuel's invitation. He's a very nice young man, you know."

Pansy pouted. "But he's not exciting like Ned."

Why was it, Cecily wondered, that young girls were attracted to the wrong kind of men? That excitement they craved was often their undoing. She could hardly accuse the man of murder without any kind of proof, yet she dreaded the thought of this innocent young woman endangering herself by being in the company of a possible killer.

"Well, now that you know the truth about him," she said, "I hope you will think long and hard before you agree to meet him again."

"Oh, I will, m'm. You can be sure of that."

She would have to be satisfied with that, Cecily told herself as she made her way upstairs. Vowing to do everything she could to hunt down Sid Porter's killer as soon as possible, she headed for her suite to join her husband.

Just before she reached the door she heard someone call out, "Madam?" Turning her head, she saw Gertie hurrying up the stairs toward her.

Panting and holding her middle, Gertie gasped out, "Oh, I'm so glad I caught you, m'm. Pansy just told me something and I thought you should know about it."

Cecily waited, fully expecting Gertie to tell her she'd heard that Pansy's boyfriend had been in prison.

Instead, she was taken aback when Gertie blurted out,

"It's that Mr. Atkins. In room eleven. Pansy heard him having a big argument with Sid Porter the other day."

"Mr. Atkins? Is she certain?"

"Yes, m'm. She said that Sid Porter had gone up to the top floor with Mrs. Fortescue. She took him up on the roof to look at the chimney. Anyway, she left him up there and Mr. Atkins came along and they had this really big argument. Pansy heard it all. I thought you should know about it, seeing as how Sid got killed."

Cecily managed to cover her surprise with a smile. "Did Pansy say what the argument was about?"

"No, m'm. I didn't ask her that. She were worrying about the carpet sweeper being missing and I told her to go and look for it."

"Well, I'm sure it was nothing, but I'll mention it to the constable when he returns. You did the right thing, Gertie. Thank you for telling me."

Gertie beamed at her. "Yes, m'm. I have to run, or Mrs. Chubb'll be breathing down my blooming neck."

Cecily watched her chief housemaid charge back down the stairs in her usual unladylike manner. The news she'd just heard disturbed her. She couldn't imagine how Desmond Atkins could be acquainted with Sid Porter, much less have a reason to argue with him.

She might have put it down to a chance encounter and Mr. Atkins's usual display of short temper, had it not been for where the two men had met.

Given that her cantankerous guest had such an aversion to climbing stairs, he must have had a compelling reason to be on the top floor. If that reason was Sid Porter, she would give a great deal to know exactly what the argument was about.

It was unlikely he would be willing to divulge that information to her. On the other hand, if she could manage to approach his wife alone, she might just find out more about his relationship with the dead man.

Until then, she had a husband waiting for her, and an evening to enjoy. Nothing would be allowed to interfere with that.

CHAPTER
❊ 9 ❊

Later that evening, while Baxter read the newspaper, Cecily did her best to concentrate on her favorite magazine. Her mind kept wandering, however, to Desmond Atkins and his mysterious argument with Sid Porter. When she could no longer calm her thoughts, she dropped the magazine in her lap. "Darling, I wonder if you'd do something for me, to-morrow," she said, as Baxter turned the page of his newspaper. "That is if you have no other plans, of course."

"The only plan I have is to make sure you stay out of harm's way." Baxter folded the newspaper and laid it down. "What would you have me do?"

"I'd like you to look through the register for perhaps the last two or three years to see if Desmond Atkins has ever stayed at the Pennyfoot before this."

Baxter drew his brows together. "Desmond Atkins? Isn't he that bad-tempered fellow you were talking about?"

"Yes." Knowing he would not let the matter rest there, she went on to explain. "He insisted we had given him the wrong room, but it isn't like Philip to make a mistake. He's always so careful to accommodate our guests in their special requests."

"Everyone makes mistakes now and then."

"I suppose so. But I wondered if he's stayed here before in a first-floor room.

Baxter narrowed his gaze. "Does this have anything to do with Porter's murder?"

She did her best to look innocent. "Whatever makes you think that?"

"I know you too well, my darling wife. What makes you think this Atkins fellow could be involved with Sid Porter?"

"Pansy heard Mr. Atkins arguing with him."

"It was my understanding that Mr. Atkins has a penchant for arguing with just about everyone."

"Well, that's so, but I couldn't help wondering if his limp is due to a recent injury." She paused, then added delicately, "Perhaps during a climb over a roof?"

Baxter stared at her, then growled, deep in his throat. "Cecily, you are incorrigible. Your devious mind can find more ways to condemn a man than I can imagine. Just because the man has a short temper and an ugly disposition doesn't make him a murderer."

"Nevertheless, I should like to know if he's stayed here before, and if he specifically requested a first floor room at that time."

"Why don't you simply ask him if he recently injured himself?"

"I don't want to give him the opportunity to lie, and I'd rather he not know I suspect him."

"Well, at least with that I'm in complete agreement." Baxter picked up his newspaper again. "Very well, first thing in the morning I'll go through the ledger."

"Thank you, darling. You are such an accommodating husband."

Baxter merely grunted, letting her know he knew quite well she was humoring him.

Satisfied for the moment, Cecily reached for her magazine. Nothing more could be done until tomorrow. If Sid Porter's ghost was indeed wandering around the hotel, he would have to wait another night for justice to be done.

Phoebe arrived early the next morning, followed soon after by Madeline. Both ladies seemed anxious to begin the rehearsals and took up almost an hour of Cecily's time while they rounded up the performers.

Phoebe, as usual, fretted about her dance troupe, who straggled in at various intervals and continually disrupted the proceedings. Doris and Elise appeared midmorning, just as Cecily prepared to escape from all the chaos.

"You are not going to watch the rehearsal?" Elise asked, as Cecily greeted them both.

"I'm afraid my duties take me away." Cecily gave the woman a cool smile. "I shall be in the audience tonight, of course." She turned to Doris. "I certainly would not want to miss an opportunity to hear you sing. I'm proud to be so well acquainted with someone who has actually sung in front of the king."

Doris laughed. "If you could have seen how hard my knees were shaking you would not be so proud. I could hardly get a word out I was so overwrought."

"I'm sure you sang beautifully."

"She sang like an angel," Elsie said, linking her arm through her friend's. "We both did, *non*?"

"Until Colin Masterson came on stage." Doris giggled. "Then we were both struck dumb."

Cecily pricked up her ears. "You've met Colin Masterson? Oh, how fortunate you are! He is such a wonderful baritone. I have been absolutely dying to hear the man sing. I mentioned his name once or twice to Baxter, in the hopes he would take me to see him, but Baxter, poor dear, is so jealous if I show the slightest affection for another man." She slid a sideways glance at Elise. "I shall just have to put aside my wishes to appease my dear husband, I'm afraid."

Elise exchanged a significant glance with Doris, then said warmly, "I'm quite sure your husband has nothing to worry about, Mrs. Baxter. You seem devoted to him."

"We are devoted to each other," Cecily assured her. "I look forward to tonight, but now I must be on my way. I do hope the rehearsal goes well."

Just then Phoebe's voice echoed shrilly across the ballroom. "Doris! Do come over here this minute. The pianist needs to see your music."

Doris made a face at Cecily, then sang out, "Very well, Mrs. Fortescue!"

Cecily left them to deal with Phoebe's fussing and closed the ballroom doors behind her. Walking down the hallway, she wondered just how convincing she'd sounded when she'd declared how devoted Baxter was to her.

As she reached the lobby she saw Desmond Atkins limping across to the main doors. She waited just long enough to see him depart; then she headed for the stairs. With a little luck, she'd find Mrs. Atkins alone in her room.

She tried to decide how she would phrase the questions she needed to ask the woman without arousing her suspicions, but the memory of that silent exchange between Doris and Elise Boulanger left a niggling ache of anxiety under her ribs, disturbing her concentration.

Much as she loathed to admit it, there was no doubt in her mind that both Doris and Elise were hiding something from her. The thought that it might have something to do with Baxter was like a knife in her heart.

Her husband had never given her cause to be jealous, but any man might be forgiven for having his head turned by such a beautiful woman. Even a man as solid and reliable as Hugh Baxter.

She reached the first floor, determined to put her worries aside for now. She had a delicate task to perform, and she needed her full attention. Lifting her hand, she knocked on the door of room eleven.

The woman who greeted her must have once been a great beauty, but age had robbed her of the freshness of youth.

Obviously surprised by Cecily's visit, she opened the door wider and invited her in.

"I wanted to assure myself that you are satisfied with your accommodations," Cecily said, as she entered the elegant room. "Since your husband appeared to be so upset about the mix-up with your reservations, I thought it wise to verify things myself, just in case you needed something."

"That is so kind of you, Mrs. Baxter." Mrs. Atkins gestured to a chair and sat down herself. "I must apologize for my husband's ill temper. He can be rather impatient if things don't go as he planned."

Cecily crossed the floor and seated herself. "I suppose he had reason to be annoyed, if he specifically requested a room on this floor. It must be quite difficult for him to manage the stairs."

"He manages quite well, all things considered."

Cecily longed to ask how the woman's husband had acquired the limp, but good taste prevented her from posing an outright question. "I'm so very glad to hear it," she murmured, casting about in her mind for a subtle way to obtain the information she needed.

Mrs. Atkins glanced around the room. "This is a very nice room, however, and we are most comfortable here. Of course, the news of the two deaths is unsettling. I understand an employee of yours was responsible for stabbing that poor man. That must have been so distressing."

"Yes, it was." If that was what everyone believed, Cecily thought with relief, then she'd let them rest with that assumption for the moment. She fully intended to clear Roland's name, but if the guests thought the matter was settled, there would be less chance of panic and a mass exodus from the hotel. "I do hope the tragedy won't spoil your enjoyment of the Christmas festivities," she added. "We have so much planned for entertainment this year."

"Not at all. Though I must admit, Desmond thought we should move to another hotel. I managed to persuade him to stay. After all, we'd already moved once since we arrived here."

"I apologize for the inconvenience. My clerk must have misunderstood your husband's request when he made the reservations."

Mrs. Atkins inclined her head. "I'm afraid my husband can be quite difficult at times. You might be surprised to learn that he is actually a very considerate and affectionate man. Most people don't understand him. My family certainly harbors the wrong impression of him."

"I'm sorry to hear that."

"Well, one doesn't need the approval of one's family to fall in love. Though it saddened me when they refused to attend the wedding." She sighed. "I wish they could see how happy we are together."

"That's all that matters, isn't it." Still unable to find a way to broach the subject of Desmond Atkins's argument with Sid Porter, Cecily reluctantly rose. "I must attend to my duties, Mrs. Atkins. I'm pleased that the room is satisfactory. Please let us know if there is anything we can do to make you more comfortable."

"I certainly will." The woman sprang to her feet and accompanied Cecily to the door. "Thank you for being so concerned. Desmond will be gratified, I'm sure, to hear of your visit."

Cecily rather doubted that. She turned to go, then paused. "By the way, I understand your husband was acquainted with Mr. Porter."

Mrs. Atkins gave her a blank look. "Mr. Porter?"

"The man who was stabbed."

The woman's shock seemed genuine. "Are you sure? He has never mentioned it to me."

"One of my maids happened to hear your husband arguing with Mr. Porter a few days ago."

Mrs. Atkins shook her head. "Desmond most likely lost his temper over something or other. He tends to flare up quite quickly, and then just as promptly calms down again and forgets why he was angry in the first place." She smiled. "Men are difficult to live with, and every bit as difficult to live without."

"They are indeed." Frustrated by her failure to find out anything useful, Cecily had no choice but to leave the woman and return to her office.

She found Baxter still leafing through the ledgers in an apparently fruitless search for an earlier reservation by Desmond Atkins.

"I should have simply asked Mrs. Atkins if they had stayed here before," she said, when she caught sight of Baxter's bored expression. "Except that wouldn't have told me if he'd requested a first-floor room."

"Well, you could have saved me a great deal of time." Baxter shut the heavy book with a loud thud. "As far as I can tell, the Atkins have never stayed at the Pennyfoot. At least, not in the last six years."

"Goodness. You went back that far?" Cecily felt guilty. "Well, it's not as if you had anything pressing to do."

"Doing nothing would have been more interesting than wading through all those signatures." Baxter leaned back and opened his mouth in a yawn.

"I've had a wasted morning, too." Cecily sat down opposite him. "Mrs. Atkins is quite sure her husband was not acquainted with Sid Porter."

"Then it must have been a chance encounter, after all. That man sounds so unpleasant, I imagine he'd argue with anyone who looked at him the wrong way."

"I suppose so." She sighed. "Though I'd still like to know why he'd gone to the trouble of climbing all the way to the top floor."

"Well, I did come across something interesting in my perusal of the ledgers." Baxter opened the book up again and started turning pages. "Do you remember that article in the newspaper last month about the young woman who walked into the ocean and drowned herself?"

"I remember you mentioning something about it." Cecily leaned forward and reached for the pile of bills sitting at his elbow. "I didn't actually see the article. I never seem to have time to read the newspaper these days."

"Well, I thought at the time her face seemed familiar." Baxter flipped another page. "Ah, here it is! As I went through the register I recognized her name as that of the one in the article. She stayed here at the Pennyfoot last September, with her family. Her name was Felicity Rotheringham."

"Oh!" Cecily raised her head. "I do remember the Rotheringhams. Wasn't he something to do with banking?"

"I believe he was, yes."

"She was a pretty little thing. Whatever possessed her to drown herself?"

Baxter shook his head. "Tragic story. She was supposed to marry this Christmas. With so much to look forward to, it seems very strange that she would take her own life."

"How sad. I suppose we'll never know the reason."

"Well, I merely mentioned it because I remembered her name after reading the article. Then I saw it in the ledger and realized she'd actually stayed here."

"Do you still have the article?"

"I believe I did keep it somewhere, yes. I meant to show it to you at the time, for some reason, but then I forgot about it until now."

"I'd like to see it."

"I'll try to dig it up."

Sensing a mystery behind the senseless death of one so young, Cecily resolved to delve further into the incident. Before she did anything about that, however, she had a murder to solve. A murder that had become more confusing than she'd anticipated.

She had to make some headway soon, or time would run out and P.C. Northcott would be back to complicate matters once more. Once Inspector Cranshaw, her immortal adversary, became involved, the investigation would be taken out of her hands and she was quite determined that should not happen. No matter what risks she had to take.

"Isabelle! What on earth are you doing!" Phoebe's voice rose to a shriek, causing everyone in the ballroom to cease talking and stare in the direction of the stage. Even the pianist faltered and gradually came to a halt, his fingers still hovering over the keys.

Phoebe marched to the stage and stared up at the group of women standing there. "What is the matter with you, Isabelle! I have told you fifty times at least that you turn left as you come out of the circle. *Left*." She nodded for emphasis and the wide brim of her hat flopped up and down like a giant fan. "Now, show me your left arm."

Isabelle lifted an arm and the rest of the women giggled behind their hands.

"That," Phoebe said coldly, "is your right arm. Good heavens, after all these years, do you still not know your right from your left?"

"She can't remember which is which," Dora piped up, giving the young woman next to her a nudge with her elbow. "She's always putting her shoe on the wrong foot and her glove on the wrong hand."

More giggles followed. Phoebe bristled. She had the distinct impression that Isabelle knew quite well her right arm from her left, and simply delighted in making things difficult for her.

For years she'd done her best to teach these ungrateful fools how to perform onstage. Why she wasted her time with them she just couldn't imagine, though possibly it had a lot to do with the fact that local talent was not exactly abundant in Badgers End. In fact, it was nonexistent, which left her to deal with a collection of dunderheads who couldn't tell a pas de deux from a pirouette.

Settling her hat more firmly on her head, she called out,

"Once again, please. From the beginning." Ignoring the exaggerated groans, she added, "And this time, Isabelle, *left* as you leave the circle. *Left!*" She waved her left hand at the young woman, who promptly waved back with her right.

Phoebe resisted the urge to rush up there and shake the annoying woman by the shoulders. Oh, for the days when all she had to worry about was placing them in position for a tableau. At least they could hold their places without moving, and she could relax.

Of course, now and then someone would slip and the tableau would collapse, sending everyone sprawling. That didn't happen very often. Unfortunately tableaux had gone out of fashion and nowadays one was expected to present dancers for a successful revue. Which meant she had to be constantly on guard as her protégés pranced and cavorted around the stage like rampaging elephants instead of the ethereal sylphs she'd imagined.

Signaling to the pianist to begin, she braced herself for another debacle of the Fire Dance. The crashing chords startled the dancers. Taken unawares, they leapt into position several beats behind the music, then skittered about trying desperately to catch up.

Isabelle turned the wrong way again, causing Dora to slam into her. Both women clung to each other, tottered for several breathless seconds, then collapsed to the floor. The rest of the dancers gathered around them, loudly applauding.

Furious, Phoebe waved a hand at the pianist to stop. Either he hadn't seen the confusion onstage, or he'd become tired of constantly pausing in his rendition of the stirring music. He went on crashing chords.

Phoebe yelled, "Stop the music!" twice. When that didn't produce any effect, she marched over to him and cuffed his ear. "I said to stop," she said through her teeth.

Her slap dislodged the man's spectacles and they slid sideways down his nose. He straightened them, smacked down the lid of the piano and stood. "Madam, I regret to inform you that you and your mélange of boorish amateurs will never reach a margin of competence that will in any way, shape, or form be considered entertainment. I refuse to be part of this outrageous insult to my profession."

"I'll double your stipend," Phoebe said bluntly.

The pianist flipped his coat tails and reseated himself at the piano.

Out of the corner of her eye, Phoebe detected yet another disturbance onstage and turned to confront it. Her eyes widened when she saw her husband amble over to center stage, scattering the dance troupe left and right.

"Frederick!" Once more her shrill voice echoed to the rafters. "For heaven's sake, what on earth do you think you are doing?"

"I, my dear, am reciting." The colonel swayed back and forth, one hand stuck inside the lapel of his coat. "I waz-z on the road to Mafeking . . ."

Realizing her husband had been indulging heavily in his favorite refreshment, Phoebe sprung toward the stage. "Frederick, get down from there this instant."

"Guns blazing and ships sinking . . ."

Phoebe opened her mouth to scream another order, then closed it again. The group of women standing behind her husband appeared to be staring at the balcony behind her, pointing and muttering among themselves.

Curiosity overcoming outrage for the moment, Phoebe spun around, blinked, and blinked again. Unable to believe what she saw, she started forward, her gaze glued to the object hanging from the first floor balcony. No, her mind hadn't deceived her. She really could see a carpet sweeper hanging by its handle several feet above the ballroom floor.

Even Frederick had ceased his ridiculous recitation, and for once the women onstage were speechless. Then the silence was shattered, pierced by a horrendous crash and an ear-splitting scream.

Pansy stood in the doorway of the ballroom, a tray of sandwiches scattered at her feet. Her hand shook as she pointed at the balcony. "It's the ghost! He hung it there! We're being haunted by a clown!"

CHAPTER
❄ 10 ❄

Cecily received the disturbing news early that afternoon. A delicious aroma of spiced fruits had wafted into the lobby, and she realized Michel had begun boiling the plum puddings, one of the traditions she adored.

Drawn by the promise of sampling the batter, she'd made her way to the fragrant warmth of the kitchen. As she entered, three of the maids scuttled by her, their faces drawn with tension.

"They seem a trifle jittery," Cecily observed, as she joined Mrs. Chubb at the kitchen table. "I do hope we're not overworking them."

"Of course we're not. Girls that young used to work twice as hard in my day. No, it's that carpet sweeper that went missing. It turned up this afternoon, hanging from the balcony in the ballroom."

Cecily stared at her. "The *balcony*? How on earth did it get there?"

"No one seems to know. According to Pansy, they had a terrible time getting it off the railings. Luckily Mr. Baxter was there. He and Mrs. Fortescue's pianist managed to haul it up."

"Goodness. Thank heavens it didn't fall. Someone could have been hurt. No wonder everyone's upset."

"Well, it's more Pansy's fault the maids are upset. She's putting crazy thoughts in their heads." Mrs. Chubb rolled her eyes. "She keeps telling everyone it's a ghost moving everything around. If there's a ghost floating around the hotel, how is it that Pansy is the only one that's seen it? That's what I'd like to know."

Cecily caught Michel's eye, and he picked up a bowl and brought it over to her.

"Thank you, Michel." She took the bowl from him. He'd left the mixing spoon in it and she took it by the handle, scraped the side of the bowl and brought the delicious batter, with its wonderful mixture of dried fruit, spices, brandy, and rum, to her mouth.

Mrs. Chubb shook her head, obviously disapproving of Madam behaving in such a juvenile way.

Unabashed, Cecily scraped the bowl once more, then handed it back to Michel. "Delicious," she pronounced. "I don't know why it tastes so much better before it's cooked."

"Ze cooking destroys ze alcohol, m'm," Michel said, grinning.

He returned to his station and she dabbed her mouth with the serviette Mrs. Chubb handed her. "Well, anyway," she said, "I'm quite certain these incidents have nothing to do with a ghost. I suspect it's someone playing a rather elaborate hoax. Though I must say, whoever is doing this has gone to a remarkable amount of trouble. It couldn't have been an easy task to suspend a carpet sweeper from the balcony."

"Nor move that blooming great plant, neither."

"Well, we must impress upon the maids that there are no such things as ghosts, and that they have absolutely no reason to be afraid."

"I'll make sure I do that, m'm." Mrs. Chubb turned her head as the two new waiters Cecily had hired rushed by her, balancing dishes of fruit and cheese on their arms.

Cecily watched them nimbly manipulate the door with their feet as they passed through. "How do you like those young men?" she asked the housekeeper. "It's the first time we've employed waiters at the Pennyfoot. I must say, they are quite impressive."

"Oh, they do the work all right, m'm." Mrs. Chubb picked up a serviette from the pile on the table and began folding it expertly into the shape of a swan. "Though I'm not altogether convinced they're a good choice for the Pennyfoot. They tend to distract the girls. That Reggie is a bit of a rake, and Lawrence likes to lord it over everyone."

Cecily sighed. "I heard the Bayview hired waiters. I thought if we hired some ourselves it might help us keep up with the modern times."

Mrs. Chubb grunted. "I don't know as how we need to keep up with the times, m'm. The Pennyfoot has always been favorable among the higher-class people, and I don't think they'd want to see us change too much."

"Perhaps you're right." Cecily moved to the door. "Sometimes it's difficult to know what to do for the best. The world is changing so fast, and I'm afraid if we don't keep up with it, we may lose our business to those who do."

"We're full to capacity this Christmas, aren't we?"

Cecily smiled. "You, Mrs. Chubb, as well as my husband, are quite right. I do tend to worry too much." She let the door swing behind her and hurried back up the hallway.

All this talk of ghosts was nonsense, of course, but Pansy had seemed convinced she'd seen a clown on the top floor. She heard Pansy's voice again, pitched high with dread. *What was it she'd said? One minute it were there, and then it weren't. It disappeared right before me eyes.*

That wouldn't be impossible. There were plenty of cupboards and corners where a man could slip inside in a flash. Pansy mentioned that she'd closed her eyes for a second or two. That's all it would have taken for a man to dive into a closet and close the door. When Pansy opened her eyes again, the man would have seemed to disappear.

She crossed the lobby, struggling with her tangled thoughts. Perhaps Sid had brought a partner along. But if so, what happened to the clown after Sid was stabbed and Roland fell to his death?

There seemed only one logical answer to that. Pansy had seen her ghost about the same time Sid Porter had descended the chimney with a knife in his chest. It would seem that Sid Porter had been stabbed by a man wearing a clown suit. After all, what better disguise than a face covered in greasepaint.

Taking advantage of a lull at the reception desk, she paused in front of it. At first she didn't see Philip, who had bent double with his head hidden behind the counter. He shot up when she spoke his name, dislodging his spectacles. "Madam! I didn't see you there. I do beg your pardon." He pushed the specs back up his nose. "What can I do for you?"

"I was just wondering, Philip." She glanced over her shoulder and lowered her voice. "Have you by any chance seen a clown wandering in and out of the hotel?"

Philip's sparse eyebrows lifted. "A clown, m'm? I don't believe so. I think I certainly would have remembered if I'd seen a clown in the lobby." His face grew a little pale. "You don't mean that ghost everyone's talking about, do you? I thought that was just Pansy's imagination." He pulled a large handkerchief from his pocket and mopped his brow. "Oh, my, oh, my. I don't like ghosts. I really don't. I really, really don't like ghosts."

"Don't worry, Philip. I'm convinced there's a real live man behind all that paint. If you should spot a clown, however, I'd like you to inform me at once."

"Oh, yes, m'm. I certainly will. Yes, indeed." Philip nodded his head so hard his specs fell forward again. Once more he pushed them up his nose.

"One more thing. Has anyone moved out of the hotel during the past two days?"

Her desk clerk appeared confused. "Moved out, m'm?"

"Yes, Philip. Vacated their room."

"Not to my knowledge, m'm. I was under the impression that everyone is here for the Christmas festivities."

"Quite so. I just wondered if anyone had changed their minds, that's all."

His frown cleared. "Oh, I see. You mean because of Father Christmas being murdered."

"Well, it's bound to make some people nervous. I just hope no one will let the tragedy spoil their holiday plans."

"Not so far, m'm."

"Well, that *is* good news. Thank you, Philip." Cecily left him muttering to himself and headed for the stairs. The hotel was usually quiet at this time. This might be an ideal opportunity to carry on a little investigation.

If the clown had hidden inside the broom cupboard when Pansy saw him, as she suspected, there might be something in there to help her.

She began climbing, and as she turned the corner, she happened to glance down. Her stomach took a nasty turn as she caught sight of Elise standing half hidden inside the hallway. She was talking earnestly to a tall man, and Cecily could tell by the furtive manner in which the singer kept turning her head that she didn't want to be overheard.

Cecily might have dismissed the matter entirely if she hadn't recognized the man standing back in the shadows. She would have given anything at that moment to know exactly what secrets her husband shared with Elise Boulanger.

On her way back to the kitchen that afternoon, Gertie decided to take an extra minute or two and peek at the rehearsal for the variety show. She'd be too busy that evening to watch it, and she hoped to catch Doris doing her song.

She could hear music drifting down the corridor as she headed for the ballroom, and a voice that carried the tune so clearly, she knew it had to be Doris.

She hurried forward and pushed open the doors. They bumped against something and she heard Pansy's voice utter a sharp, "Ouch!"

"Sorry." She slipped inside and closed the doors behind her.

Pansy stood just in front of her, rubbing the back of her head. She gave Gertie a reproachful look, then directed her attention back to the stage.

Doris had on a lovely gown in pale blue, and danced across the stage as she sang. Gertie stood entranced. She'd never had any ambitions to be on the stage, but right then she envied the fragile singer her dainty dance steps as she floated back and forth in the spotlights.

Not that she could ever be dainty, Gertie thought wistfully. She'd always be too hefty and too clumsy to ever look like Doris, but just once it would be nice to know what it felt like to stand up there in front of an adoring crowd and hear them all clapping for her.

Caught up in her daydream, she failed to notice the man standing beside her, until he gave her a hefty nudge with his shoulder. She turned to see Reggie grinning at her.

"So what are you going to do in the show tonight, Humpty Dumpty? Will you fall off a wall and break into a hundred pieces?"

Doris's song came to an end, allowing Gertie to raise her voice. "I'll bloody break your head into a hundred bleeding pieces if you call me that again."

Still grinning, Reggie started prancing around her, poking her in the back painfully with his finger while he recited the nursery rhyme.

Pansy cried out in protest. "Stop that!"

Gertie spun around and lifted her hand to give Reggie a slap, but he caught her wrist and twisted it until she cried out. Just then a shadow moved swiftly from the back of the ballroom and materialized at Reggie's side.

In the next instant Reggie let go of her and grunted in pain, his right arm twisted back and helpless in the firm grip of Jeremy Westhaven.

"If I see you so much as touch this woman again, or any other woman for that matter, I'll break your arm right off," Jeremy snarled.

Reggie whimpered. "I was just having a bit of fun, that's all."

"I suggest you find your amusement somewhere else." Jeremy gave his arm a vicious twist that brought a yell of pain. "Do I make myself clear?"

"All right, all *right*!" Reggie snatched his arm free and hugging it, backed away.

Gertie didn't see him leave. She had her full attention on Jeremy, gazing at him with unabashed adoration. No man had ever come to her rescue like that. She'd remember this moment forever. "Thank you, sir," she said, her voice breathless with emotion. "I'm much obliged."

Jeremy gave her a slight bow. "My pleasure. I hope he didn't hurt you too much?"

She rubbed her wrist and smiled at him. "No, it's all

right. That was very kind of you to step in and tell him off like that."

Jeremy shook his head. "I won't tolerate anyone ill-treating a woman. Any woman." .

Somewhat deflated that he hadn't done it just for her and her alone, Gertie held her smile. "Well, I'm much obliged, anyway."

"Entirely my pleasure." He inclined his head again. "I do want to thank you for your choice of wine last night. Excellent. I thoroughly enjoyed it."

"It were more Michel's choice than mine." She hadn't seen Jeremy in the dining room, and assumed he'd taken his meal in his room. Dying to know if he'd entertained a lady friend, she added demurely, "I hope your friend enjoyed it, too."

Jeremy raised his eyebrows. "My friend?"

Now she felt silly. "Oh, I thought you might have wanted the wine for a friend."

His smile seemed sad. "No, I drank it all myself. I didn't feel like company last night. I preferred to be alone."

Her heart ached at the misery in his eyes. "I'm sorry," she said softly. "I hope you'll feel better tonight. Will you be watching the show?"

"I don't think so." He glanced at the stage, where every-one stood around pretending to listen to Phoebe's final or-ders. "In fact, I've been considering the idea of returning to London for Christmas."

Her heart seemed to crack right open. "Oh, no! I hope it doesn't have anything to do with the murder."

He gave her a sharp look. "Murder?"

She could have cut out her tongue. "Oh, sorry, I thought you would have heard. Everyone's been talking about it. I mean, it isn't a secret. I just thought you might have—" her words ended in a gasp as she caught sight of something moving along the balcony.

At the same time, someone in the group on the stage must have seen it, too. A scream, raw and shrill with terror, echoed up to the rafters. Almost at once, several of Phoebe's dance troupe joined in the screaming.

Gertie put her hands over her ears, her gaze still fixed on the figure of a clown. Its grotesque face seemed to be grinning at her as it hovered over the seats in the balcony. Then Reggie yelled, loud enough for everyone to look at him. "It's the ghost! It's the ghost! Run, everyone, run!"

Panic-stricken women broke from the group and charged toward Gertie. Afraid of being mowed down by the frantic mob, she took one last look at the balcony before she leapt for the doors.

The clown had disappeared.

Cecily reached the top floor, thankful to find herself alone. She might well have some difficulty explaining to a curious guest why the hotel manager would be rummaging around in a broom closet.

She should have asked Pansy where she stood the night she saw the ghost. Looking up and down the hallway, she assumed Pansy had been close to the stairs, which meant the rest of the hallway would be in shadows.

Cecily imagined seeing a figure standing there. Then she closed her eyes for a moment or two before opening them again. The broom cupboard was situated on her left, toward the end the hallway. It would have taken someone no more than two or three seconds to slip inside and close the door.

Advancing toward the cupboard, she passed the narrow steps that led up to the roof. It would have been so simple for someone to jump down from the roof onto the ledge and drop into the roof garden.

The door at the top of the steps would have been unlocked, since Sid Porter and Roland would have gone through it to reach the roof. Roland had fully expected to return that way, after he'd lowered Sid down the chimney.

Except he hadn't returned. He'd crashed to the hard ground below, leaving Sid Porter to die in the chimney. Someone else had used that knife, she was convinced of it now. Someone who had worn a clown suit for a disguise.

The killer could have easily entered the hotel through one of the rear doors, into either the library or the ballroom. All doors were kept unlocked during daylight hours to accommodate the guests.

Even if someone had seen a clown wandering around, at Christmastime he would not have seemed out of place. With all the festivities taking place, he would simply have been mistaken as one of the performers.

Cecily paused in front of the broom closet. If she knew exactly why Sid Porter had been killed, it might help in her quest to find the murderer. As it was now, she had to work completely in the dark.

She sent a quick glance up and down the hallway, then

opened the cupboard door. The shadows made it difficult to see inside. Leaving the door open, she knelt down and began feeling around the floor.

The carpet sweeper had not yet been returned, which made her task a little easier. No doubt Pansy was still sweeping the floors since she'd had a late start, thanks to the antics of the prankster, whoever he might be.

It seemed that although the maids kept the hotel floors well swept, apparently they neglected to clean the actual cupboard. She found a pencil, a screw that had most likely fallen out of the carpet sweeper, several hairpins, and a small round object about the size of a snooker ball.

Intent on her search, she had no idea someone approached until she heard a slightly hysterical voice behind her. "There you are, Cecily! I've been looking all over the place for you. What on earth are you doing down there?"

Cursing under her breath, Cecily backed out of the cupboard and climbed to her feet. Brushing dust from her skirt, she turned to face Phoebe. "Oh, hello Phoebe. I was just looking for something, that's all."

"If you're looking for the carpet sweeper," Phoebe said crossly, "I saw it hanging from the ballroom balcony."

"So I heard." Cecily closed the broom cupboard and slipped the objects she'd found into the pocket of her skirt. Her search would have to wait until later.

"Well, you haven't heard the worst." Phoebe clutched her chest as if she were in the throes of heart failure. "I've never seen anything so utterly terrifying in all my born days. I would have fallen in a dead faint had it not been for that new waiter of yours. Reggie, I think his name is."

"My goodness." Well used to Phoebe's hysterics, Cecily refused to become alarmed. "Whatever did you see? It must have been harrowing, for you to climb all the way up here to tell me about it."

"I thought you should know at once. Everyone is talking about it. No one seemed to know where you were. Your husband is quite beside himself looking for you. If Philip hadn't mentioned you were up here—"

Cecily interrupted her. "Baxter is looking for me?" Now she felt a pang of anxiety. "What's happened, Phoebe? Tell me at once."

"It's the ghost." Phoebe flapped a hand in the direction of the stairs. "I saw it for myself. Dreadful it was. It had a huge red mouth grinning from ear to ear, wild eyes and a shock of bright red hair standing on end. If I hadn't seen it with my own eyes I would never have believed anything could be so utterly ghastly."

"You saw the ghost? Was it a clown?"

"Uglier than any clown I've ever seen before." Phoebe shuddered. "I hope and pray I never set eyes on that . . . thing again."

"Where did you see it?"

Phoebe seemed to be struggling for breath, her mouth opening and shutting like a hungry fledgling. "Floating." In her agitation, she grasped Cecily's sleeve and gave it a tug. "Actually *floating*, Cecily. Above the seats in the balcony. If it hadn't been for that nice young man escorting me from the ballroom I am quite, quite sure I'd still be lying on the floor down there. Heaven knows what would have become of me. I doubt I would be alive to talk about it."

Gently Cecily freed her sleeve. "That was very good of the young man."

"Yes, it was." Phoebe's face grew stern. "I have no idea what happened to Frederick. He should have been the one to rescue me. Instead, he simply wandered off somewhere. I shall have some strong words to say to him when I see him again, I can assure you."

Cecily took her friend's arm and led her back to the stairs. "I'm sure the colonel is extremely worried about you," she said firmly. "You know how he is. He just became befuddled as usual, that's all. Once he sees you again he'll be vastly relieved, I'm quite sure."

Phoebe muttered something in response, but Cecily paid her scant attention. If her theory about the ghost was correct, that meant the killer was still on the premises. Though why he should deliberately draw attention to himself she couldn't begin to fathom.

On the other hand, there was always the possibility that she had been searching up the wrong path, and the clown really was a ghost. As incredible as that seemed, if it were so, she had more trouble on her hands than she'd first imagined.

CHAPTER
❈ 11 ❈

Cecily had barely reached the bottom of the steps before Baxter rushed toward her. "Where the devil have you been?" he barked, completely ignoring Phoebe's plaintive attempts to ask him if he'd seen the colonel. "I've been looking for you everywhere."

"I was upstairs." Feeling decidedly cool toward him, Cecily had no intention of enlightening him further.

"On her knees in the broom cupboard," Phoebe muttered, obviously piqued at being so rudely dismissed.

Baxter's eyebrows shot up. "What . . . ?"

"I'll explain later." Cecily released her friend's arm. "Phoebe, I suggest you take a look in the lounge. Knowing the colonel, he is no doubt soothing his shattered nerves with a jigger of scotch."

"You are probably right." Phoebe tugged her gloves over her elbows. "I shall look for him there." She flounced off, the wisps of lilac chiffon on her hat drifting after her.

"Who else saw the clown?" Cecily asked, avoiding her husband's shrewd gaze.

"I have no idea. The first I heard of it was when a flock of screaming women ran past the library. All I could get out of them was a garbled string of words that made absolutely no sense at all."

"What about the staff? Did any of them happen to see the ghost?"

"I understand Gertie was there. I don't know how much she saw."

Cecily nodded and started for the kitchen.

"I say, Cecily?"

She paused, and turned back to him.

"Have I done something to distress you?"

She tightened her lips. "I do not have time to discuss the issue at this moment. It can wait until later."

His brow darkened. "If you don't mind, I prefer that we discuss it now."

"I do mind. I need to talk to Gertie first."

"I'm afraid I must insist."

She opened her mouth to protest, then closed it again when she realized that two of the maids were close by, supposedly intent on straightening cushions on the chairs. Inwardly fuming, she allowed her husband to take her arm and march her down to her office.

Once inside, however, she snatched her elbow from his

grip. "How dare you lead me here like some disobedient child! In front of the staff, no less."

His expression remained annoyingly calm. "I demand to know what has driven you into such a huff. If it's some offense of which I am unwittingly guilty I deserve to know what it is. How else can I apologize or explain myself?"

Faced with such a rational plea, Cecily's anger deflated. Now she'd been placed in an awkward position. She needed, quite desperately, to know why her husband had been whispering in the corridors with an attractive young singer, and why he'd engineered a meeting with her in London.

He could, of course, simply deny everything. On the other hand, if she voiced her concerns and they were unfounded, he would most likely chide her for her imaginative suspicions, and she'd be rendered the guilty party. Either way, knowing her husband, she would not win this dispute. She had to find another way to learn the truth.

"You have done nothing, Bax." She managed a sweet smile. "My bad humor is due entirely to the adverse events taking place in this hotel. I'm concerned that with the murder of Sid Porter and rumors of a ghost, we may very well lose our customers to the Bayview Hotel."

She met his gaze and held it. She knew quite well that he was not convinced, but for the moment she hoped to win a reprieve. She would tackle him on the subject when the time was right. Until then, he would simply have to have patience and trust in her judgment.

"I saw Gertie on her way to the kitchen a short while

ago," he said, his tone warning her he was still displeased. "Perhaps you should have a word with her."

"I shall."

She was almost at the door when he stopped her again. "By the way, you never did explain what you were doing in the broom cupboard."

"Looking for something." She left, disturbed to be at odds with her husband, and even more concerned for the reasons behind it.

She found Gertie in the midst of an argument with Mrs. Chubb. Their raised voices had reached her even before she'd opened the door.

"He was poking me in the back, he was." Gertie flung out her hand, narrowly missing a jug of milk on the table beside her. "He twisted my wrist and all. I tell you, those two are nothing but flipping trouble. I don't know why Madam hired them, I really—" She broke off as Cecily entered the kitchen.

Gertie and the housekeeper were alone in there, Cecily saw at once. Michel was nowhere to be seen. The maids were most likely in the dining room, preparing the tables for the evening meal. Cecily wasted no time taking advantage of that. "To whom were you referring?" she asked Gertie, who immediately assumed a look of innocence.

"Who, me, m'm? No one. I was just telling Mrs. Chubb about the ghost, that's all."

The housekeeper seemed apprehensive. She glanced at Cecily muttering, "I don't know what to think, m'm. I really don't. Gertie says she saw a clown floating in the balcony, but I find that hard to believe."

"Tell me exactly what you saw, Gertie." Cecily settled herself on a chair and crossed her ankles.

Gertie exchanged a worried look with Mrs. Chubb. "All I know is that it were a clown, only it didn't look very funny, if you know what I mean. It looked . . ." She shuddered. "It looked *evil*, m'm. Honest it did."

"And it floated?"

"Yes, m'm. Above the seats it were."

"It must have been dark up there. Are you quite sure it wasn't just a simple trick of light that made it appear to be floating?"

"No, m'm. I'm as sure as you're sitting there. It were floating. Just like a great ugly balloon."

"I see." Cecily reflected on the image for a moment. "I heard you say someone poked you in the back. Tell me, who was that?"

"Oh, it were just one of the lads horsing around." Gertie fidgeted with the skirt of her apron.

"She means Reggie, m'm," Mrs. Chubb said. "He's been tormenting her. Calling her names and poking her, he has. I'm afraid those two are turning out to be a lot more trouble than they're worth."

"Well, it turned out all right," Gertie said, her cheeks turning pink. "Mr. Westhaven came to my rescue. Proper gentleman he was. Told off Reggie, he did. Said for him to stay away from me."

Mrs. Chubb beamed at the housemaid. "Mr. Westhaven is a very nice gentleman, indeed. How nice of him to step up for you."

"I thought it was very nice of him." Gertie looked at Cecily.

"I don't want to get nobody in trouble, m'm. Now that Mr. Westhaven took care of it, I don't think Reggie will bother me no more."

"I'll have a word with both of them," Cecily promised. "I'll make sure they behave in the future, or they can find work elsewhere."

"Thank you, m'm." Gertie glanced at the clock. "I'd better get off to the dining room and see if them maids have got the tables ready. If I don't keep an eye on them, they forget half of what they're supposed to be doing."

"Perhaps you should do something special for Mr. Westhaven's table tonight," Mrs. Chubb said. "To thank him, I mean. Maybe some flowers."

Gertie snorted. "Blokes don't like flowers. That's women's stuff."

"Well, then, tie a couple of balloons or something to his chair. Just to show your appreciation."

Gertie headed for the door. "Nah, he doesn't like balloons."

Mrs. Chubb raised her eyebrows. "Now how would you know that?"

"He told me." Gertie shot a guilty look at Cecily. "Thank you, m'm." She disappeared in a flurry of skirts.

"Well!" Mrs. Chubb crossed her arms, her gaze still on the door. "Did you hear that? Looks as if our Gertie has had more than one conversation with Mr. Westhaven. She's moving up in the world."

"I wouldn't put too much importance into that little exchange." Cecily got up and went to the door. "In my experience, gentlemen such as Jeremy Westhaven seldom waste their time on lowly servants. He's simply passing a pleasant moment or two, that's all."

"I hope Gertie knows that." Mrs. Chubb sounded worried. "I wouldn't want her hurt again. She's barely got over losing Ross."

"If she is over it," Cecily said quietly. "I think Gertie is looking for something to help her forget. I just hope she keeps a clear head on her shoulders."

Mrs. Chubb nodded, though she still wore a frown. "I don't think we need to worry about Gertie, m'm. She knows better than to barge in where she's not wanted. She knows her place."

"I expect you're right." Cecily glanced at the clock ticking away on the shelf above the stove. "I'll be in the library for a spell if anyone needs me."

"Very well, madam."

Cecily left the kitchen, her brow furrowed. With all the problems she faced right now, worrying about Gertie only complicated matters. She had to trust her chief housemaid wouldn't lose her head over someone who was so obviously out of reach.

A few minutes later she entered the library to find a group of guests standing about in front of the fireplace. For an uncomfortable moment she thought there might be something there to disturb them. Perhaps something else incriminating had fallen from the chimney.

She hurried forward, but her anxious glance discovered nothing out of place on the hearth. She greeted the guests with a nervous smile. "Dinner will be served shortly. I hope you all enjoy your meal."

One woman flicked her feather boa across her shoulder. "The food here is excellent," she said. "Please convey my compliments to the chef."

Murmurs of "Here, here," from the rest of the group followed her comment.

"Thank you." Cecily beamed in relief. "I shall be happy to pass your kind words along to Michel. He . . . is . . ." Her voice trailed off as she stared across the room.

Small wonder everyone stood about like little lost lambs. Something was missing. No, not something. Several things. All of the armchairs in fact. All five of them had completely disappeared.

Cecily shook her head, convinced her eyes played tricks on her. The armchairs failed to materialize. Aware that the guests watched her with great interest, she uttered a light laugh.

"Good heavens. The maids must have forgotten to bring back the chairs. I . . . er . . . thought we might need them for the variety show tonight, but as it turns out, we won't be needing them after all."

She began backing toward the door, nodding and smiling. "I can assure you they will be replaced right away. Meanwhile, perhaps you would all care to sit in the lounge until dinner is served?"

"Quite all right," one of the gentleman assured her. "We'll be sitting all evening watching the concert. It won't hurt us to stretch our legs for a bit."

"Thank you for being so understanding." Cecily felt the door frame against her back and fumbled for the doorknob. "Enjoy the concert. And your meal." She almost fell out the door and had to steady herself out in the hallway with a hand against the wall. Enough was *enough*. Ghosts didn't move things. Certainly not five heavy armchairs.

Her temper rising, she pushed her hand into her pocket to find her handkerchief, and yelped when something stabbed her finger. She'd forgotten all about the items she'd picked up in the broom cupboard.

She started toward the kitchen, intending to hand everything over to a maid to drop into the dustbins outside. As she emerged into the lobby, she glanced down at the objects in her hand. Seeing the clump of hairpins, she realized one of them must have stabbed her.

The shiny red snooker ball nestled in the middle of her palm. She turned it over in her hand, and realized at once it could not be a snooker ball after all. It weighed far less and had a large hole in one side of it.

Curious now, she held it up to the light, turning it this way and that. Then it came to her, and she lowered her hand quickly. She knew now what she held in her fingers. Not a snooker ball at all, but a ball that would fit perfectly over the end of a nose. The clown must have dropped it when he hid in the broom cupboard.

So her assumptions had been correct. Not a ghost, but a flesh-and-blood killer. Why did he linger in the hotel instead of making good his escape? She could think of only one reason. His evil work had not been fully accomplished. He intended to kill again.

Gertie sent a nervous glance up at the balcony as she entered the ballroom. To her intense relief, she could see no sign of a ghost. Her knees still shook whenever she thought about that ugly face grinning down at her.

The concert was supposed to begin in less than an hour, and she still had to get the chairs lined up. At the moment they were stacked along the wall, and more behind the stage. Muttering to herself, she pulled out two of the chairs and dragged them across the floor.

Being alone in the ballroom at night gave her the creeps. Especially since she knew a ghost might still be floating around. Any minute now the performers would start arriving, and she'd feel a lot better. She just hoped they'd hurry up.

On her third trek back to get some chairs she paused, aware she'd heard something. Tiny trickles of ice slid down her back when she heard the light tapping, somewhere at the back of the ballroom.

She shot another nervous glance at the balcony. The tapping came from that direction. Nothing in the world could lure her over there to have a look. Nothing.

Heart racing, she stared at the main doors. *Please, please let someone come through them now. Anyone.* Even fussy Phoebe would be better than her being all alone in a haunted ballroom. *Please.*

The door remained stubbornly closed. And the tapping continued. Louder, and more urgent.

Gertie lifted a chair and held it in front of her like a shield. She had no idea if it would give her protection against a ghost, but it was better than nothing. She called out, her voice quivering as if she had fallen into an icy pond. "Who's there? What do you want?"

The tapping continued.

Gertie frowned. Maybe the sound didn't come from the balcony, after all. It seemed to be coming from the side of the room, near the windows. She squinted into the shadows, but could only see chairs lined up along the wall.

It dawned on her then. She could hear tapping on the window, all right. Only *outside* the window. For a moment courage failed her again. If it was the ghost, it could tap all night as far as she cared. As long as it bloody well stayed outside.

Wait a minute. She put the chair down. Why would a ghost bother to tap on a window, when all it had to do was pass through it? There had to be someone out there.

Cursing under her breath at whoever was playing this stupid joke on her, Gertie marched over to the nearest window. Not there. Further along.

She moved to the next window. Then the next. The black night made it impossible to see outside. She reached the end window, and still the tapping sounded further along.

Either the bugger moved along with her, or else . . . She stared at the French windows that led to the rose garden. Could there be someone out there trying to get in?

The thought raised goosebumps along her arms. Two people had died already, she didn't want to be the third. Obeying the desperate urge to turn her back on the doors and run like mad, she twisted around. At the same instant the tapping intensified into a pounding.

Shocked, she turned back to the doors. A man's face pressed against the glass, the light from the gas lamps spilling on his white whiskers. Her eyes widened, and her mouth opened to let out a terrified yell.

Then he raised his hand, and Gertie's scream collapsed into a groan. "Silly old bugger," she muttered, as she pulled back the bolts. "What the flipping 'eck is he bleeding doing out there?"

She pulled the doors open and Colonel Fortescue stumbled in. "Thank God," he said, running a hand through his hair, which already stood on end. "I thought I would have to spend the whole blasted night out there."

"Why didn't you come around to the front doors," Gertie said crossly, remembering belatedly to add, "sir."

"What? What?" The colonel shook his head. "Couldn't see a blasted thing, old bean. Reminds me of the time I was stuck in the jungle all night. There I was—"

"If you'll excuse me, sir, I have to finish lining these chairs up or no one will have nowhere to sit tonight to watch the concert."

Colonel Fortescue shook his head in disappointment. "Well, I suppose I could tell you the story later. Dashed funny, actually. At least it is now. Wasn't at the time, of course. I remember—"

"Colonel, your wife is looking for you. I think she's in the bar." Gertie smiled hopefully at him.

"The bar?" The colonel looked around as if hunting for something. "Where is it? Have they moved it again?"

"No, sir. It's out those doors and down the hall." Gertie pointed at the doorway.

Just then, the door flew open. A group of chattering young women surged in, followed by Phoebe. Layers of lace covered her pearl pink gown, making her look like a badly iced wedding cake. Her hat perched on the side of her head in the latest Paris fashion and seemed about to fall off as she rushed toward Gertie and the colonel.

"Frederick! Where in the world have you been? I've been out of my head with worry. The show is about to begin and I have enough on my mind without you wandering off and causing me all this distress. Really, Frederick. This is most inconsiderate." She jerked her head for emphasis, and the wide brim of the hat dipped up and down, sending wisps of pink ostrich feathers floating to the ground.

The colonel seemed unaffected by this display of wrath. "I have been sitting on the bowling green, my dear." He waved a hand vaguely in the direction of the French windows. "Very comfortable for lawn chairs, I must say."

"What on earth do you mean?" Phoebe looked at Gertie for help.

"He were outside, Mrs. Fortescue," Gertie said, doing her best to hide a grin. "He were tapping on the doors to come in. I think he got lost out there."

"I most certainly did not get lost!" The colonel twirled the end of his mustache with a gesture of annoyance. "I have led an entire regiment through a blasted jungle, by Jove. I do not get lost."

"Yes, sir," Gertie said demurely.

"Then pray tell us what you were doing on the bowling green in the dark." Phoebe thrust her hand at the windows. "It's freezing out there."

The colonel followed the gesture with a puzzled gaze. "Oh, that! Well, I saw the armchairs and thought I'd enjoy a quiet moment or two. Must have nodded off."

"In the middle of the lawn? What are you talking about, Frederick? There are no armchairs on the lawn."

"I beg your pardon, my dear. There were quite a few of them." He pulled a watch from his pocket and stared at it. "Good Lord. Is that the time? I'm dashed well missing my brandy."

"You've actually missed your whole dinner," Phoebe said, rolling her eyes. "Come along, I'll take you to the dining room. There might be time for you to eat something, though now you'll be late for the concert." She led her husband by the arm and headed for the doors, still quietly nagging him.

Gertie shook her head, then turned to Phoebe's dance troupe, who stood about as if waiting for instructions on what to do next.

Gertie knew exactly what to tell them. "Here," she called out, "if you want a bleeding audience watching your concert tonight, you'd better bloody help me get these flipping chairs lined up!"

CHAPTER

❦ 12 ❦

To Cecily's relief, and no doubt that of the audience that evening, the show went quite well. Since King George had now made the music hall acceptable entertainment for everyone, Phoebe had followed the successful format.

Tasteful skits were intermingled with modern-day songs, and the audience was invited to join in the singing, which they did with great gusto, though they were lacking somewhat in musical talent. Both Doris and Elise, however, performed with a flair that delighted everyone.

Except Cecily. She would have vastly preferred that Elise Boulanger had never set foot in the hotel. Had she not done so, however, Cecily might never have known that her husband had more than a passing acquaintance with the flamboyant entertainer. To be aware of such things, she assured herself, was halfway to solving the problem.

The knowledge tempered her enjoyment of the proceedings, and she vowed to tackle her husband on the subject once they were alone.

As the guests filed out of the ballroom, Baxter accompanied her backstage to congratulate the performers. She kept one eye on him while she talked to Phoebe, and noted sourly that he paused to exchange a few words with a glowing Elise.

"I can't imagine what possessed him," Phoebe said, forcing Cecily's attention back to the conversation at hand. "Sitting out there in the middle of the lawn in the dark, and all this talk about armchairs. I'm really quite concerned about him these days."

Cecily started. "Did you say armchairs? What exactly did the colonel say?"

Phoebe tutted as two of her dance troupe jostled her in passing. "When will these girls ever learn to behave like young ladies. As for that Isabelle, she can't even remember her left from her right. Did you notice her make a wrong turn in the middle of the Fire Dance? Thank heavens the others covered up her mistake. I was mortally embarrassed."

Cecily had noticed the disturbance in the routine, but refrained from saying so. Considering past mishaps, such as the time one of the girls kicked a sword during the sword dance and nearly stabbed a matron in the heart, a misstep here and there hardly caused a ripple.

"You were saying something about armchairs," she reminded Phoebe.

Her friend seemed confused. "Was I? Oh, yes. Of course I was. It was Frederick who kept rambling on about the armchairs. He actually said he'd sat down on one in the middle of the bowling green and had fallen asleep. Can you imagine that? Now I ask you, what in the world would armchairs be doing in the middle of the bowling green?"

Cecily stared at her for a moment, then said abruptly, "Please excuse me, Phoebe. I have something that needs my immediate attention." Darting across to where Baxter stood talking to Samuel, she placed a hand on her husband's arm. Keeping her voice low, she murmured, "I need both of you to follow me."

The ballroom had emptied out, except for two gentlemen deep in conversation by the main doors. Cecily led Baxter and Samuel to the French windows, which she opened and then stepped outside.

"May I ask where we are going?" Baxter inquired, as he joined her in the frosty night air.

Samuel stepped out, too, and closed the doors behind him. Looking at Cecily, he said with an air of someone about to commit a crime, "Madam?"

"We are going over to the bowling green," Cecily said. "Come."

Baxter sounded a little impatient when he answered her. "Isn't it a trifle cold to be playing bowls? In any case, I was under the impression the equipment had been put away for the winter."

Samuel said nothing as he followed the two of them through the rose garden and out onto the lawn.

Cecily took several steps onto the smooth turf, then

stopped. "There," she said, pointing with a triumphant hand. "Over there."

Both men followed her direction and peered into the darkness.

Although thick clouds hid the moon, the shadows couldn't quite obscure the unusual sight. There they sat in all their glory, placed in a ring on the damp dark grass like ghostly thrones in some strange ceremony.

"Good Lord," Baxter muttered. "Aren't they the library armchairs?"

It took Baxter and Samuel more than half an hour to return all the chairs to the library. By that time Cecily had made herself ready for bed and had retired to the boudoir.

Pulling a brush through her long tresses, she peered at her reflection in the mirror. The dull ache under her ribs refused to go away, and she laid down the brush. She had to know the meaning of her husband's interest in Elise Boulanger, and she had to know tonight.

Until now she'd avoided the issue, afraid of what she might learn, but she could no longer continue with suspicions and assumptions. If Baxter had transferred his affections to another woman, she would have to face the fact and try to find a way to resolve the problem.

She leaned forward, examining her face with a critical eye. Despondent, she tried to see herself as her husband would see her. There were crow's feet at the corners of her eyes, but then Baxter had them as well. He was the younger by two years, but he had gray threads in his hair, especially at the temples, while she had none.

Could it be true that a man grew more handsome with age, while a woman simply aged, as the saying went? She'd never thought of Baxter as growing old. He would always remain young and undeniably handsome in her mind, no matter how many decades passed by.

Perhaps he felt neglected. Her duties in the hotel kept her busy, and perhaps she didn't have enough time to spend with him. She would have to remedy that.

Picking up the brush, she once more stroked her hair. She had already decided to pay a visit to Sid Porter's home the next day. P.C. Northcott hadn't had time to search it yet, and she hoped to find some clue as to who might have wanted Mr. Porter's life to end so abruptly.

She planned to ask Baxter to accompany her. Perhaps they could enjoy lunch at the George and Dragon. The Pennyfoot could do without her for a short while. Pleased at the prospect, she had almost forgotten about her intention to talk to him about Elise.

His sudden entrance into the boudoir gave her memory a nasty nudge. "I'd like to get my hands on the pesky blighter who took all those armchairs outside," he said, as he flung his coat onto the bed. "I'd give him a good thrashing. The legs were covered in mud. We had to take every one of them into the kitchen to be cleaned before we could carry them back to the library. My back will never feel the same again."

"How annoying for you," Cecily murmured. "Obviously someone is having an enormous laugh at our expense."

"The maids think it's the work of a ghost." He sat down on the edge of the bed and looked at his wife. "What do you make of all this?"

She laid down her brush and swung around on her stool to face him. "I must confess, I'm baffled. I felt quite sure the clown that Pansy saw had killed Sid Porter and pushed Roland from the roof." She picked up the clown nose from her dressing table. "Look, I found this in the broom cupboard upstairs, where Pansy said she saw him."

Baxter shook his head as he reached for the nose. "So that's what you were doing in the broom cupboard."

"I thought I might find something that would help me find out what happened. At least this tells us the clown is real, and not a ghost."

Baxter handed her back the nose. "But he was seen again today, in the ballroom."

"Exactly. That's what I don't understand. Why is he drawing attention to himself, and more importantly, why is he still here in the hotel?"

Baxter pulled at his bottom lip. "He's planning another murder?"

Cecily sighed. "I must confess, the idea occurred to me. That is what worries me the most."

"Then we have to hunt him down and hand him over to the constabulary."

"Precisely." She looked hopefully at him. "Perhaps you'd like to accompany me tomorrow, when I go to search Sid Porter's room? I'm hoping to find something that might help the investigation."

A frown appeared on his face, drawing his brows together.

"I don't like this, Cecily," he muttered. "I don't like this one little bit."

"Neither do I, Bax. But I really don't know what else we can do."

"I suppose we could contact the inspector and ask for his help."

"No!" Aware she'd spoken too sharply, she softened her tone. "You know very well that the inspector has been looking for an excuse to shut us down for years. He hates the card rooms, and the fact that we have gambling in the hotel. Any investigation on his part could unearth a reason for him to do so. I would prefer to leave him out of this situation until we know exactly what happened and who was responsible."

"And if someone else dies in the meantime?"

Cecily shuddered. "We shall just have to hope that won't happen."

"What does all this business with the clown have to do with objects being moved to odd places?"

"That's what baffles me. I can't imagine a killer going to all that trouble, and what would be his purpose? It doesn't make any sense at all."

"Murder seldom does."

She held out her hands to him. "Will you come with me tomorrow to Sid Porter's house?"

"Of course." He rose, reached for her hands and pulled her to her feet. "Where did this fellow live?"

"I don't know. We'll have to ask at the George and Dragon. I'm sure someone there will be able to tell us. I thought we might have a bite to eat while we're there."

"A good idea." He drew her to him and kissed her soundly on the mouth. "Now, enough of this talk of murder and mayhem. I need a sound night's sleep if I am to guard you against unknown villains."

She waited until they lay side by side in bed before broaching the delicate subject. "Bax?"

His mumbled reply told her he was already on the brink of sleep.

"Bax, I happened to see you talking to Elise Boulanger this morning."

She felt his tension when he answered. "Yes, I did exchange some words with her."

"I couldn't help wondering why you didn't want to tell me you met her in London."

She held her breath, feeling her heart pound in her ears, while she waited for his reply.

Sighing, he turned on his side to face her. "I wondered how long it would take you to question me about that."

"Well, I hesitated to mention it. I didn't want you to think you had a prying wife." She couldn't see his face in the dark, and wished now that she had brought up the subject while the lamps were still alight.

"Would your burning curiosity be satisfied if I told you that if you knew the reason it would spoil a surprise?"

"Oh!" Intrigued, and faintly relieved, she murmured, "Well, in that case, I suppose I can contain myself. What sort of surprise?"

"I refuse to say any more. You will simply have to wait until I tell you."

"Is it a Christmas present?"

"Not a word, Cecily. Now go to sleep. We both need our rest."

As an elderly woman needs a rest, perhaps? She pinched her lips together. She had to stop indulging in this petty jealousy. Much as she disliked the idea of her husband sharing secrets with a glamorous young singer, she must trust him and believe that he meant only to surprise her in some way. She could only hope the revelation would be a pleasant one.

CHAPTER

❈ 13 ❈

Midway through the following morning, Cecily's agitation had reached fever pitch. Anxious to be on her way, she had little patience with the numerous obstacles that popped up to prevent her from leaving.

The first, in the form of Desmond Atkins, occurred shortly before the scramble to serve breakfast. Visiting the library to inspect the traveling armchairs, Cecily was relieved to find no one there, thus allowing her to delve into the back of the cushions for possible clues.

After a thorough search of each armchair yielded nothing that could help, she sank down on one in frustration. Somehow someone had managed to transport five chairs from the library to the lawn outside without anybody noticing. She would have given a great deal to know just how that was accomplished.

She had spoken to the staff earlier that morning. No one had seen the maneuver take place. Without exception, every maid she spoke to seemed convinced the ghost had spirited the chairs to their grassy spot. Even Gertie, usually so down to earth and logical, seemed reluctant to let go of the idea. In fact she had described, in lurid detail, seeing the ghost hover over the balcony seats. It was a feat, Cecily had to admit, that would have been difficult for a mortal.

The idea came to her in a flash of inspiration. Of course. Why hadn't she thought of it before? She needed to talk to Madeline—the expert on ghostly manifestations. She could probably answer her questions and possibly tell her whether or not the ghost was real.

Madeline's so-called trances disturbed Cecily, but she had to admit, there had been many times when her friend's visions had revealed some interesting insights. There had even been a time or two when she had saved Cecily's life by sensing danger with a means far beyond Cecily's capabilities. Or anyone else's for that matter.

Thinking about the night before, Cecily remembered seeing Kevin Prestwick engaging Madeline in conversation at the variety show. Aware that matters had not been going well between the two of them she'd refrained from disturbing them. She rather hoped their little talk would help patch things up. Perhaps Madeline would be willing to talk about it.

In fact, she decided now, she had more than one subject

to discuss with her friend, and what better time than that morning. Although she still had duties to take care of, her appointment with Baxter was not until one o'clock, which would leave her plenty of time to have a nice long conversation with Madeline.

Deciding she had better get started, she rose to her feet, just as the door opened and Desmond Atkins rushed in. He seemed surprised to see Cecily, and stammered a greeting.

"I've come to borrow a book for my wife," he said, heading for the bookshelves. "She needs something to keep her mind off this murder business. I don't mind telling you, I wanted to get her out of here, but she insisted on staying for Christmas, at least. I just hope she doesn't live to regret it."

Since the opportunity had presented itself, Cecily felt perfectly justified in seizing it. "Speaking of the murder," she said, as Desmond reached for a book, "I understand you were acquainted with Mr. Porter. It must have been quite a shock for you to hear of his untimely demise."

She had expected him to deny any knowledge of the man. Instead, Desmond dropped the book. It landed with a thud on the floor, and he stared down at it as if mesmerized.

After a moment or two, Cecily said quietly, "Mr. Atkins? You did know Mr. Porter, didn't you?"

"Never heard of the fellow in my life." Desmond bent down and scooped up the book. "Ah, this one will do very well, I think."

He started across the carpet, but she stepped in front of him. "I understand you were arguing with him on the top floor of this establishment a day or two before he was killed."

Desmond's eyes flicked one way then the other. "Oh, was that who that was? I had no idea—"

"On the top floor, Mr. Atkins. I find that rather strange, since you were so adamant about the difficulty of climbing the stairs."

He stared at her for a moment or two, then all the resistence faded from his eyes. "All right, all right. I suppose you'll find out about it eventually anyway, if I don't tell you."

He limped over to a chair and sat down. "It's true, I did know Porter. I hadn't seen him in years. That is, until a week ago." He coughed, and fiddled with the blue silk cravat nestled at his throat. "I wasn't always a gentleman, you see."

Personally Cecily found it difficult to class him as a gentleman now, but that was beside the point. "Really? I'm not sure I understand."

He shook his head. "No, no, of course you wouldn't." He sent a furtive glance at the door, as if to make sure no one would enter and overhear him. "I don't usually admit this to anyone," he said, speaking in a low voice she could barely hear. "But under the circumstances . . ." Again he hesitated.

"You don't have to concern yourself," Cecily said, growing impatient. "Whatever you tell me will be held in the strictest confidence. Unless you've broken the law, of course."

She'd added the last as an attempt to lighten his anxiety, and was taken aback when he answered, "Well, that's just it, you see. I have broken the law. Many times. I used to . . . ah . . . manipulate the locks on safes."

Her eyes widened. "You were a safecracker?"

He wriggled on his chair. "Ah, you are familiar with the term. I wasn't sure—"

"Mr. Atkins." Cecily leaned forward. "Are you telling me you were a professional thief?"

Desmond tucked his cravat more securely inside his coat. "I suppose I was, yes." He wagged a finger at her. "But I'm not anymore, you understand. I gave all that up long ago." He patted his knee. "Got kicked by a horse when I was running from the bobbies one day. Put an end to that career, as you might well imagine. Not much future in being a robber if you can't run from the law, is there."

"No, I suppose not." She frowned. "But what does all this have to do with Sid Porter?"

"Ah, well, you see, we were in partnership once." He shook his head. "Not for long. Couldn't trust the blighter. He'd rat on his best friend to save his neck, that he would."

As indeed, it seemed he had betrayed Ned Barlow, Cecily reflected. "I see. So I assume Mr. Porter saw you and recognized you."

"Yes, Mrs. Baxter. Not only recognized me, but wanted me to go back into the business with him." He made a sound of disgust in the back of his throat. "Seems things hadn't been going too good for old Sid. When you get low enough so you have to sell balloons on the beach to make a ha'penny, things are bad. Anyway, Sid knew about this safe at the bank in the high street. He kept insisting it would be just once more for old time's sake."

"And you refused."

"Well, of course I did." Desmond leaned forward. "Look,

Mrs. Baxter, you've seen my wife. I'm sure you can tell she's a proper lady. I don't know why she agreed to marry someone like me, but from the very first moment I set eyes on her I knew she was the one who could change my life. I knew how hard I would have to work to make that happen, and I spent every waking moment learning how to be a gentleman. Even then, I didn't think she'd have me."

Cecily smiled. "She must have seen something commendable in you."

Desmond shrugged. "I don't know. I only know she fought tooth and nail with her family over me, until they had to agree to the wedding. She knows nothing about my past. I made up another one. If she had any idea of who I really was, she'd be gone in a flash."

Cecily pursed her lips. "So Sid Porter was a threat to you."

"You bet he was. He threatened to tell Bernice about our partnership if I didn't help him crack that safe."

"You realize, of course, that this gives you a motive for murder?"

"Which is why I'm telling you all this. If I'd killed him, I'd keep my mouth shut, wouldn't I. I didn't kill Sid Porter, Mrs. Baxter. I swear it on my mother's grave." He paused. "Mind you, I'm not saying I didn't threaten him. I told him one word out of his mouth and he was a dead man."

"What did he say to that?"

"He just shrugged his shoulders, said I was a fool to pass up an easy take, and walked away."

"And you never saw him again."

"Never." Desmond pushed himself up from the chair.

"Mrs. Baxter, I'm trusting you to keep my secret. I'm sure you don't want to destroy a happy marriage."

Cecily rose to her feet. "I promise not to divulge your secret on one condition."

"And what's that?"

"If I find out you were involved in any way with Sid Porter's death, I shall feel it my duty to inform the inspector of our conversation."

"Fair enough." He gave her a sharp nod and crossed the room to the door. "You won't find anything on me, Mrs. Baxter. I can promise you that."

The door closed, leaving her staring after him. He had seemed sincere, but she had learned long ago to trust her instincts, and she didn't feel fully convinced that Desmond Atkins's hands were as clean as he professed. Perhaps her search of Sid Porter's room would tell her something. She certainly hoped so. Only two more days until Christmas Day and she was no closer to solving this puzzle.

She left the library and headed for the kitchen. She had to go over the menu with Michel, and confer with Mrs. Chubb about the table settings for the Christmas dinner. After that perhaps she could find the time to visit Madeline.

Hurrying down the hallway, she went over in her mind her conversation with Desmond Atkins. Something he'd said had struck a bell somewhere. She'd grasped at it when he'd said it, but the words had slipped away from her before she could understand their significance.

As she entered the lobby, Phoebe came charging through the front door, and Cecily had to give up her attempt to recall the elusive message in her head. Maybe later she'd remember, when she had a quiet moment to herself.

"I had to come by and see you," Phoebe said, gasping from her exertion. "I stopped in Dolly's tea shop this morning to pick up some Banbury cakes, and Dolly told me you'd found a dozen armchairs sitting in the middle of the tennis court."

Cecily sighed. "Only five armchairs, Phoebe, and they were in the middle of the bowling green. Not the tennis court."

Phoebe dismissed the discrepancy with a flap of her hand. "So Frederick was telling the truth, after all. Do tell, Cecily. Was it the ghost? How utterly dreadful! Did anyone see them floating through the air? Imagine a ghost being able to move heavy furniture that way. Terrifying, my dear." She patted Cecily's arm with her gloved fingers. "You must be beside yourself with worry. It could be the Christmas tree floating around next. Just imagine."

Cecily shuddered at the thought. "I doubt very much if a ghost could transport a feather, much less five armchairs," she said grimly. She glanced over her shoulder at a couple descending the stairs. "I do hope you won't repeat any of this to anyone," she added. "I don't want to have our guests needlessly frightened away."

"Oh, of course, Cecily." Phoebe placed a delicate hand over her mouth. "I shall say nothing." Her eyes grew wide over her fingers. "If it's not a ghost, then who would do such a silly thing?"

The couple passed them by, smiling a greeting at Cecily. She waited until they were out of earshot, then murmured,

"Phoebe, I'm sorry, but I have something I must attend to in the kitchen. Perhaps we can meet later, when I have more time to discuss all this?"

"By all means." Phoebe's frown disappeared. "Why don't we meet for refreshments at the tea shop? Dolly asked about you this morning. She said she hasn't seen you in far too long. I'm sure she'd love it if you pop in today."

Tempted, Cecily considered the idea. It had been some time since she had enjoyed one of Dolly's scones spread with strawberry jam and thick clotted cream. Her mouth watered at the memory. "Very well," she said quickly, before she could change her mind. "I'll do my best to be there at half past eleven."

"Wonderful!" Phoebe clapped her hands. "We can have a nice long talk."

"I won't be able to stay for long," Cecily warned. "I promised Baxter I'd go with him to the George and Dragon at one o'clock."

Phoebe smiled, and waved happily as she trotted back to the door.

With a glance at the grandfather clock in the corner of the lobby, Cecily quickened her pace to the kitchen. If she were to pay Madeline a visit, that would leave no time for breakfast. Already the maids had returned from the dining room for the tea trolleys.

Michel had disappeared when she entered the warm kitchen, and she found Mrs. Chubb in the pantry, making a list for the grocer.

"We'll have to order some additions to the willow china soon, m'm," she said, when she saw Cecily. "The maids are all fingers and thumbs this morning. Lost three plates and a cup and saucer. That's not counting the plates Gertie dropped the other day."

"Well, please make a list of what we need and I'll send one of the footmen into town to buy some more." Cecily looked along the shelves at the stacks of china. "What about the rose pattern? Do we have enough for the tables on Christmas Day?"

"Yes, m'm." Mrs. Chubb pointed with her pencil. "You bought extra of those last summer."

Cecily nodded her approval. "Where is Michel? I must go over the menu with him for tonight's dinner. It should be something simple, since the carol singers will be arriving shortly after dinner is served. We don't need maids running around the dining room while the singers are performing."

"Michel didn't say where he was going." Mrs. Chubb lowered her voice. "He's been acting strange, ever since young Doris and that singer got here. I think he's got it bad, m'm."

Cecily frowned. "Got what?"

"Oh, sorry, m'm. That's Gertie's talk. It rubs off on me sometimes. No, I mean Michel has taken a fancy to that singer friend of Doris's. He's been disappearing every now and then, and I think he's meeting her somewhere."

Cecily pinched her lips together. "She certainly likes to attract attention."

"That she does, m'm. But then she's on the stage. What can you expect."

Just then a disturbance in the kitchen distracted the

housekeeper, and she rushed out to see the cause of all the commotion.

Cecily left her to restore order among the maids, and went in search of Michel. She eventually found him in the ballroom, talking to Elise, as Mrs. Chubb had suspected. He seemed flustered when she entered, and Elise quickly left his side, murmuring a soft greeting as she slipped past Cecily and out the door.

"You were looking for me, madame?" Michel's accent seemed even more pronounced.

Assuming it was for the benefit of the singer, Cecily gave him a sour look. "The menu, Michel. Did you forget?"

"Pardonnez moi!" Michel dug in his pocket and drew out a slip of paper. "I had meant to leave this with Mrs. Chubb." He handed it to Cecily, who quickly scanned it.

"The pheasant and ptarmigan pie will do very nicely," she murmured. "I think, however, that we should dispense with the blood pudding this evening. I want to keep things as simple as possible."

"Oui, madame. As you wish."

"Blancmange for dessert, with the glazed cherries." She handed the menu back to him. "The rest I'll leave for your choice."

"Merci, madame."

Unable to help herself, she murmured, "Michel, I saw you talking to Elise Boulanger. I hope she doesn't have any complaints?"

"Complaints, madame? I do not think so. She is . . . how you say . . . anticipating the Christmas dinner with great excitement. That is all."

"Hmmmm." Cecily gave him a shrewd look. "Be careful, Michel. These stage people can be quite unpredictable."

"I shall bear it in mind, madame."

He gave her a sweeping bow, but before he straightened, she turned her back on him and hurried to the door.

She would not have time now to visit with Madeline, unless she could persuade her friend to join her and Phoebe. She would send a carriage to fetch her to the tea shop, she decided, and that would give her time to visit with them both.

It also meant she would have to put up with the squabbling between her two dearest friends. No one would ever dream that the two of them were genuinely fond of each other behind all that petty bickering.

Still, Madeline could certainly advise her as to how to handle the problem of the ghost, and right then Cecily needed all the help available. She had a horrible feeling that things were about to spiral out of control, and with Christmas just two days away, she could not afford to let that happen.

Phoebe was sitting in her usual spot by the fireplace when Cecily entered the tea shop. A carriage had been dispatched to Madeline's house, with a message that Cecily desperately needed to discuss something with her. She hoped Madeline's curiosity would persuade her to accept the invitation to join them.

Madeline didn't care much for formal appointments. She tolerated them when necessary, and avoided them whenever possible. Phoebe, on the other hand, adored being out in public and always made certain she was immaculately dressed for the occasion.

Today she wore a white and black gored skirt with a lacy white blouse, and had covered it with a black coat trimmed in white fur. Her black hat sported several white roses, and for a dash of color, a robin with a bloodred chest sat among them.

"Oh, there you are," she called out, as Cecily approached the table. "I took the liberty of ordering tea and crumpets for us both. I hope that's all right?"

"Quite all right." Cecily seated herself, and took a moment to breathe in the delicious aroma of freshly baked bread. "Thank you, Phoebe. We shall have to add to the order, however. I've asked Madeline to join us."

"Oh." Phoebe's face dropped. "Well, I suppose, since we don't get too many opportunities to meet . . ." Her voice trailed off, giving Cecily the impression that Phoebe would tolerate Madeline for Cecily's sake.

Dolly chose that moment to bear down on them with a large tray. She somehow managed to maneuver her enormous girth between the tables without sweeping everything off in her wake. It seemed to Cecily that Dolly added an extra roll or two of fat each time she saw her.

Dolly's chins wobbled in delight as she greeted Cecily. "Mrs. Baxter! I was beginning to think you'd gone off my baking!" Her hearty laugh rang out, turning the heads of the half dozen customers in the tiny dining room.

She dropped the tray on the table, rattling the cups and

saucers. Lowering her voice, she whispered, "I heard about the murder up at the Pennyfoot. Can't believe young Roland would do such a thing. He seemed such a nice lad."

"Yes, we are all very upset by the tragedy." Cecily looked at the tray. "My, Dolly, those crumpets look delicious. I can't wait to taste one. Your baking is such a delight. I've sorely missed your wonderful scones."

"Then you shall have some to take home. My treat."

"That's most kind of you." Cecily smiled up at the woman. "I wonder if we might bother you for another pot of tea and some more crumpets. Madeline will be joining us shortly."

"It will be my pleasure." Dolly lumbered off in the direction of the kitchen.

Turning to Phoebe, Cecily opened her mouth to speak, then closed it again when she saw the shocked expression on her friend's face.

"Murdered?" Phoebe's lips barely moved. "Are you telling me Mr. Porter was *murdered*? And *Roland* was responsible?"

Cecily glanced over her shoulder, but the other women in the shop all seemed engrossed in their own conversations. Leaning forward, she said softly, "I'm sorry, Phoebe. I thought you would have heard the news by now. I'm afraid Sid Porter had been stabbed."

"Oh, my!" Phoebe slapped a hand over her mouth. "I don't believe it. Roland was a nice boy. So helpful. I can't believe . . ." Tears welled in her eyes, and she hunted in her sleeve for a handkerchief.

"If it's any consolation," Cecily murmured, "neither do I believe that Roland was the cause of Mr. Porter's death. I'm doing my best to find the real culprit."

Phoebe delicately blew her nose. "Well, I can't say I was particularly impressed by Mr. Porter. No gentleman, that's for certain. Then again, a gentleman would never agree to slide down a chimney dressed as Father Christmas. A man like that was bound to have enemies. Who do you think killed him?" Phoebe shuddered.

"I really can't say at this point." Cecily thought about the clown's nose she'd found. "There are so many disturbing elements to this puzzle." Several of which, she decided, she needed to keep to herself.

"If anyone can solve a puzzle, Cecily, it's you."

The mellow voice had spoken from behind her, and Cecily turned her head to see Madeline smiling down at her.

"Madeline!" Cecily waved her to a seat. "This is so nice. The three of us here at Dolly's again. It's been far too long." She smiled at her friend. "I haven't had an opportunity to tell you how wonderful the Christmas decorations are this year. I've had so many compliments on them. The ballroom looks magnificent."

Madeline's pink muslin frock floated about her ankles as she sat down. "Thank you, Cecily." She shook her dark tresses back from her face, earning a frown of disapproval from Phoebe, whose sense of decorum did not allow for unbound hair at a dining table.

"I just wish I'd had more time," Madeline added. "The balloons looked a little sparse, don't you think? We just didn't have the time to blow up enough of them." She nodded at Phoebe, who gave her a faint smile back.

"I thought the room looked fairly presentable," Phoebe said. "After all, not everyone likes balloons. Especially when they burst. Those loud popping noises can be quite startling if one isn't prepared."

Madeline ignored her. "So what do we need to discuss that is so desperate, Cecily? I have to admit, I am intrigued by all this mystery."

"Well, I'm sure you've heard we're being haunted by a clown ghost." Cecily reached for the teapot and began pouring tea into the cups. "I need your expert opinion. Are ghosts able to move something heavy around, such as an armchair or an aspidistra, for instance?"

Madeline's laugh rippled across the table. "Highly unlikely. Why do you ask?"

"Several large objects have been mysteriously whisked from their homes and deposited in very unusual places."

Phoebe nodded. "Frederick found some armchairs from the library in the middle of the bowling green. The silly man actually fell asleep out there. Can you imagine?"

"Well, that's what happens when one has as loving a relationship with a bottle as your husband does," Madeline said, in a silky tone that warned Cecily she was in a cantankerous mood.

As usual, Phoebe rose to the bait. "Well, at least I have a husband."

"Some of the time," Madeline murmured.

The roses of Phoebe's hat quivered. "Just what do you mean by that?"

Sensing an imminent battle, Cecily broke in. "I saw you talking to Dr. Prestwick last night. It's nice to see you two getting along so well."

Phoebe sniffed. "Not well enough to make an honest woman of you, apparently."

Madeline smiled. "I don't need a man to make me honest. Not like some people I could mention."

"Will you be spending Christmas with the doctor?" Cecily asked, before Phoebe's outrage could explode.

Madeline shrugged. "We plan to attend the carol singing in the library tonight. Beyond that we haven't made any firm arrangements."

Phoebe opened her mouth to say something, but Cecily forestalled her. "I hope while you are there, you can use your wonderful powers to find out if we have a ghost in our midst, or if all this moving about of furniture is someone's strange idea of a joke.

"No need," Madeline murmured. Her green eyes half closed as she focused on Cecily's face. She raised a hand, flattening it as if pushing against air. Her voice dropped to a monotone, making Cecily's skin prickle. "The ghost does not exist and you will soon be rid of the clown forever."

Phoebe uttered a nervous laugh. "Really, Madeline. Do you think you can be rid of a ghost just like that? I saw it myself, yesterday. I saw it with my own two eyes."

"Your eyes deceived you."

Madeline's voice had returned to normal, and Cecily relaxed. "Then you're saying the clown is not a ghost?"

"All I'm saying," Madeline said, as she stole a crumpet from Cecily's plate, "is that you do not have a ghost in the hotel. Not at the present time, anyway." She picked up a knife, expertly scooped a dab of butter onto the end of it and began smearing it over the crumpet. "What you do have, however, is a devious killer who will stop at nothing to cover his tracks." Her gaze met Cecily's. "Beware, my friend. Even you are no match for this one."

CHAPTER
❈ 14 ❈

Cecily had asked Samuel to return to Dolly's with the trap at noon, giving her plenty of time to take Madeline back to her house and continue on to keep her rendezvous with Baxter.

Her stable manager was waiting outside when she stepped through the door of the teashop, and she could tell at once he had something of importance to tell her.

Wisely he held his tongue until Madeline had been safely deposited at her front door and had drifted inside in a cloud of muslin.

Settling back on her seat, Cecily waited for Samuel to speak. She didn't have long to wait. He had barely urged the horses into a trot before calling back over his shoulder, "I found something this morning, m'm. Thought I should tell you about it."

She leaned forward again. "You did? What is it?"

Holding the reins with one hand, he passed an envelope back to her.

She took out a length of strong twine and stared at it in confusion. "Where did this come from?"

"I thought I'd take a look around the balcony, just to see if I could find anything to do with that ghost everyone saw yesterday. I found that tied to one of the pillars. I knew it didn't belong with any of the Christmas decorations, so I thought you might want to take a look at it. I found this up there, as well."

He fished in his pocket and came out with a handful of straw. He let go of it, allowing it to fly back in the wind. "Straw, m'm. From the stable, I reckon."

A piece of the straw had been trapped by Cecily's arm. She picked it off and held it while she examined the ends of the twine. Both had been neatly cut.

"I don't know what you'd make of it, m'm, but I didn't think that belonged there. I know the maids cleaned the balcony yesterday morning."

Cecily stared at the piece of straw. "Samuel, the moment we return to the hotel, I'd like you to search the stables."

"Yes, m'm." Samuel flicked the reins, and the horses tossed their heads and snorted. "Perhaps you'd better tell me what I'm looking for, m'm?"

"I think," Cecily said slowly, "that we're looking for a scarecrow."

Samuel shot her a startled look over his shoulder. "A scarecrow, m'm?"

"Yes, Samuel. A scarecrow with the face of a clown." She

leaned back again, still fingering the piece of straw. So that's how the culprit managed the illusion. He'd stuffed straw into clothes to make up the figure of a clown, and had used twine, probably slung over the chandelier, to suspend the "ghost" above the chairs. Then he must have cut the twine and carried off the clown, disappearing before anyone had time to get up there.

That still left the question of why he'd gone to all that trouble to move the furniture. There seemed no purpose in frightening everyone into thinking the hotel was haunted, unless he hoped everyone would blame Sid Porter's death on a ghost. A bit far-fetched, even for the most gullible.

Cecily sighed. The further she delved into this business, the more confusing it became. Perhaps her visit to Sid Porter's house would unearth something that would help shed light on the mystery. Until then, she would do her best to enjoy the outing with her husband.

Baxter had already arrived at the George and Dragon, having been met at the train station by one of the footmen and transported to the pub. He had arranged for a table in the private bar, where Cecily's presence would be acceptable. Ladies were not allowed in the public bar. That was reserved for the men alone.

Bernie Milligan waited on them himself, and brought each of them a ploughman's lunch. Cecily surveyed the array of cheeses, ham, apple slices, pickled onion, and thick bread with regret for having eaten too many crumpets earlier.

Baxter had no trouble at all tackling the feast, and seemed content to listen to her talk while she picked at her meal. "I have a theory about the ghost in the balcony yesterday," she said, as Baxter tore off a piece of the bread and thrust it in his mouth.

He raised an eyebrow at her and she explained how she thought the clown had been suspended with the twine above the balcony chairs.

"So you think the clown was just a rag doll?"

"I think the one in the balcony might have been, yes."

"What about the one Pansy saw on the top floor?"

"I suppose that could have been a dummy as well. It lost its nose, though. Before the ghost in the balcony appeared. I wonder if it had a new nose."

"From the sound of it, I don't think anyone would have noticed."

Cecily picked up a slice of Gorgonzola and bit into it. The tangy cheese stung her tongue and she took a sip of her ale. Putting down the glass, she said, "I suppose you're right. I've asked Samuel to search the stables when we return to the hotel. Just in case someone happened to hide our ghost in there somewhere."

"So Porter wasn't killed by a clown after all."

"It would seem that way." She sighed. "Perhaps there's no connection there at all, and I've simply been following the wrong trail all this time."

Baxter gave her a smug smile. "Which is a very good reason to leave sleuthing to the constables."

That was a sentiment with which she would never agree, Cecily thought, as she speared a pickled onion with her fork. Deciding the time had come to change the subject, she asked, "Did you ever come across that article you talked about?"

"Oh, the one with the woman drowning herself?" Baxter shook his head. "I've looked for it, but so far it remains hidden. One of those maddening instances of putting something in a safe place and forgetting where I put it." He pushed his empty plate away and sat back. "I must be getting old."

"Never!" She patted his arm. "You've had a lot on your mind lately."

Frowning, he fiddled with his dessert spoon and fork. "I've been thinking about it. I seem to remember she'd survived an attack of some sort. I believe it was while she stayed with her family at the Pennyfoot. Something to do with balloons, if my memory serves me well, though I have to admit it hasn't done so lately."

"She was attacked by balloons?" Cecily burst out laughing. "Really, Baxter, you have to find the article now. My curiosity knows no bounds."

"Does it ever?"

She wrinkled her nose at him. "If you are finished with your meal, I'd like to visit Sid Porter's house now. I must return to the hotel in good time to attend to the carol singers when they arrive."

"Very well." Baxter dabbed his mouth with his serviette and rose. "I'll have a word with Milligan and find out where the fellow lived."

"You'll find Samuel in the public bar. He's waiting to take us there."

She watched her husband stride from the room. It was really no wonder that Elise Boulanger found herself attracted to him. He presented a fine figure of a man, and wore his age extremely well. She could hardly blame the young woman for paying attention to him.

Depression settled on her like a dark cloak, but she shook it off. She had to trust that her husband's intentions were honorable, though she knew quite well her mind would not settle until she understood exactly what kind of surprise he had planned for her.

She smiled at him when he returned and allowed him to assist her in rising. "Did you find out where Mr. Porter lived?" she asked, as she led the way out into the cold wind.

"I did." He led her to the trap, where Samuel waited, reins in hand.

Cecily stepped inside and seated herself. Climbing in after her, Baxter gave Samuel the address and then settled himself beside her. "Exactly what do you hope to find at this residence?" he asked, as the horses clattered down the road.

"I really don't know." Cecily tied her warm scarf over her hat and nestled closer to her husband for warmth. "Anything that might help us discover who wanted Mr. Porter dead."

"That could be any number of people, judging from what I've heard about the fellow."

"Perhaps, but how many of them hated him enough to actually kill him?"

Baxter pursed his lips. "I see what you mean. It's simple enough to wish someone dead, but actually doing the deed yourself would be taking extraordinary measures."

"Exactly. So, what we need to find out is who had reason to go to those lengths." She paused. "I do have one suspect." She told him about her conversation with Desmond Atkins.

"You think he's capable of murder?"

"Everyone's capable of murder, if the urge is strong enough. I think Mr. Atkins's motive was strong enough, but I'm not so sure the urge to kill was there. Then again, I've been mistaken before, but I can hardly accuse the man without any proof. That's what I'm hoping to find in Sid Porter's house. Some sort of proof that will convince the inspector."

Baxter groaned. "Don't even mention that supercilious oaf to me. The less we have to do with him, the better."

"Which is precisely why I want to solve this case before he has a chance to interfere."

"Which is the reason I've agreed to this search, against my better judgment."

She smiled up at him. "I do appreciate your help, Bax. I feel so much more secure with you by my side."

He grunted in reply, but she could tell by the tiny quiver to his mouth that her compliment had been well received.

A few minutes later they entered the high street. Samuel reined in the horses at the end of a narrow alleyway. "This is the address, Mr. Baxter," he called out.

Frowning, Baxter peered down the dark passageway. "I don't see any houses."

"No, sir. The address is a flat above the greengrocer's. You get to it down that alley and up the stairs."

Baxter looked with distaste at the broken cobblestones and expanse of mud. "Cecily, I think you should wait for me here," he said, as he prepared to step down.

"Piffle. I'm coming with you." Before he could protest further, she scrambled out of the trap. "Samuel, please wait here for us."

"Yes, m'm." Samuel touched his cap with his whip and settled back on his seat.

To Cecily's relief, Baxter gave her no further argument. She followed him down the alleyway, being careful not to step into the mud and soil her shoes. The odor of decaying refuse from the filthy buildings made her wrinkle her nose, and she tried not to breathe too deeply as they reached the door.

Baxter turned the handle, but the door refused to budge. "It's locked." He actually looked relieved.

Disappointed, Cecily glanced up to the street. "Then we must ask the greengrocer for the key." She looked expectantly at her husband.

Baxter sighed. "Why do I allow myself to become involved in your misadventures?"

"Because you care enough about me to want to protect me," she answered, hoping she had spoken the truth.

He grimaced. "Sometimes I think it is I who needs protection." He glanced about, but they were alone in the alleyway. "Wait here until I return. I shall be no more than a moment."

She nodded, thankful she didn't have to traipse up and down that dreadful passage any more than necessary. Instead, she flattened herself in the doorway and hoped no one would approach until her husband had returned to her side.

She waited several moments, then growing impatient, she stuck her head out of the doorway to peer up the alleyway. Right in front of her stood a grubby little urchin with ragged hair and torn clothes, one muddy hand outstretched toward her.

With a gasp, Cecily drew back. "What do you want?" she demanded sharply.

"Just a ha'penny, mum?"

"I haven't any money with me," Cecily said, softening her tone. "I'm sorry."

"What about the gent with you? Would he happen to have a ha'penny?"

"He's more likely to give you a cuff around the ear than a ha'penny," Cecily said, beginning to feel sorry for the lad. "I suggest you find someone else with whom to do your begging."

Looking dejected, the boy dropped his hand. His gaze moved from her to the door behind her. "Watcha want with Sid?"

Now he had Cecily's attention. "You knew . . . ah . . . know Mr. Porter?"

The boy nodded. "I see him on the sands in the summer. He sells balloons, and sometimes he's a clown. He thinks I don't know it's him, but I can tell as soon as he opens his mouth who it is."

Cecily narrowed her eyes. Balloons. A clown. There it was again. That little voice that told her she had all the pieces of the puzzle and just needed to fit them all together. "Well," she said, "if you can answer a question or two for me, perhaps I can persuade my husband to give you a penny."

The boy's eyes lit up. "I'll be happy to tell you anyfink I know."

"Do you know if Mr. Porter had visitors to his home?"

"Not many. I know one of 'em, though. It's a bloke wot

just got out of the clink. I heard Sid yelling at him all the way down the street."

"You mean Ned Barlow?"

The boy eagerly nodded his head. "Yeah, that's his name. Ned. I heard him say he was going to get Sid for what he did to him."

An image of Ned Barlow's cruel face popped into Cecily's mind. She saw him lurking in the doorway, his fingers carefully stroking his nose as if it hurt to do so. She remembered noticing a small round cut on it. The sort of cut, perhaps, that might have been caused by the bright red nose of a clown.

A shout from further down the alleyway brought up her head. Baxter hurried toward her, anxiety creasing his face. His shout echoed through the buildings. "Here, you! Get away from my wife!"

"It's all right, darling," she cried out. "He just wanted to tell me something."

Baxter puffed out his chest as he reached them and glared at the boy. "What is it he wants?"

"I promised this young man a penny if he could tell me something useful, and he did. So would you please pay him for me?"

She smiled sweetly at Baxter, who now seemed angry with her. "What did he tell you?"

"I'll explain in a moment." She smiled at the boy who had nervously backed away from Baxter. "Thank you," she said. "You've been most helpful."

Grumbling, Baxter dug in his pocket and gave the urchin two pennies. "Here. Now leave us alone."

A huge grin spread across the boy's face when he examined the change in his hand. "Cor! Thank you, sir! Much obliged, I am."

"All right, be off with you." Baxter flapped his hand as if brushing off a fly. Still grinning, the boy spun around and fled up the street.

"Thank you, darling." She looked down at his hand. "Did you get the key?"

"Yes, I did. The chap was reluctant to give it to me, until I mentioned the Pennyfoot, and that we might have need of some of his produce. He was quick enough to hand it over then."

"I imagine he was." She waited eagerly for Baxter to fit the key in the lock and turn it.

Inside the building, the smell of rotting vegetables seemed overpowering and again she attempted to hold her breath for as long as possible as she made her way up the stairs with Baxter close on her heels.

Daylight filtered through dusty windows as she reached the top landing. A sitting room lay on her left, with a broken down chair and table, and a chipped, stained sink in one corner.

Baxter followed her into the room, complaining bitterly about the smell. "This place hasn't been cleaned in years by the look of it."

"Well, let's hurry with our search. Then we can leave." Cecily opened a cupboard and peered inside. A few cracked cups and glasses stood amid a half dozen or so chipped plates and a bowl.

"I don't know what I'm supposed to be looking for," Baxter muttered.

"Letters, scraps of paper, maybe a scribbled address. Perhaps someone we can ask about Sid's acquaintances." *Especially one in particular,* she added inwardly.

"Nothing in here," Baxter announced, a short time later. He walked into the hallway. "I'll take a look in this other room."

She heard a door open and guessed he'd found the bedroom. A few minutes later he returned to find her hunting through a coat she'd found hanging on a hallstand.

"Nothing." He sounded disgusted. "I searched through drawers, cupboards and a wardrobe. Even under the bed. The dust is so thick under there you could make a horse blanket out of it."

Cecily hung the coat back on its hook. "Well, I'm satisfied."

"Satisfied with what? We found nothing."

"Exactly. It's not what we found that's significant, but what we didn't find."

He stared at her. "What are you up to now?"

"Think, my darling husband. What is the one thing we know about Sid Porter?"

"That he was no Father Christmas?"

She smiled. "That, and the fact that he dressed as a clown to sell balloons on the beach."

"Right, but what does that have to do with anything?"

"Where is his clown suit? I assume you didn't see it in the wardrobe, or you would certainly have told me."

"Perhaps he gave it away."

"I rather doubt that. After all, the clown suit was an integral part of Mr. Porter's livelihood. He could hardly pursue his summer vocation without it."

Baxter gave her a speculative stare. "You're saying someone stole it?"

"I'd say that's entirely possible."

"To do what? Pretend to be a ghost and frighten Sid Porter to death?"

She sighed. "I know it all sounds ridiculous right now, but I can't help feeling that all this is connected somehow. There's the cut on Ned Barlow's nose, for instance."

"Cut?"

"Yes, a round cut on the end of his nose. It could have been caused by the clown nose I found in the broom cupboard. Perhaps he bumped into the wall and knocked it off his nose, giving him a nasty cut in the process."

Baxter shook his head in disbelief. "So we're back to the clown killer theory again?"

"I don't know." She headed for the door, anxious now to be out of those miserable surroundings. "I suppose the suit could have been used for the fake ghost in the balcony, and the cut on Ned's nose was just a coincidence."

"If you ask me," Baxter muttered as he followed her down the stairs, "this entire scenario sounds like a bad farce."

"I couldn't agree more." Cecily stepped back into the street, welcoming the chill of the wind on her face. "But let us not forget that two people are dead, and someone is responsible. He must be found and made to pay for the crime."

Baxter's grunt of disagreement unsettled her. "Don't be too surprised if the killer proves to be Roland, as Northcott contends, and your efforts have been a complete waste of time."

She refrained from answering him. Although her conviction of Roland's innocence refused to be swayed, she still lacked proof of any kind that could suggest someone else was responsible.

A clown nose, that's all she had. Not enough to cast suspicion on anyone, much less convict them. The inspector would dismiss her suspicions and Roland's parents would have to bear a stain on their son's name.

Cecily tightened her lips as she climbed into the trap. One way or another, she must uncover the truth. And soon.

CHAPTER

✿ 15 ✿

"Are you going to listen to the carol singers tonight?" Gertie asked, as she carried a pile of dirty plates to the kitchen sink.

Mrs. Chubb finished counting the silverware before answering. "Of course I am! Wouldn't miss it."

Gertie dumped the plates into the soapy water. "I wonder if all the guests will be there."

"You mean you wonder if Jeremy Westhaven will be there, don't you?"

Gertie twisted her face into a wry grimace. "Why does everyone think I've got any interest in a toff? Fat lot of bloody good that'd do me. I might as well have romantic feelings for the king." She giggled. "Come to think of it, I might have better luck with him."

"We don't speak that way about members of the royal family, Gertie, so mind your tongue."

Gertie grinned, and headed back to the door. "I remember when King Edward were here. Right bleeding Casanova he were. I bet his wife never knew how many ladies he entertained in his boudoir, or how many maid's arses he pinched."

"That's enough, young lady!"

Mrs. Chubb's sharp reprimand followed Gertie out into the hallway. Still chuckling, she hurried to the dining room. Her smile faded as she threaded her way through the tables.

Several people had already left the room, but Jeremy Westhaven still sat at his table, his chin resting on his hands. She'd been happy to see him come down for the evening meal, but he'd barely summoned a smile when she'd spoken to him, and seemed disinclined to speak.

He needed cheering up, that's what he needed. And she was just the person to do it. Squaring her shoulders, she marched right up to his table. "Is there anything else I can get for you, sir?"

His glance skimmed her face. "What? Oh, no. Nothing. Thank you."

She tried again. "There's going to be carol singing in the ballroom in a few minutes. They're rather good. I heard them last year. I think you'd like that, if you don't mind me saying."

He blinked at her. "I'm not in a very good frame of mind to enjoy Christmas carols."

"Oh, I'm sorry to hear that." She leaned closer. "Not poorly, are you? I could ask Mrs. Chubb for a powder if you need to settle your tummy."

"Thank you, no. I'm quite well." He seemed to make an effort to smile. "In fact, I think I might listen to the carol singers after all." He rose from his chair and pulled a watch from his waistcoat pocket. "In the ballroom, you say?"

"Yes, sir." Gertie nodded and smiled. "They should be starting any minute now."

"Then I'd better dash along. Thank you for your kind concern."

He hurried off, and she stared after him. Something was wrong with him. She could feel it in her bones. Something really bad. She hoped, with all her heart, he wasn't really, really ill, like dying or something. That would break her heart right in two.

Despondent now, she helped the maids finish clearing the tables, then made her way to the ballroom. Now she needed cheering up, and listening to Christmas carols seemed a good way to do it.

The lilting music rang in her ears as she slipped through the doors and took up a position behind one of the pillars. Servants weren't allowed to have a seat in the audience, but Madam let them stand in the back and watch.

A group of singers stood on the stage, their red cloaks making a splash of bright color against the gray background. Madeline had suspended huge white snowflakes above the performers' heads, and a Christmas tree stood in the corner of the stage, its candles unlit.

Gertie shivered at the memory of the fire in the library last year. The smell had hung around for weeks, reminding them all how close they had come to losing the Pennyfoot.

To most of the staff, the hotel was home, the place where they lived and worked.

Except for the two twerps Madam had hired for Christmas. Gertie gazed around but couldn't see Reggie or Lawrence anywhere. What she did see, however, raised her eyebrows clear into her forehead.

Baxter stood behind a pillar across the room, hidden from the people seated in front of the stage. Elise Boulanger stood next to him, and judging by the way she gazed up at him, the two of them were a lot more cozy than was proper.

Gertie scanned the audience and spotted Madam seated in the front row, an empty chair next to her. Gertie got a sick feeling in her stomach. There weren't nobody what loved each other like Madam and Mr. Baxter did.

If Madam knew he was skulking about behind the pillars with Elise Boulanger, there'd be bloody hell to pay. She could only hope and pray that whatever Mr. Baxter was whispering in that painted tart's ear wouldn't offend Madam.

Cecily watched the group of carol singers without paying attention to the words they sang. Baxter had promised to join her, yet she'd waited for him through three of the carols and he still hadn't appeared.

The nasty niggling worry in her chest seemed to spread throughout her body. She couldn't deny that her husband had behaved quite strangely lately, and with no real explanation for his actions. He had been secretive, evasive, and had far too many conversations with Elise Boulanger.

She could no longer accept his excuse of surprising her. She didn't want to be surprised. She wanted her husband back where he belonged, at her side, with a full accounting of his behavior.

Perhaps she should look for him and demand he tell her what she wanted to know. She sent a furtive glance left and right to make sure she hadn't missed him waiting in the aisle for an opportunity to slip into his seat.

Having convinced herself he hadn't arrived, she made a movement to stand, then paused as a lithe figure slipped into the seat beside her. She stared at Samuel, taken aback by the uncharacteristic display of bad manners.

"Begging your pardon, m'm, but I need to have a word with you." Samuel jerked his head in the direction of the doors. "Outside, if you don't mind."

With a stab of concern, she gave him a brief nod. Just at that moment the carol came to a flourishing finish. Cecily politely applauded, then bent double and slipped out of her seat to make her way into the aisle.

Just as she did so, she saw Baxter step out from behind a pillar and head her way. She was about to lift a hand in greeting when she saw another figure slip out from the same pillar and disappear into the darkness on the other side of the room. She recognized her at once. That red hair was identifiable anywhere. Elise Boulanger.

A knife turned in her heart. Staring straight ahead, she walked right past her husband and marched toward the door. She heard him speak her name, urgently under his breath. She chose to ignore it, and as the opening strains of

"God Rest Ye Merry Gentlemen" rang out, she pushed open the doors and stepped through them.

Samuel must have darted ahead, since he waited for her at the end of the hallway. "I have to show you something," he said, as she joined him. "It's in the stables."

In spite of the ache under her ribs, she felt a stir of anticipation. "You found something?"

"Yes, m'm."

Since people were milling about the lobby, she held back her questions. "Wait here until I fetch my cloak," she told Samuel, then hurried up the stairs to her suite.

It took her but a moment to wrap the warm cloak about her shoulders, and then she rejoined Samuel in the lobby. Beckoning him to follow, she stepped outside into the cold night air.

The salty sea mist clung to her face and hair as she did her best to keep up with Samuel's quick steps while they crossed the courtyard.

Rounding the end of the stables, Samuel paused. "It's in here, m'm," he said, in a low voice. He stepped inside the first stable and she followed, picking up her skirts to avoid sweeping straw along with her.

Cecily waited until Samuel lit a lamp and held it aloft. "Oh, my." She stopped short at the sight of what appeared to be a dead body. "Please don't tell me we have another murder on our hands."

"No, m'm." Samuel walked up to the body and gave it a hefty kick. "It's the scarecrow clown, m'm."

She hurried forward, and stared down at the heap of clothes and straw. "My goodness. Not a very good one, is it."

"No, m'm."

The clown's head had been badly shaped with straw stuffed inside a flour sack. A garish red mouth covered half the lower face, and a painted red nose sat above it, below two black eyes. A tangled mop head, soaked in what appeared to be red ink, stuck out the top. The rest of the body had been tied to the mop handle.

Up close it looked ridiculous, though Cecily could well imagine how frightening the scarecrow must have seemed suspended in the air above the balcony seats. "Well, that at least clears up the matter of the ghost," she said. "Be sure to tell the maids about this. It will help settle their minds."

"Yes, m'm." Samuel hesitated, then added, "But I don't think a straw clown could have killed Mr. Porter."

"No, Samuel. I think we can safely rule out this bundle of rags as a suspect."

"Then Roland must have killed him after all."

Cecily frowned. "I don't think so. I believe we are dealing with two clowns. One of them this monstrosity." She poked the straw dummy with her foot. "The other, I'm afraid, quite real."

Samuel's eyes widened. "Two clowns?"

"Yes. I think this one was made to throw us off the scent. I found a clown nose on the top floor in the broom cupboard. It certainly didn't belong to this one, so I must assume there is another clown prowling around the hotel."

"I think it might be better if I didn't mention that to the maids, m'm."

"Quite right. Just tell them you found the scarecrow, and

leave it at that. With any luck, we shall find the other clown before he makes any more ghostly appearances."

"Or bumps off someone else."

"That, too." Picking up her skirts she turned toward the door. "Please get rid of that thing, Samuel. I suggest you burn it."

"Yes, m'm. I'll be sure and see to it first thing in the morning."

She left him to pick up the ragged dummy and made her way back to the hotel. She had barely stepped inside the front doors when Baxter stormed across the lobby, his face a mask of resentment.

"Where in blazes have you been?" he said, his voice low with suppressed anger.

"To the stables." She slipped past him and headed for the stairs. "Samuel had something he needed to show me."

"In the middle of the night?"

"It is hardly the middle of the night. It is barely time for bed."

She began mounting the stairs, behind a couple of elderly guests, who were taking their time with each careful step. She could feel Baxter's body close behind her, and hear his furious breathing, but fortunately he had the good sense to hold his tongue until they were alone in their suite.

Pulling off her gloves, Cecily marched into the boudoir.

Baxter followed her, pausing in the doorway to glare at her. "What was so damnably important you had to leave me sitting in that blasted ballroom without so much as a word as to where you were going?"

"You weren't exactly pining for my company," Cecily retorted.

"What the hell does that mean?"

Ignoring him, she threw her gloves onto the bed and sank down on the edge of it. Her shoes had picked up a fair amount of mud and bits of straw still stuck to the soles, despite the fact she'd wiped her feet upon entering the hotel.

Sighing, she got up and walked over to her dressing table.

"I insist you explain that cryptic remark." Baxter took a few steps toward her.

Cecily picked up her button hook and carried it to her favorite Queen Anne chair. Seating herself, she began undoing the buttons of her shoes.

"Cecily, I will not tolerate—"

Her temper finally unleashed; she jerked up her chin. "You will not tolerate what? It is I who will not tolerate your behavior any longer. It is bad enough that you find it necessary to sneak around in the shadows to talk to your dear Elise, but when you display your indiscretions in full view of the guests and staff of this hotel, then I must put my foot down. There will be no more clandestine conversations with that woman in this hotel. I hope I make myself quite clear."

Heart thumping, she watched her husband thin his lips, his face white with temper. "Quite clear." He stuck two fingers in his waistcoat pocket and withdrew something small, square, and white. Marching over to her, he threw it down on the bed beside her. "Here. This is what Elise and I have been discussing. She went to a great deal of trouble to get these for you, at my request."

Her fingers trembling, Cecily picked up the envelope. "What's this?"

"It's part of your Christmas present. Open it."

She did so, and withdrew two cards. Tickets, she saw, to a concert at the Whitney Theater in London. A concert featuring her favorite singer, Colin Masterson. With an invitation to visit him backstage.

A shocked gasp left her lips, and she looked up at her husband. "I had no idea!"

"Of course you didn't. You assumed the worst, and I am sorely disappointed in you. I was under the impression you trusted me."

Stung by the injustice of his accusation, she struck back. "Exactly what was I to think, I ask you? Everywhere I looked, there you were with your heads together, whispering like two guilty lovers. I'm quite sure I was not alone in my suspicions, either. Heaven knows what the staff must think."

"I couldn't care less what the staff might think!"

His roar made her jump, but she faced him with her own righteous indignation. "Surely you could have managed this transaction without all that skulking around? After all, Elise Boulanger is an attractive woman, and associated with the stage. And, as such, her reputation is not exactly one of notable respect."

"It is not my fault if people have evil minds."

"People will gossip, Hugh, no matter how innocent the situation might be. With that in mind, you should have taken pains to spare me the embarrassment."

"Embarrassment of what, may I ask?"

"The embarrassment of giving people the false impression you had a personal interest in Miss Boulanger." She paused, then allowed her own resentment to get the better of her by adding, "That's if it *is* a false impression."

For a moment he stood staring at her, his jaw twitching in anger. Then he spun on his heel, muttering over his shoulder, "Elise Boulanger is not you, Cecily. You would do well to remember that in the future."

"Where are you going?"

He didn't answer her, and a few moments later the door slammed behind him.

Left alone, Cecily stared down at the tickets in her hand. True, she had jumped to the wrong conclusion. But, he had given her just cause.

She tugged at the buttons of her shoe with renewed vigor. Then again, Baxter had gone out of his way to obtain the tickets for her. He had no interest in the baritone himself, and he hated to ask anyone for a favor.

With a grunt of frustration, Cecily threw the button hook across the room. Although she felt a certain amount of justification, she could understand Baxter's outrage. His feelings had been hurt because she had doubted him.

Men. Piffle. Why did they have to be so infuriating with their logic and their rationalized behavior? It was enough to turn her hair gray. And she hadn't even had the chance to tell Baxter about the scarecrow Samuel found.

Well, it would just have to wait until the morning now. Knowing her husband, he would return far too late and in no mood for conversation.

She could only hope that by the morning he would have

recovered his temper. After all, it would be Christmas Eve. She couldn't bear the thought of being at odds with him at such a wonderful time of the year.

Sighing heavily, she prepared herself for bed and lay aching for a long time before she finally fell asleep with an empty space beside her.

She awoke the next morning, relief flooding through her when she saw Baxter sleeping at her side. Debating whether or not to wake him up, she deliberately tossed herself around on the bed until he stirred.

"Bax—" she began, but he interrupted her.

"I'm sorry, Cecily. I was unduly harsh last night. After thinking things through I can see where you might have formed the wrong impression. Thoughtless of me, but I wanted to surprise you and I was afraid you'd guess that I'd asked Elise if she could procure the tickets."

"I'm sorry, too." She smiled at him, and smoothed back his tousled hair with a loving hand. "I should have known you would not conduct yourself in that manner for the wrong reasons."

He raised his head to kiss her, which banished the ache in her heart. Resting her head on his shoulder, she said carefully, "What I didn't understand is how you could be on such friendly terms with Elise, without telling me that you were even acquainted with her."

"I didn't make her acquaintance until a few nights ago. I left the office early, intending to buy the tickets at the theater. I arrived there just as Doris and Elise were leaving, after their rehearsals. Doris introduced us, and when I mentioned the tickets Elise explained she was a good friend of Colin

Masterson's and could possibly arrange for us to visit him backstage. I thought it would make a wonderful surprise for Christmas."

"And it was, darling. Thank you." Cecily sighed happily. All was explained; her husband still loved her and she had an exciting event to look forward to after Christmas.

Now all she needed was to find out who killed Sid Porter and caused the death of her footman. Then, perhaps, she could put all this upheaval behind her and enjoy the celebrations.

That, she reflected, with a stab of anxiety, would not be quite so easily resolved.

CHAPTER

❧ 16 ❧

Pansy stood in front of the broom closet, struggling to find the courage to open the door. Ever since the carpet sweeper had been found hanging from the ballroom balcony, she'd been afraid to touch it. Just knowing that the ghost had moved it around gave her the willies.

She felt quite sure that once she grabbed hold of that sweeper handle she'd be whisked away to the middle of the woods somewhere, or even dumped into the icy depths of Deep Willow Pond.

It was not yet light outside, and the gas lamps flickered with a feeble glow along the walls. Out of the corner of her eye Pansy thought she saw something move. Sick with fright she flicked a quick glance down the hallway, certain she'd see the ghostly figure of that hideous clown hovering about in the shadows.

Only half reassured by the empty passage, she snatched the door open and dragged out the carpet sweeper. She still had to sweep the stairs and the lobby before Madam came down from her suite. Then she had to collect the dirty wash from the laundry chute and take it to the laundry room before getting back to the kitchen in time to start serving the breakfast meal. If she didn't get a move on, she'd be late again and in hot water with Mrs. Chubb.

Hurrying down the hallway she dragged the sweeper after her to the top of the landing. How she hated cleaning the stairs. If she wasn't careful the sweeper bumped against the wall or the bannisters, disturbing the guests. Mrs. Chubb wouldn't be too happy if she got complaints about her maids making noises this early in the morning.

Carefully, Pansy slid the sweeper back and forth on each stair, stepping down before lowering the heavy machine to the next one. As quietly as she could, she cleaned each narrow strip of carpet.

Reaching the landing of the first floor, she picked up the sweeper and carried it around the bend to the next flight of stairs. That's when she heard it. The soft sound of tinkling bells.

For a moment she froze, unable to move or even breathe. The tinkling sounded louder. Closer.

Pansy didn't wait to see if the clown hovered in the hallway. She didn't even wait to clean the rest of the stairs. She picked up the sweeper and bounded down the steps as if a pack of wolves were at her ankles.

* * *

"I'm bloody glad I don't have to look after the twins all day," Gertie said, as she held up the knife she'd just polished to inspect it for smudges. "They can't keep flipping still. Jumping all over the place they are. Keep asking me when Father Christmas is coming. I told them, after they go to sleep tonight and not bleeding before."

"I hope you didn't use those exact words," Mrs. Chubb muttered, wincing as one of Michel's saucepan lids hit the floor with a resounding crash.

" 'Course not. I want my kiddies to grow up proper." She sighed. "I know they're going to miss Ross this Christmas. I've tried to buy extra for them this year to make up for him not being here."

"Well, I've got a couple of little things for them in my room." Mrs. Chubb picked up her grocery list and ran her finger down it. "I hope I've got everything on here we need for the banquet tomorrow."

"That's really nice, Chubby." Gertie threw her arms around the housekeeper's shoulders. "I don't know what I'd do without you, and that's the truth. You're the best friend anyone could want."

"How many times have I told you not to call me Chubby." She sounded cross, but Gertie could tell the housekeeper hid a smile. "Besides, the twins remember when I was taking care of them before we came back to the hotel to work. They'd be disappointed if they didn't get a present from their Nanna."

"Well, I'll make sure they thank you when we have our Christmas dinner tomorrow night." Gertie laid down the knife and picked up another. "I'm looking forward to that.

It's always nice to eat dinner in the dining room. Specially when all the guests have gone and we have it all to ourselves."

"Except we still have to do the washing up after," Mrs. Chubb reminded her. "It takes us nearly all night to get all those glasses and dishes washed and put away."

"It's worth it. Think of all the lovely grub we'll be enjoying tomorrow."

Mrs. Chubb glanced at the clock. "Where is that Pansy? I sent her to pick up the dirty laundry and take it to the laundry room. The maids have to get everything washed and out on the lines by ten o'clock or they won't be dry and ironed by tonight. Pansy should have been back here by now."

"Still chatting with the maids more'n likely." Gertie dropped the knife onto the table. "I'll go look for her and bring her back here."

"Tell her to hurry. Breakfast is less than half an hour away."

Gertie nodded and hurried from the kitchen, glad to be out of hearing range of Michel's banging and crashing. She could tell the chef had the jitters about cooking the Christmas dinner. He had always been a bit of a butterfingers, but whenever he got worried about his cooking he dropped just about everything he picked up.

Funny thing was, no matter how nervous he got, his food was always perfect, and people never stopped raving about the meals at the Pennyfoot.

Gertie smiled to herself. Michel was one of the reasons the hotel did so well, and even the posh hotel across the downs couldn't take the Pennyfoot's guests away as long as Michel cooked for them.

She rounded the corner of the corridor that led to the laundry room. Pausing in front of the door, she pushed it open. The room smelled of soap, and little rivulets of water ran down the white walls from the steam that curled above the boilers. Raising her voice, she called out, "Is Pansy in here?"

A chorus of voices answered her. "No!" "Haven't seen her!" "She's not here!"

Gertie muttered a curse under her breath. Silly cow probably got her head stuck in the laundry chute or something. She closed the door and hurried down the hallway. They were all going to be late for breakfast if Pansy didn't hurry up and get back to the kitchen.

Gertie rounded the corner and squinted down the narrow passage. A single gas lamp flickered on the wall, sending faint shadows dancing along the stripe-papered walls. The light didn't quite reach to the end of the passage, and at first Gertie thought that a bundle of clothes had fallen out from the chute onto the floor.

As she approached, however, she saw a pair of oxford shoes and then a white cap. She halted, one hand over her mouth as she stared at the still figure of Pansy. Finding it too difficult to see clearly in the dim shadows, she crept forward. Her voice wavering like a crummy singer she called out, "Pansy? Are you all right?"

She could see no movement from the figure lying on the floor. She inched closer, one hand outstretched to touch the maid. Then her heart jumped in relief as Pansy stirred and uttered a soft moan.

"Bloody hell," Gertie muttered. "I thought you was bleeding dead. What're you doing down there?"

Reaching the girl, she dropped to her knees beside her. "What's the matter? Are you ill?"

Pansy moaned again, her eyes shut tight as if she were afraid to open them. With a shaking hand she pointed a finger at the chute.

Gertie followed the gesture to the dark square opening in the wall. Shock slammed into her when she saw a face peering back at her. An ugly, horrifying face with bright orange hair, a thick grinning red mouth, and white eyes that stared unseeingly at nothing.

With a low moan, Gertie joined Pansy on the floor.

"I think we should serve mulled wine and hot cider around the Christmas tree tonight," Cecily said, peering over Mrs. Chubb's shoulder at the list the housekeeper held in her hand. "And some of those little sausage rolls you bake so well. They are utterly delicious and the guests love them."

"Yes, madam." Mrs. Chubb scribbled on her list with a worn-down pencil. "What about mince pies, and perhaps some cheese twists?"

"Excellent." Cecily turned to Michel, whose crashing around had punctuated the conversation for the past ten minutes. "What are you cooking, Michel? It smells divine."

"Bacon rolls, madame." Michel stuck the prongs of a fork into the frying pan and came up with a sizzling round object on the end of it. "You would like to taste, *oui?*"

"I would indeed."

"Careful. It is hot." He handed her the fork.

Holding the roll close it her nose, she sniffed at it. "What's inside it?"

"Chestnut, madame, and a little liver paste."

Cecily raised her eyebrows. "How intriguing." She took a careful bite. "This is absolutely scrumptious." She beamed at the chef. "I hope you've made lots. The guests will devour them."

"I have made plenty," Michel assured her.

"The guests will be going hungry if those girls don't get back here soon." Mrs. Chubb sent a worried look at the clock. "I sent Gertie to look for Pansy, who was supposed to take the dirty wash to the laundry room, and now they're both late. Looks like I'll be serving breakfast myself."

"I'll go and see what's keeping them." Cecily licked her fingers then wiped them dry on the serviette Mrs. Chubb handed her. "Mmm, these are good. Please save some for Baxter, Michel. I'm quite sure he'll adore them." She left the kitchen, still enjoying the taste of the tidbit in her mouth.

The maids in the laundry room informed Cecily that Gertie had been in earlier asking for Pansy and that they had seen neither girl since. Frowning, Cecily headed for the laundry chute.

As she rounded the corner she heard someone sobbing and quickened her pace. In the dim light at the end of the passage she saw Gertie with her arm around Pansy, whose shoulders shook with the force of her weeping.

"Whatever's the matter?" Cecily hurried toward them, and Gertie held up her hand.

"Wait there, m'm," she called out. "Don't come down

here." She gave Pansy a little shake. "Come on, let's get out of here. Mrs. Chubb is waiting for us."

Cecily ignored the warning and rushed forward. "What's the matter with her? Is she ill? Does she need a doctor?"

Something in Gertie's face made her pause. "No, m'm," Gertie said. "But I reckon he does." She jerked her thumb back at the open chute. "I wouldn't go down there, m'm. It ain't a pretty sight."

At her words, Pansy wailed. "It's horrible, m'm. Really horrible!"

"Whatever are you talking about?" Cecily marched past them and halted in front of the chute. In the next instant she regretted tasting Michel's bacon rolls as her stomach heaved. "Oh, my goodness."

She slammed down the chute door and turned to the maids. Their white faces stared back at her.

"Gertie, Pansy, I must ask you not to mention this to another living soul. At least until I've had time to find out what happened. The very last thing we need is for the guests to hear about this latest calamity. I won't have Christmas spoiled for them."

"Yes, m'm," Gertie said, while Pansy nodded, her teeth chattering. "It might be a little hard to explain to Mrs. Chubb why Pansy's in such a dither, though."

Cecily looked at the young girl. "Gertie, get back to the kitchen and tell Mrs. Chubb Pansy's not well and that I'm taking care of her. Pansy, you come with me."

Gertie handed over her charge. "What shall I say kept us so long?"

"Just tell Mrs. Chubb that you brought Pansy to me

because you were worried about her and that I'll explain everything to her later. You'll be far too busy to say much else for the next hour or so."

"Yes, m'm."

Gertie still seemed shaky, and Cecily peered at her. "Will you be all right, Gertie?"

"Yes, m'm. I'm a lot tougher than I look."

Cecily managed a wry smile. "I'm quite convinced of that. Just remember, both of you, not a word about this for now. You must give me your word."

"You can count on me, m'm," Gertie said. "Not a bloody word, I swear."

"Me, neither," Pansy said faintly.

"Good. Thank you both. Now get along, Gertie."

"Yes, m'm." The housemaid scurried down the hallway and disappeared around the corner.

Cecily escorted Pansy back to her room and ordered her to stay there until she felt able to carry on as normal. Then she went back to the lobby and rang Dr. Prestwick. She had to leave a message for him as he was in his surgery, attending to a patient. After that she went in search of Baxter.

She found him in the lounge, reading a newspaper. He looked up when she walked in, as if sensing her agitation. After one look at her face, he quickly folded his newspaper and rose to his feet. "What is it now?"

"I need you in my office," she said quietly.

He followed her down the hallway, saying, "Don't tell me we have another crisis on our hands."

She paused at her office door and looked back at him. "We have another crisis."

"I asked you not to tell me that."

She sighed. "Much as I appreciate your good humor, this is nothing to joke about. I've sent for Dr. Prestwick."

His expression changed at once. "Is someone ill? Not you, I trust?"

"I'm afraid it's worse than that." She opened the door, stood aside to let him in, then closed it behind him. "There's a dead clown in the laundry chute."

He blinked, then said slowly, "I suppose it's too much to hope that this is a joke, after all."

"I'm afraid so." She sat down rather heavily on a chair. "At least now I know the identity of the other clown."

Baxter sat down, too. "The other clown? There's more than one?"

Belatedly, she realized she still hadn't told him about Samuel's find in the stables. Quickly she explained about the dummy clown, and her theory that it had been used by the killer to confuse everyone. "Of course," she finished, "that was when I thought the killer was the second clown."

Baxter leaned his elbows on the desk and steepled his fingers. "What about all those objects disappearing and appearing in odd places? Was he responsible for that?"

"I don't know." She gave him a helpless shrug. "If so, I can't imagine the purpose behind it all."

"Perhaps he did it to confuse us all further." He shook his head. "I must say he's having remarkable success at that."

"It's possible, I suppose." Cecily frowned. "I should have suspected him when I first saw the cut on his nose."

Baxter stared at her. "I was under the impression that Ned Barlow had the cut on his nose."

"Yes, he did. That's what I'm trying to tell you. The dead clown in the chute is Ned Barlow."

Baxter's eyebrows lifted. "I see," he said, in a voice that sounded as if he didn't see at all.

"I didn't recognize him at first." Cecily shuddered at the memory. "He had all that ghastly clown paint on his face. I really don't think I'll ever be able to enjoy a clown again after this."

"So how did you recognize him?"

"By the cut, of course. He has rather a prominent nose, you know. As soon as I saw that little round cut I knew him." She rubbed her forehead with two fingers. "I had just about concluded that he was responsible for Sid Porter's death, but now I'm not so sure."

"Perhaps he was, and then he was killed by someone else who wanted revenge for Porter's death."

"I'd say that was possible, except I have yet to hear of anyone who had a kind word to say about Mr. Porter, much less want revenge on the person who killed him. The people I spoke to didn't seem at all upset that he'd died. I'd say it is much more likely he had to be silenced because he knew too much."

Baxter leaned back in his chair. "So then, what is your theory?"

"What gives you the idea I have a theory?"

"I know my wife. Your mind has been working feverishly ever since you found that body, am I not right?"

"Well, yes." She lifted her hands and let them drop in her lap again. "I've considered all kinds of possibilities, and can settle on only one."

"And what is that?"

"Let us go back to the beginning. I assume that Roland was with Mr. Porter when he was attacked by the killer on the roof. The murderer seized his chance to stab his victim at his most vulnerable, halfway inside the chimney and unable to defend himself. Roland saw it happen and had to be silenced. It would have been a simple enough matter to push the boy off the roof. Roland wasn't exactly robust."

"True. But where does Ned Barlow fit into this macabre picture?"

"Well, he knew Sid Porter, and presumably, his enemies. Let's suppose that somehow he discovered who had killed Sid Porter. Perhaps, when he heard that Roland had been blamed for Mr. Porter's death, he saw his chance to make some money."

Baxter's eyebrows rose again. "Blackmail?"

"He could have taken Mr. Porter's clown suit from the flat, and disguised himself when he confronted the killer, so that the killer would not know his true identity."

"But why here, in this hotel?"

"Well, that's the disturbing part." Cecily crossed her ankles and stared at her shoes. "If I am right, then Ned Barlow had to approach the killer where he knew to find him. Which means that one of our guests is guilty of murder." She let out her breath in a sigh. "What's more, I think I know who it is."

"More bacon rolls, Michel!" Gertie sang out as she shoved open the door of the kitchen. "The guests are going bloody barmy over them."

"Zay can go as barmy as zay like," Michel snapped. "I do not have ze four pairs of hands, *non*?"

"Come on, ducky." Gertie handed him an empty platter. "Can't keep the guests waiting, can we."

"I will have ze bacon rolls ready when they are ready." Michel straightened his chef's hat, which tended to slip sideways when he got irritable. "So they will have to wait, *oiu*?"

"I bet you'd have them ready quick enough if I told you Miss Boulanger were asking for them," Gertie mumbled, as she dropped the platter on the counter next to his elbow.

Michel's flushed face darkened. "Shut up," he said through his teeth.

"I know all about you and Miss Fancy Pants." Gertie tossed her head. "If you think you'll get anywhere with her, you're barking up the wrong bloody cliff. She's too fancy for the likes of you. She could have any toff she wanted, being on the stage. Why would she want a common chef?"

Michel's eyes flashed fire. "Tree."

"What?"

"You mean barking up a tree, not a cliff. In any case, *mon petit cochon*, it is none of your business."

"Here!" Gertie dug her fists into her hips. "You swearing at me?"

"You would do well to watch your tongue." Michel crashed the heavy iron frying pan down on the stove, making two of the maids at the sink squeal in fright. "Perhaps you say these things because you 'ave been disappointed yourself, n'est-ce pas?"

Gertie narrowed her eyes. "What's that supposed to bloody mean?"

"You favor a certain gentleman, *non?*" Michel threw strips of bacon into the pan, wincing as the sizzling fat spat back at him.

"I don't know what you mean." Gertie turned her back on him and picked up a tray of poached haddock. "I'll be back for the bacon rolls so have them ready for me."

"You do not give me ze orders!" The maids squealed again as Michel accompanied his roar with a loud clashing of saucepan lids.

Gertie sniffed and kicked the door open. It swung back quicker than she expected and caught her in the spine on the way out. Cursing, she carried the tray down the hallway and into the dining room.

After depositing the haddock on the sideboard, she made her way to Jeremy Westhaven's table. He held a newspaper in front of his face, and all she could see of him was his hands. "I'm sorry, sir," she said, "but the bacon rolls are not quite ready. I'll bring them in just as soon as our chef has finished making them."

"Thank you."

Disappointed that he wasn't even looking at her, she left him to his reading. Moody bugger, she thought, as she hurried back to the kitchen. One day he was all smiles and pleasant talk, and the next he didn't want to utter a word to her. Good job she didn't have a chance with him. She wasn't sure she'd have him even if he offered.

How she missed her Ross. Christmas wouldn't be the

same without him. Why did he have to go and die and leave her all alone?

Fiercely, Gertie dashed an unaccustomed tear from her eye. She'd promised herself she'd keep cheerful for her twins and that's what she'd have to do. Even if it killed her.

CHAPTER
❈ 17 ❈

Having left Baxter in her office to wait for Dr. Prestwick, Cecily made her way upstairs to Desmond Atkins's room. She got no response from her tapping on the door and was about to descend the stairs when she saw Bernice Atkins climbing up toward her.

Cecily waited until the woman reached the landing before approaching her. "Good morning, Mrs. Atkins," she called out as she drew near. "I trust you and your husband had an enjoyable breakfast?"

"It was lovely, thank you," Bernice replied. "Those bacon wrapped chestnuts were absolutely delicious. Desmond ate far too many of them."

"They are rather good, aren't they. Michel is so innovative."

"He is indeed. How fortunate you are to have such a

creative chef." Bernice clasped her hands together. "How I would adore to have a cook like that in my house. It must be so wonderful to enjoy such an excellent meal every time you sit down to eat."

"And so devastating for the waistline." Cecily glanced down the stairs. "Where is your husband? I was hoping to have a word with him."

"Oh, I'm afraid you've just missed him." Bernice shook her head. "He went to join in the fox hunt. He left a few minutes ago."

And he won't be back until the early afternoon, Cecily thought ruefully. Her questions would have to wait. "Thank you, Mrs. Atkins. You will be attending our little ceremony around the Christmas tree this evening, I trust? It's a tradition in the Pennyfoot. Just a few carols and good things to eat and drink."

"I know Desmond is looking forward to it," Bernice assured her. "As am I. Though I suspect we have different reasons for doing so."

She laughed, and Cecily laughed with her. "I look forward to seeing you both this evening." She smiled, then headed down the stairs to the lobby.

It would be a great shame, she reflected, if her suspicions about Desmond Atkins proved to be accurate. Bernice Atkins was such a pleasant woman and seemed devoted to her husband. She would take it very hard indeed if she discovered she had married a cold-blooded murderer.

Reaching the office, Cecily pushed the door open to find Baxter seated at her desk reading a torn page from a newspaper. "Has Dr. Prestwick arrived?" she asked him.

"Yes. I sent him down to the laundry chute. I thought it would seem less obvious if he went by himself. I warned him you were trying to keep this as quiet as possible."

"I don't know how long we can keep this from the guests," Cecily said, sinking onto a chair with a sigh. "We'll have to remove the body, of course, though Dr. Prestwick may want it to remain there until P.C. Northcott returns."

"Until after Christmas?" Baxter shook his head. "The smell would be intolerable."

"Yes, I suppose you're right." She clasped her hands in her lap. "I suppose we shall have to send for the inspector after all."

"I can't see any alternative." Baxter gave her a sympathetic smile. "I'm sorry, my dear. I know that is the last thing you want to do, but we can't have dead bodies lying around for days on end. Besides, I'm extremely uncomfortable with the thought that this killer may very well still be in the hotel. The sooner we find him and hand him over to the constabulary, the more secure I'll feel."

"I agree."

"Good. Then would you please tell me the name of your suspect?"

"I was hoping to have a word with him first. Unfortunately he's left the hotel."

She jumped at Baxter's harsh growl. "Once more you rashly invite danger. Thank heavens you didn't have a chance to accuse him. Heaven knows what he would have done to you. You could well have been the fourth victim."

"I was prepared to question him in the presence of his wife. I hoped to catch him unawares so that he'd let something slip.

242

I wouldn't have accused him outright. I know enough to leave that to the inspector."

"Do you really," Baxter said, his voice heavy with irony. "Well, if your suspect has left the hotel, it doesn't seem as if the inspector will have a chance to apprehend him."

"He's only gone for the day. He'll be back sometime this afternoon. By then perhaps Dr. Prestwick can tell us how Mr. Barlow died."

"And if you insist on questioning this person yourself, you can do it with me beside you."

She smiled at him. "Very well."

"Who is it, anyway? Why do you think he could be the killer?"

She told him about her conversation with Desmond Atkins. "He swore he had nothing to do with Mr. Porter's death, of course," she said, "but his motive was very strong. I shall certainly mention him to the inspector when he arrives."

"I suppose I'd better give the inspector a ring," Baxter said. "By the way, I found that article I told you about." He picked up the newspaper page and handed it to her. "You'll never believe who else it mentions."

Cecily took the page from him and began to read. Apparently Felicity Rotheringham's body was found on the sands in the early dawn. Her shoes and stockings were found at the base of the steps leading down from the Esplanade. The reporter was sad to inform his readers that Miss Rotheringham had taken her own life, after leaving a note for her betrothed. . . . Cecily gasped. "Did you read all of this?"

"Not all of it, no. I was about to when you came in." Baxter eyed her warily. "What does it say?"

Cecily started to read out loud. "Miss Rotheringham had taken her own life, after leaving a note for her betrothed, Jeremy Westhaven. They were due to be married the week before Christmas, and planned to spend their honeymoon at the Pennyfoot Hotel."

Baxter nodded. "Ah, yes, I read that last month. Now I remember why I kept the article to show you. Poor devil. I feel for him. He must be going through hell right now."

"I imagine he is. Perhaps that's why Gertie has been paying him extra attention."

Baxter looked startled. "What? You mean he's here?"

"Yes, he is. I suppose, since he had the room booked for the honeymoon, he decided to come by himself."

"Good Lord." Baxter shook his head. "The poor fellow must be here to mourn his lost love. How tragic."

"It is, indeed. Little wonder he always looks so sad. Gertie said—" She broke off as a sharp tap on the door interrupted her. "Come in!" she called out, then smiled as Kevin Prestwick stepped into the room. "How nice to see you again, Kevin."

"The pleasure is entirely mine, Cecily."

Baxter coughed. "If you two have quite finished exchanging greetings, I'd like to know how Ned Barlow got into our laundry chute."

"I don't know how he got in there," Kevin said, as he advanced into the room. "I can tell you how he died, however. His neck is broken."

"Oh, my." Cecily clutched her throat. "Just like Roland. What do you think happened?"

"He has a severe bump on his head. That could have been caused by the fall, but I'm more inclined to think it was administered before he went into the chute."

"In other words, you think he was murdered."

"I'll know more when I get him to the morgue and can take a better look at him." Kevin glanced at Baxter. "I didn't want to get him out of the chute until I knew how you wanted to handle it, but I'm afraid it does look rather as if you have another murder on your hands."

"We have to get the body out of there," Baxter said, getting up from his chair. "We were hoping to avoid calling in the inspector until after Christmas. Now it appears we have no choice."

Cecily appealed to the doctor. "Is there anything you can do?"

Kevin stroked his chin. "I suppose, since we don't know for absolute certain that he was killed, I could take charge of the body and examine it at the morgue. I could tell Inspector Cranshaw that I thought the deceased might have fallen into the chute by accident and had broken his neck in the fall."

Cecily clasped her hands together. "Oh, would you, Kevin? We would be so obliged, wouldn't we, Baxter."

Baxter frowned. "I suppose there's no chance that could actually have been what happened?"

"Fallen in by accident?" Kevin shook his head. "Sorry, old chap. It's extremely unlikely. Ned Barlow was a big man. I could smell no alcohol on him and unless he was staggering drunk, or climbed in for some obscure reason, I can't see him falling down there by accident."

"In any case," Cecily pointed out, "the door would be closed.

"In fact, it would have taken a strong man to heave a chap that size into the chute." Kevin glanced at the clock. "I'll need some help getting him out of there."

"Oh, dear." Cecily looked at her husband. "You'd have to carry him through the kitchen to get him outside. You can't very well take him out through the lobby."

"We'll have to pick a time when it's quiet in the hotel." Kevin looked at Cecily. "What do you suggest?"

Cecily thought about it for a moment. "I suppose the best time would be after the evening meal, when everyone's in the library for the Christmas Eve ceremony. There shouldn't be anyone in the kitchen, since most of the staff will either be in their rooms or in the library."

"Yes," Baxter agreed. "I should say that's the best time. I'll have Samuel give us a hand to get the body out to the carriage. He can take you both down to the morgue."

"Oh, dear!" Cecily looked at Kevin in dismay. "That means you will miss the ceremony. Madeline was so looking forward to sharing the evening with you."

"I still plan to attend the ceremony," Kevin assured her. "I don't think Mr. Barlow will mind waiting for me in the carriage."

"No, I don't suppose he will." Cecily rose, laying a hand on her husband's arm for comfort. "I do hope this won't cause trouble for you with the inspector, Kevin. I wouldn't want to be responsible for you breaking the law."

"Under the circumstances, with the constable being away, no doubt the inspector is hoping he won't be called in for duty while he's enjoying the festivities." Kevin smiled. "He'll probably thank me for waiting until after Christmas to contact him."

"I hope so." Cecily looked up at Baxter. "Now all we have to hope is that no one sees you taking the body out."

"We'll be as discreet as possible." Baxter patted her hand. "But I suggest you lock the door to the laundry chute, before some unsuspecting maid tries to remove the contents to wash them."

"Heavens, yes." Cecily headed for the door. "Please excuse me, Kevin. We'll see you tonight, then? Perhaps you and Madeline would like to join us for dinner?"

Kevin looked embarrassed. "Ah . . . actually, Madeline is preparing a meal for me at her house, before we attend the ceremony here."

Cecily beamed at him. "How nice! I'm so happy to see you two on such good terms."

"Yes, well, at the present anyway. There is no telling how long it will last. I'm afraid Madeline and I don't always see eye to eye on important subjects."

Only too aware of that, Cecily had no comment. She left Baxter to make the final arrangements with the doctor and hurried down the hallway to the kitchen. She needed the key from Mrs. Chubb to lock the laundry chute door, and she would have to find some excuse for doing so. That is, if Gertie and Pansy had kept their promise not to mention the dead body.

She found the kitchen in its usual uproar, with Michel and Mrs. Chubb arguing above the sound of clattering dishes and Gertie's strident voice issuing orders.

The main breakfast rush was over, but the hustle to get the dishes washed, the dining room cleaned, and the tables laid for the midday meal kept the maids running.

Relieved to see Pansy scurrying about the kitchen and apparently over her nasty shock, Cecily made her way over to Mrs. Chubb.

The housekeeper's face glowed with temper as she waved a rolling pin in Michel's face. "I need the cheese for my twists," she yelled at him, "so keep your sticky fingers out of the pantry."

"It is my pantry, too, you old bat," Michel snarled, all traces of his French accent disappearing entirely.

The housekeeper caught sight of Cecily and immediately lowered her voice. "Madam. So sorry. I didn't see you standing there."

Cecily raised her eyebrows at the irate chef. "You have a problem, Michel?"

For a moment it seemed as if Michel would explode into a torrent of words, but then he gave a slight shake of his head and turned away.

"We were just discussing the refreshments for tonight, m'm, that's all." Mrs. Chubb tucked a stray gray hair under her cap. "Michel wasn't sure if we had enough cheese for the twists, but I think we have it sorted out now, don't we, Michel?"

Michel mumbled something under his breath, but his face suggested it was just as well no one could hear what he'd said.

Mrs. Chubb turned to Cecily. "I'm sorry, m'm. Busy time in the kitchen, that's all. What can I do for you?"

"I will be needing the key for the laundry chute for just a short while, Mrs. Chubb."

Cecily tried to keep her expression bland while the housekeeper scrutinized her face. "Is something wrong with the chute, m'm?"

Cecily laughed, though it sounded a trifle forced to her. "Wrong? Of course not. What makes you ask?"

"Well, if you remember, Pansy was supposed to take the dirty wash to the laundry room this morning, and then Gertie went to look for her and then when Gertie came back she said Pansy wasn't well and then Pansy came back and when I asked her about the wash she looked at me like I'd asked her to drown herself and I couldn't get another word out of her and I just wondered if something was wrong."

The housekeeper paused for breath, and Cecily said quickly, "It's the hinges on the door, actually. One of them is damaged and the door won't close properly. I've arranged for someone to repair it, but until then I want to keep it locked."

"Oh, is that all." Mrs. Chubb looked relieved. "Well, don't you worry yourself, m'm. I'll send one of the maids down there to lock it."

"No!" Cecily hastily lowered her voice as Mrs. Chubb stared at her. "That's really not necessary. I can see how busy everyone is, and I'd like to take care of it myself."

Looking slightly offended, Mrs. Chubb reached for the keys on her belt. "Very well, m'm." She detached a key from the ring and handed it to Cecily. "I'd be obliged if you see that it gets returned to me right away. We don't want the wash piling up in the chute, now do we."

"No need to worry." Cecily slipped the key in her pocket. "The chute has been emptied and the wash taken care of for now. I'll return the key as soon as possible."

Turning her back on the surprised housekeeper, she fled the kitchen. Mrs. Chubb knew her well enough to know when she wasn't telling the truth.

She'd simply have to avoid being alone with the housekeeper, Cecily told herself as she hurried down the passage to the laundry chute. To her relief, the door remained closed. Apparently no one besides Dr. Prestwick had been there to open it again, or surely she would have heard about it from Mrs. Chubb.

Quickly, she locked the door and pocketed the key. The secret was safe for now, at least. Pansy and Gertie had kept their word.

On her way back to the lobby, Cecily thought how hard it must have been for poor Pansy to keep quiet about the body in the chute. No wonder she'd looked at Mrs. Chubb as if she'd been asked to drown herself.

That reminded Cecily of the newspaper cutting. She'd left it on her desk in the office. Kevin had interrupted her before she'd had a chance to finish reading it.

Later, she promised herself; when the Christmas Eve ceremony was over, the body was disposed of, and everything was peaceful again. After she and Baxter had a word with Desmond Atkins.

Now that it seemed likely that the man had actually killed three people, she was happy Baxter had insisted on being with her when she questioned Desmond. She still had trouble picturing the man as a cold-blooded killer. Then again, as she'd learned from past experience, one could never tell what evil lurked in some people's minds.

Not that she had much hope of solving the murders before the inspector arrived on the scene, anyway. It looked very much as if this could be one crime that would prove to be beyond her capabilities.

CHAPTER
❈ 18 ❈

Desmond Atkins arrived back at the hotel later that afternoon. Cecily, who had been watching anxiously for him from her boudoir window, hurried down to alert Baxter of the man's return.

Together they went up to the Atkins's room and tapped on the door. Baxter had agreed to allow Cecily to do the questioning, though he'd cautioned her to avoid accusing the man of any wrongdoing.

Bernice opened the door and invited them inside. "Desmond has just returned from the fox hunt," she told them after inviting them to seat themselves. "He's changing his clothes at the moment but will be with us shortly."

"Thank you," Cecily murmured. "I assure you we won't keep him long."

"May I ask what this is about?" Bernice looked worried. "My husband isn't in any trouble, is he?"

Cecily met her gaze. "Why would you think so?"

Bernice looked down at her hands. "Mr. and Mrs. Baxter, may I be frank?"

Cecily interpreted a warning look from her husband and gave him a brief nod. "By all means. I can assure you whatever you wish to say to us will be kept in strictest confidence. Unless, of course, it concerns the constabulary, in which case we should be forced to pass on any information that might be considered relevant."

"I understand." She heaved a deep sigh. "This is about the recent deaths, is it not? You suspect my husband of having a hand in it."

Whatever Cecily had expected her to say, it wasn't that. She exchanged glances with Baxter, who looked as if he wanted to bolt from the room.

"It's quite all right," Bernice added. "I understand why you suspect him. Desmond and I had a long talk last night. He told me the truth about his past, and about the conversation you had with him."

"I'm sorry," Cecily said quietly. "That must have been difficult to hear."

"Yes, it was. I admire my husband, however, for being truthful with me. It must have been every bit as difficult for him."

"I'm sure it was."

"The point is, I understand that the two men were killed during the children's Christmas party, is that correct?"

"Quite correct."

"Then I can assure you my husband was not responsible. He was here with me that entire afternoon. I was not feeling well, and he stayed by my side. We did not leave the room until we went down for the evening meal. Desmond was with me the rest of the evening." She looked straight into Cecily's eyes. "My husband had nothing to do with the death of those two men, Mrs. Baxter. I'm willing to swear to it on the Bible."

Cecily held the woman's gaze for a moment or two, then nodded. Getting to her feet, she said briskly, "Well, I see no reason to disturb you and your husband further. I apologize for any inconvenience we might have caused you. I hope you still plan to join us this evening for the Christmas Eve ceremony in the library?"

Baxter leapt to his feet as Bernice rose. "Indeed we shall," she said, smiling. "Desmond has a good voice. He will enjoy singing the carols."

Baxter said nothing until they had descended the stairs and reached the door of the office. "Do you believe her?" he asked, as they entered the room.

"I see no reason to doubt her word." Cecily sank into a chair and passed a hand across her brow.

"She could be lying to cover up for him."

"She could, but I don't think she is." Cecily sighed. "I give up, Bax. This is beyond my powers of deduction. My mind is so confused, I can't think straight anymore."

Baxter frowned. "Are you not well? It isn't like you to give up so easily."

She smiled wearily at him. "Perhaps it is time I stopped interfering in police business and concentrated on running the hotel."

"Now I know you're not well." He got up and laid a hand on her forehead. "You have always loved the challenge and excitement of solving a seemingly impossible puzzle."

"But not the worry of it all." Cecily yawned. "I'm tired, and we still have the evening event to struggle through before I can retire."

"Not to mention the disposal of a dead body." Baxter reminded her.

"Well, I'm leaving that little problem in your capable hands."

"I just hope Prestwick remembers he's supposed to help me with the body. That man can be a fool when he's in the company of a woman."

"I rather think it's the other way around," Cecily said, smiling. "But a cryptic reminder when he arrives should help stir his memory."

Baxter shook his head. "This is a terrible time to be dealing with a murderer."

"Is there ever a good time?"

He frowned at her. "You know what I mean. Here we are, celebrating a birth, while someone is out there indiscriminately taking lives."

"I don't think it's indiscriminate. I think he's desperately trying to cover his tracks."

"Then why is he still here?"

"We don't know that he is." Cecily got up and moved to the door. "He might well have left, now that he's disposed of the one person who could have pointed him out as a killer."

"Always supposing that's why Barlow was killed."

"Exactly, which is why this whole situation is giving me

a brutal headache. There are just too many questions yet unanswered and nothing seems to be coming together. And yet . . ." She paused, her hand on the doorknob.

"Yet what?"

"I can't dismiss the feeling I know something that might help solve this whole puzzle. The problem is that I can't quite grasp it."

"You've had these feelings before," Baxter reminded her.

"And they have always proved to be significant in some way." She shook her head. "I don't know why I can't bring this one to the forefront where I can examine it."

"Perhaps subconsciously you don't want to know what your mind is trying to tell you."

She stared at him for a moment, then murmured, "You know, Bax, I hate to admit it, but you could possibly be right. That's what worries me most of all."

She opened the door, then turned back to him. "Of course, if our killer is one of our guests, he could hardly leave now without arousing suspicion. Which means he most likely is still in the hotel."

"Well, let's hope his killing spree is over, at least. The good thing is, the longer he's here, the more chance Cranshaw will have to catch him."

"Amen to that." She left him then, closing the door gently behind her. Part of her wished Christmas was over. As much as she hated to call in the inspector, she did not enjoy the knowledge that a desperate killer still lurked amongst them. It put a damper on the festivities, to say the least.

*   *   *

Leaning across the table, Gertie piled dirty dishes onto her tray and balanced two wine glasses on top of them. She glanced across the dining room, to where Jeremy Westhaven sat with his chin buried in his hands, apparently unaware that the room had emptied out.

He'd barely spoken to her when she'd fetched his fruit and cheeses a few minutes ago. It was obvious to her he'd been drinking quite a bit. In fact, the bottle of wine she'd brought him looked as if it were just about empty.

Sidling over to him, Gertie murmured, "Is there anything else I can get for you, sir?"

He glanced up at her, his glassy eyes telling her he'd drunk more than enough for one evening. "Yes," he said, giving her a wide smile. "You can fetch me another bottle of this excellent wine."

She hesitated, concerned that any more of the stuff would put him on the floor. "You still have some left in this one, sir." She lifted it up. "Let me pour it for you." She tilted the bottle, but her hand shook, spilling dark red splotches on the white tablecloth. Chubby would have her hide for that.

Quickly she mopped it up with the serviette that Jeremy had thrown carelessly onto the table. "Sorry," she muttered. "Me nerves are a bit dodgy at the moment."

"Bit too much excitement, is that it?"

Charmed by his smile, and thrilled that at last he was actually talking to her again, she forgot to be discreet. "Too much is bloody right. What with all the fuss over Christmas, we don't need all this nasty business messing us about, that's for sure."

Jeremy nodded in sympathy. "Must be troubling for you.

Three poor souls on a dead man's chest." He lifted his glass and toasted her. "To you, my dear, and another bottle, if you please."

She stared at him as he swallowed the wine then smacked the glass down on the table so hard she was afraid it might break.

He looked up at her, and all traces of a smile had vanished from his face. In fact, his eyes glinted in the candlelight like the steel that sharpened Michel's knives. "Be quick about it, my girl."

"Yes, sir." She backed away from him. "I'll fetch it from the cellar this instant."

"Good." He shoved back his chair and stood. "Bring it to my room. I'll drink it there."

"Yes, sir." She hurried to the door, her thoughts in a whirl of misgivings. He was drunk, she told herself. Didn't know what he was saying. Even so, she couldn't shake the uneasiness she felt when she remembered the awful look in his eyes.

Mrs. Chubb stood at the kitchen table, fitting silverware into velvet-lined boxes. She looked up when Gertie burst in. The housemaid looked frazzled, with her cap on sideways as usual and hair all over her face.

Mrs. Chubb opened her mouth to scold her, then shut it again. It was Christmas. Let the girl alone, for once. There'd be plenty of time to straighten her out once Christmas was all over and done with.

Instead she glanced up at the clock. "Where have you

been? The ceremony's about to start in the library. Everyone's already gone in there."

"You haven't," Gertie pointed out.

"I'm going just as soon as I finish this. Can't trust those maids to put the knives and forks in their proper places. When I opened the boxes this morning the silverware was all over the place."

"I'll have a word with them about that tomorrow," Gertie promised.

"Well, get along with you to the library then." Mrs. Chubb frowned at her. "I'll be along in a minute."

"I have to go down to the cellar first. I just stopped by to get the key. Mr. Westhaven wants another bottle of that wine he likes. The one I can't pronounce proper."

"Beaujolais." Mrs. Chubb clicked her tongue. "He's a bit late with that, isn't he?"

"He wants it in his room." Gertie shrugged. "I suppose he doesn't feel like singing carols tonight."

"Well, here you are." Mrs. Chubb took the key off the ring at her belt and handed it to her. "I showed you where it is. You can go and get it. That reminds me. Madam hasn't given me back the key to the laundry chute. I suppose I'll have to go and get it from her."

Gertie took the key and turned it over in her hand. "You know, he said something to me just now that didn't seem quite right."

Mrs. Chubb fitted the last spoon in its pocket. "Who did?"

"Mr. Westhaven."

Her attention caught by something odd in Gertie's voice, Mrs. Chubb looked up. "Why, what did he say?"

Gertie stared back at her, looking for all the world as if she badly wanted to say something, but didn't know if she should. Finally, she shook her head. "Oh, never mind. I'll go and get the wine for the toff."

The door closed behind her, leaving Mrs. Chubb to stare uneasily after her.

Cecily stood just inside the door to the library, greeting each guest as they entered the room. The string quartet she'd hired to play for them was in place and awaiting her signal to begin.

It seemed as if most of the guests had chosen to attend the ceremony. Normally Cecily would have been delighted to have such a crowd, but this evening her apprehension kept her from enjoying the spectacle of ladies in elegant gowns on the arms of their debonair escorts.

Bernice Atkins looked particularly radiant as she swept into the room. At her side Desmond actually smiled as Cecily greeted them. The man seemed quite presentable when he was being pleasant, she thought, as she watched them join another couple on the other side of the room.

Baxter edged up to her during a lull in the arrivals. "Prestwick isn't here yet," he hissed in her ear.

"I know," she whispered back. "They should be here any moment now."

"I certainly hope you're right. Samuel is waiting by the laundry chute to make sure no one is roaming about down there. He'll be wondering what's keeping us."

"I'm sure he'll wait for you." Cecily nodded and smiled as yet another couple entered. "Good evening. I'm so glad you decided to join us this evening. The carol singing will begin very shortly."

She waited until the man and his wife had moved out of earshot, before saying to Baxter, "Why don't you wait for Kevin in the lobby. It will save time. Just send Madeline down here so I will know he has arrived."

Baxter nodded. "Good idea. I can't settle into anything here anyway until we've taken care of Barlow."

"Cecily darling! Isn't this utterly exciting!"

The voice came from the hallway, and Cecily looked up to see Phoebe smiling at her, one hand holding grimly on to the colonel's arm.

"That's it. I'm off." Baxter nodded at her and rushed out the door, answering the colonel's gruff greeting with a wave of his hand.

"Oh, dear." Phoebe looked flustered as she sailed into the room in a cloud of lavender water, dark blue ostrich feathers drifting after her. "I do hope it isn't something urgent. It would be such a shame for your husband to miss the singing. Frederick loves to sing, don't you, lovey?"

Cecily stood back to allow Colonel Fortescue plenty of room. "Baxter just has an errand to run, Phoebe. He'll be back very soon."

"Good." Phoebe looked around the room, her gaze resting on one of the ladies every now and then to study her gown. Apparently satisfied no one outshone her, she smiled at Cecily. "Is Madeline here yet?"

"Not yet." Cecily peered down the hallway. "She should be here soon."

"Well, I'm rather surprised she's late. After all, the woman does nothing to make herself respectable. She simply throws one of those dreadful frocks of hers over her head and leaves it at that. She doesn't even bother to dress her hair, for heaven's sake."

As usual, Cecily felt compelled to come to her friend's defense. "That is Madeline's way, as you well know, Phoebe. She is not one for fancy clothes and dressed-up hair."

"Well, she raises eyebrows whenever she attends one of these little soirees. You'd think that pride alone would prompt her to make an effort to dress properly. Isn't it enough that everyone is half afraid of her? What with those ungodly powers of hers and all that mumbo jumbo, people already think she's a witch. It might do her well to pay more attention to her appearance, at least."

"Madeline is dressed properly as far as she's concerned. We have to accept her as she is and not judge her choices."

"You might want to amend that sentiment," Phoebe said with a smirk, "when you see what she's wearing tonight."

Cecily turned her head to see Madeline seemingly floating down the hallway. She wore a shapeless gown in gray silk that clung where it touched and flowed around her bare feet. Tiny white flowers encircled one ankle and graced her neck. She'd pinned a sprig of mistletoe in her hair, which flowed about her slim shoulders. She resembled a sprite visiting from the woods that lay behind Deep Willow Pond.

"Look at her," Phoebe whispered. "Positively pagan. Whatever that doctor sees in her I cannot imagine."

Cecily jumped as the colonel, having apparently caught sight of Madeline, bellowed out a greeting. "Hail there, maid of the mountains! To what do we owe the pleasure of your charming and gracious company tonight?"

Madeline bestowed her beautiful smile on him. "I'm here to sing Christmas carols with you, Colonel."

"Over my dead body," Phoebe muttered, loud enough for Cecily to hear.

Madeline must have heard as well, since she laid a slender hand on the colonel's free arm. "How is the mixture working for you, Colonel? Helping matters, I trust?"

Phoebe stared up at him, color flooding her face. "Frederick! Don't tell me you're taking one of Madeline's obnoxious potions! What on earth for?"

The colonel grunted and cleared his throat, apparently at a loss how to answer his wife.

Madeline had no such trouble. "A gentleman of your husband's advanced age," she said sweetly, "needs a little help in certain . . . shall we say . . . intimate matters. The colonel asked me for assistance and I was happy to oblige."

Phoebe opened her mouth but nothing came out except a strangled sound that boded ill for the hapless colonel.

Sensing trouble, Cecily drew Madeline aside and suggested she join the group around the Christmas tree. "I trust Dr. Prestwick is with Baxter?" she whispered, as the quartet began to tune up with a wail of strings that sounded like angry cats in a fight to the death.

"I'm not sure we should leave those two men together." Madeline put her hands over her ears. "You know how hostile they can be with each other."

"We don't have much choice. Besides, Samuel's presence will prevent them from becoming too contentious." Wincing, Cecily raised her hand to give the signal for the musicians to start playing. Anything would be better than that dreadful noise resounding from their corner of the room.

"Well, I'll do my best to help with the singing." Madeline drifted off toward the Christmas tree, while Phoebe dragged her confused husband to the other side of the room. Cecily was about to join Madeline when Baxter appeared in the doorway, crooking his finger at her in a frantic signal.

Frowning, Cecily slipped into the hallway and closed the door behind her. "Is it done already?"

"No." Baxter looked up and down the hallway. "I had to take care of something."

Cecily clenched her fingers in frustration. "What in heaven's name could be more important than getting that body out of the hotel?"

"I think you'd better come down to the office." Baxter took hold of her arm.

She tugged it free. "I can't come now, I have guests that need my attention. Surely, whatever it is, it can wait until we have taken care of our little problem?" She looked past him, down the empty hallway. "Where's Kevin? I thought he was with you."

"He's in the office." Baxter took hold of her hand this time. "I must insist you come with me right away. The guests will simply have to do without you for a while."

"Can't you just tell me what this is all about?"

Baxter sent an anxious glance at the library door as a chorus of voices began singing. "Cecily, we are wasting valuable time. If you want us to get that body out of here before everyone starts leaving the library, you had better do as I ask and come with me now."

"Oh, very well." Allowing him to lead her to the office, she tried to ignore the fitful churning of her stomach. The last thing she needed right now was yet another disaster.

CHAPTER
❈ 19 ❈

Baxter reached the door of the office and paused. "I wanted you to hear their story."

Cecily looked at him in bewilderment. "To hear whose story?"

His face seemed carved in stone and she realized that anger seethed behind that stoic mask. "Those blasted waiters you hired. I wanted you to hear their explanation."

Still fumbling in the dark, Cecily waited for him to open the door, then walked into the room.

Kevin Prestwick sat with one hip perched on the edge of Cecily's desk. He gave her a faint smile of apology. "Sorry about this, Cecily. Baxter thought you should be here."

Sprawled on the two chairs, Reggie and Lawrence looked up at her with identical expressions of bored indifference.

"On your feet, both of you!" Baxter roared. "Have you no manners?"

Both men got lazily to their feet and moved to the wall, where they leaned their backs, their arms folded across their chests.

They really do look remarkably alike, Cecily thought. Another part of her mind wondered what they could have done to arouse Baxter's wrath and why he was so insistent on her hearing about it from them.

Having closed the door, Baxter advanced on the two men. "I want you to tell Mrs. Baxter exactly what you were doing when Prestwick and I met up with you just now."

The men exchanged sheepish glances, but neither of them answered.

"You have exactly ten seconds," Baxter said pleasantly, "before I start pounding the words out of you both."

Cecily made a small sound of protest, which Baxter ignored. Instead he started counting to ten.

Cecily glanced at Prestwick, who looked extremely worried. And so he should. Having seen Baxter's temper at its worst, Cecily knew quite well what her husband was capable of doing to those two men if they didn't respond.

Fortunately for them, Reggie spoke up. "We were removing the grandfather clock from the lobby," he said sullenly.

Cecily gasped. "That clock has been in my family for generations. It's in a very delicate state. If anything has happened to it I shall be devastated."

"Fortunately for these two," Baxter said grimly, "the clock appears to be unharmed."

Cecily let out a sigh of relief. "Why?" she demanded.

"Why did you do this? Am I correct in assuming you were responsible for everything else that was transferred from its rightful place?"

"Including expensive armchairs that were damaged by the mud," Baxter put in.

Reggie glanced at his brother. "We were paid to do it," he said, when Lawrence merely shrugged.

"By whom?"

"Lester Hardcastle."

Cecily looked at Baxter for help, but he shook his head, apparently as confused as she was.

"Who in damnation is Lester Hardcastle?" he demanded.

"He owns the Bayview, across the downs."

"Good Lord." Cecily sat down on one of the vacated chairs. "He was trying to shut down the competition."

"It wasn't our fault," Lawrence said, speaking for the first time. "It was our job. Lester said to make it seem that the hotel was haunted, so we started moving things around and spreading rumors about ghosts."

Cecily stared at him. "Were you also responsible for dangling that scarecrow over the balcony seats?"

Lawrence nodded, actually having the audacity to smile. "That was Reggie's idea. You see, we heard them talking in the kitchen about a clown ghost. So we decided to make our own clown ghost, just to help things along and make it seem real. We fixed up a rope over the chandelier, then Reggie went down to the ballroom to make sure everyone noticed it, while I tugged on the rope and made it look like it was floating." He nudged his brother in the side. "Clever, that."

"I'll give you blasted clever, you hooligans!" Baxter yelled, raising his fist.

Lawrence pressed back against the wall.

"We were only following orders," Reggie said, with a nervous glance at his brother. "We didn't mean any real harm."

"Except for trying to frighten our guests into leaving and destroying our business, you mean?" Cecily shook her head. "How could you. I consider the people who work for me to be part of my family. I trusted you both enough to include you in that circle. I'm deeply hurt and disappointed that you betrayed me in this despicable manner."

The two men looked at each other. "Sorry," Lawrence mumbled.

"You will be sorry by the time I've finished with you," Baxter said, taking a step toward them.

Both men shrank even farther back in alarm.

"Baxter." Cecily got to her feet. "As they said, no real harm has been done. If we find any damage, of course, then we shall expect reimbursement from you both. As for now, you are free to go."

The relief on the two men's faces almost made her smile. "I want you to give Mr. Hardcastle a message," she added.

Lawrence nodded. "Anything you say, Mrs. Baxter."

"I want you to tell your employer that his nasty little plan was doomed to fail from the start. The Pennyfoot's guests are loyal to the core, and are not easily hoodwinked."

Again Lawrence nodded. "Yes, m'm."

"I don't know what sort of people frequent the Bayview," Cecily continued. "But unless Mr. Hardcastle puts his energies into creating a hotel in keeping with our envious reputation, instead of trying to ruin his competition, he will lose all of his guests to the Pennyfoot eventually. I can promise him that."

"Thank you, m'm." Lawrence glanced at Baxter. "No hard feelings, I hope, sir?"

Baxter's mouth thinned. "Get out of here before I thrash you both."

Reggie hurried to the door with Lawrence hot on his heels. Just before the door closed, Lawrence stuck his head around it. "I can tell you one thing," he said, "we thought there really was a ghost when we saw that clown hanging around. We're not the only ones who are causing trouble in this hotel."

He started to withdraw his head, until Cecily called out sharply, "Just a minute! Where did you see this clown?"

Lawrence thought for a moment. "On the first floor. Outside room number twelve. He had his hand up to knock on the door, but then when he saw us, he ran off."

"When was this?"

"This morning. First thing. We didn't think anyone was up, yet. Gave us both a shock, I can tell you."

Cecily stared at him. "Thank you, Lawrence."

The young man lifted his hand in a salute then closed the door.

"That must have been Barlow," Baxter said. "Room twelve." He leaned over the desk and flipped open the register. His voice rose in surprise. "That's Jeremy Westhaven's room."

Cecily moved over to the desk and started searching through a pile of invoices.

Kevin jumped to his feet. "We'd better get that body out of here before people start moving around."

"Just a minute." Cecily found what she was looking for and pounced on the newspaper cutting. She scanned the lines while the two men watched her, both of them obviously impatient.

"Ah, here it is." She read it through twice, then lifted her head. "Felicity Rotheringham left a note for Mr. Westhaven, explaining that her innocence had been stolen in an attack by the Balloon Man while walking on the sands late at night. She couldn't face the shame. That was the reason she took her own life."

"Great heavens," Baxter muttered. "I'd forgotten that part. I knew it had something to do with balloons."

"There may be more than one man selling balloons on the sands," Cecily said quietly. "But only one, as far as I know, who was stabbed to death."

"Sid Porter." Baxter looked dazed. "So that's why Westhaven came down here. Not to mourn his lost love, but to avenge her death."

"Well, we don't know anything for certain, of course. I remember Gertie saying Mr. Westhaven hated balloons, but that doesn't make him a killer." Cecily moved to the door. "It does make him a viable suspect with a strong motive, however. The fact that Mr. Barlow apparently intended to visit him this morning also implicates him. I think I should have a word with Mr. Westhaven right away."

"Not without me." Baxter moved quickly to her side.

"You have a body to remove," Cecily told him. "That can't wait any longer. At the moment I just want to make sure Mr. Westhaven hasn't left the hotel. If he has, we shall have to refer him to the inspector. On the other hand, if he has stayed to avoid arousing suspicion, we can both confront him in the morning."

"Very well." Baxter narrowed his eyes. "I must ask for your promise, Cecily, that you won't attempt to question the man tonight."

"You have it." She shivered. "Rest assured, I have no desire to be alone with a man who has no reservations about taking so many lives."

"Right. Then come along, Prestwick. Let's get that body out of here while we can be reasonably sure no one will see us." Baxter opened the door for Cecily to pass through.

"You go along," she told him. "I want to read this article again."

He gave her one long look of warning then left with Kevin.

She read through the account again of Felicity's tragic death then folded the paper and tucked it in the pocket of her skirt. Now that she had time to think about it, Jeremy Westhaven seemed the logical suspect for the murders. He certainly had a strong motive—revenge on the man who had destroyed his intended wife's life.

She had only one reservation—the improbable connection between Jeremy and Ned Barlow. They certainly didn't move in the same circles. So how would Ned Barlow suspect Jeremy of Sid's murder?

That was something she'd have to work out later, she decided. Right now it was important to find out if her suspect remained in the hotel.

After pocketing the spare ring of room keys, she left the office and hurried back to the library. Most people's attention was on the quartet, who was playing a spirited version of "We Three Kings," gamely accompanied by several discordant voices.

A quick glance around assured her that Jeremy Westhaven was not present, and she closed the door. After searching the lounge and bar without seeing him, she came to the conclusion that he had retired to his room.

Crossing the empty lobby, she noted that Philip had also retired for the night. Voices of the singers echoed up the stairs as she climbed them to the first floor.

She rehearsed the excuse she would use when Jeremy opened the door. She would inquire after his health, since he hadn't attended the ceremony in the library, and would ask him if he needed anything brought up from the kitchen.

After tapping several times without a response, she felt secure enough to unlock the door and open it. One peek should be sufficient to know if he had left the room permanently.

Slowly she pushed the door open, braced to close it again should she see him asleep on his bed. Unable to see anything in the darkened room, she ventured farther inside. Light from the gas lamps in the hallway spilled far enough for her to see the dresser strewn with toilet articles—a comb, a brush, a razor. Evidently Mr. Westhaven had not left the hotel.

Opening the door wider, she saw the bed still neatly made up. The room was empty. She was about to close the door again when an idea occurred to her. As long as she was in his room, she might as well take advantage of his absence and make a swift search. Just in case she could find something incriminating that would hasten the inspector's investigation.

Quickly she made her way to the dresser and reached for the matchbox. Fumbling in the dark, she found a match and struck it, then removed the cover of the gas lamp. She touched the flame to the wick, and soft light flooded the room.

She started with the dresser drawers but could find nothing that might connect Jeremy to any of the dead men. She had the same lack of success with the wardrobe, and the empty suitcases stacked beside it.

Quickly she crossed the room to the bed and opened the drawer of the small chest. The garish cover of a penny dreadful depicting a knife dripping with blood stared up at her. She picked it up and flipped through the pages. Apparently Jeremy Westhaven had a taste for tawdry crime novels.

Putting the book back again she closed the drawer. Unfortunately, if Ned Barlow had been killed early that morning, the maids would have cleaned the room.

She gazed thoughtfully at the bed. Of course, since the occupant of the room intended to be there for a few more days, the maid would not have been as diligent as she might have been had the room been prepared for a new guest.

Throwing back the eiderdown, Cecily dropped to her knees, lowered the lamp and peered underneath the bed. The flickering light glinted on something shiny on the far side. Grunting with the exertion, she rose and walked to the other side of the bed.

Once more she knelt down and peered underneath. Stretching out her hand, her fingers closed around the small round shiny object. She heard a faint tinkling as she drew it toward her and her pulse leapt in anticipation.

Standing up, she held the lamp so that the light fell across her open palm. Sitting in the middle of it was a tiny bell. Just like the bells on Ned Barlow's clown suit.

Gertie hated it whenever she had to go down to the wine cellar at night. The damp cold chilled her bones, and the cobwebs clung to her face if she didn't look where she was going. She had to light a lamp to see down there, and the shadows bounced all over the walls, like someone was creeping after her.

Tonight, for some reason, she felt even more fearful than usual. If it had been anyone else other than Jeremy Westhaven wanting a bottle of wine, she'd have told him the wine cellar was closed for the night.

She wished now she'd told Jeremy that. He'd had too much to drink, anyway. Still, he did say he would drink it in his room so he could just lie down and sleep it off. That made her feel a little better.

She crossed the courtyard, shivering as the cold wind whipped around her shoulders. She should be in the warm library now, by the fire, enjoying all the food and drinks. Christmas was the only time the staff was allowed to mingle with the guests. Then again, if Jeremy wasn't going to be there, she didn't mind if she went or not. She had no voice for singing. It would be nice to hear Doris sing again, though.

Thinking about the singer brought back memories of the

days when Doris and Daisy were maids at the Pennyfoot. Gertie smiled to herself as she paused in front of the cellar door. Doris was such a cowardly thing, no one would have dreamed she'd end up on the stage.

Thrusting the key in the padlock, Gertie gave it a turn. She had to wriggle it about a bit before the dratted thing turned and the lock snapped open. Reaching inside, she lifted the lamp from its hook on the wall and fished in her pocket for the matches.

The wind blew the first one out, and she stepped inside the door for shelter as she lit another match. This time the wick caught and held, sending a shaft of light down the narrow cellar stairs.

Holding the lamp high, Gertie began inching down, feeling for each step with her foot. She'd fallen down there once and made sure to be careful ever since.

She let out her breath in relief when she reached the floor. The racks of wine spread out all around her, the bottles lying on their sides. The Beaujolais was on the right, at the back of the cellar. She started forward, her nerves jumping as the shadows danced along the wall beside her.

She just hoped Jeremy Westhaven would be happy she'd gone to all this trouble for him. Not that he'd notice that much, seeing as how he was halfway drunk.

She shivered again, remembering the strange look in his eyes when he'd said those weird words. She'd been talking about the nasty things that had been happening that week. What with Roland dying and Father Christmas and then the clown. *What was it Jeremy had said? Three poor souls on a dead man's chest.*

It reminded her of something she'd read somewhere, only it wasn't three souls. Yes, that was it. It was fifteen men. Not three.

She tried to ignore the buzz of warning in her head as she hunted for the Beaujoulais. There had been three murders. But Jeremy couldn't have known that. Ah, there was the Beaujolais. Thank goodness. Now get it and bloody get out of there.

As she reached for it, Jeremy's words repeated in her head. *Three poor souls on a dead man's chest.* But he couldn't have been talking about the murders. Not unless he'd seen the clown for himself.

She straightened up, the bottle in her hand. As she did so, one of the shadows detached itself from the wall and moved toward her. As she stared into Jeremy Westhaven's glittering eyes, she suddenly realized how he knew there were three dead bodies.

CHAPTER

❈ 20 ❈

Cecily hurried across the courtyard, just in time to see Baxter and Kevin load the dead body into the back of a carriage. "Wait!" she called out, as Samuel, seated on the driver's side, lifted the reins.

In the act of climbing aboard, Kevin turned to look at her, while Baxter strode toward her, his lamp held aloft.

"What is it?" he demanded, as he reached her.

Cecily paused for breath. "I'm quite sure now that it was Jeremy Westhaven who killed Sid Porter and Ned Barlow. Roland, too, I imagine."

Baxter raised his eyebrows. "What in the blazes happened to convince you of this?"

"Well, this, for one thing. I found it in Jeremy's room."

She held out her palm and he swung the lantern to take a good look.

"What is it?"

"I think it's one of the bells from the clown suit. I need to look at it to be certain."

She took a step toward the carriage, but Baxter halted her with his hand on her arm. "Wait. Give it to me. I'll take a look."

She waited while the two men bent over the carriage seat, then straightened.

Baxter walked back to her, his face grim. "You're right. One of the buttons is missing. It looks as if it had been torn off—probably in a struggle. This one matches the rest of them."

Cecily nodded in satisfaction. "I thought so. I couldn't imagine how Ned Barlow could have found out Jeremy Westhaven was the killer. But now I know. He must have been there when it happened."

Baxter stared at her for a moment then turned to Kevin and lifted his hand. "Go on, Prestwick. Take the body to the morgue. I'll handle things here."

Kevin called out a soft "Goodnight," then climbed into the carriage. "I trust you will explain things to Madeline?" He waited for Cecily's nod, then with a flick of the reins, the horses moved forward, their hooves clattering on the cold, uneven ground of the courtyard.

"Let us go back inside," Baxter said, taking his wife's arm. "You're shaking. You can tell me the rest when you are warm again."

A few moments later he closed the kitchen door, while Cecily huddled close to the boiler, where the embers of a dying fire still glowed.

"You need something warm inside you," Baxter said, walking toward her. "Can I get you some brandy, perhaps?"

"Maybe later." Cecily glanced at the clock. "The carol singing will be over very shortly. We have to find Jeremy Westhaven."

"No," Baxter said firmly. "If you're sure about this, we have to ring for the inspector."

"I am sure." Cecily sat down at the table and leaned her elbows on it. "I remembered Ned Barlow saying something when I spoke to him. He said the gent had done him a favor." She looked up at Baxter. "How many gents do you think Ned Barlow knows?"

Baxter looked skeptical. "How do we know he knew Jeremy Westhaven?"

"Why else would he be knocking on his door in the early morning hours? What was he doing in the hotel anyway? He must have intended to pay Jeremy a visit."

"So it looks as if your theory about blackmail could be right." Baxter still seemed unconvinced. "But how do you know Barlow was here when Sid was murdered?"

"Pansy first saw the ghost the day of the children's Christmas party. Since Sid Porter was presumably dressed as Father Christmas, it had to be Ned Barlow who wore the clown suit. Remember we couldn't find it in Mr. Porter's room. I think Mr. Barlow went to confront Mr. Porter, and finding the room empty, stole the clown suit."

"Why would he do that?"

Cecily thought for a moment. "I don't know. All we do know is that he was wearing it when he died. He could have stolen it to use as a disguise, if he actually planned to kill him. I think it's too much of a coincidence for there to be more than one clown suit, don't you?"

"Very well." Baxter sat down opposite her. "So Ned Barlow steals the clown suit from Sid Porter. Then he comes here? Why?"

"I think that Ned Barlow heard about Mr. Porter's intent to play Father Christmas, probably when he boasted about it in the public bar of the George and Dragon. If he intended to dispose of the man, what better opportunity than when he's inside a chimney? I believe that in the disguise of a clown, Ned followed Sid Porter up onto the roof. Jeremy Westhaven, however, was already lying in wait, also having heard that Mr. Porter would be on the roof."

"Also having heard about it in the public bar?"

Cecily smiled. "Mr. Milligan told me that more than one gent had been asking about Mr. Porter. I assume Jeremy was one of them."

"Ah." Baxter nodded. "So Westhaven finds out about the Father Christmas position and decides to get rid of Porter."

"Precisely. Ned Barlow arrives up on the roof just in time to see Jeremy kill Mr. Porter and presumably push Roland off the roof."

"Then Barlow leaves without being seen. . . ."

"And later decides to blackmail Jeremy."

"And ends up in the laundry chute."

"With one button less on his clown suit." She held up the bell and shook it.

"So now the question is, where is Westhaven now?"

"I think you're right, darling." She got up from the chair. "I think we should allow the inspector to find him and apprehend him." She turned as the door burst open.

Mrs. Chubb stood in the doorway, one hand pressed against her heaving chest. "Oh, there you are, madam. Mr. Baxter. I've been looking all over for you. I'm going to need the key back for the laundry chute. The maids are waiting to finish the washing."

"Oh, yes." Cecily dug in her skirt for the key. "Here you are."

"Thank you, m'm." Mrs. Chubb clipped the key back on her key ring. "Well, that's one returned. Now I have to get the wine cellar key back from Gertie." She glanced at the clock. "Can't think where that girl has got to. I gave her that key ages ago. She was supposed to get a bottle of wine for that nice Mr. Westhaven and take it to his room." She shook her head. "She should have been back a long time ago. She missed the whole ceremony in the library. It's not like her to miss that, I must say."

Cecily exchanged an uneasy look with Baxter. "Did you say Gertie was supposed to take the wine up to Jeremy Westhaven's room?"

"Yes, m'm."

"But he's not in his room." Cecily frowned. "Why would he ask her to take it there if he's . . ." She started for the door. "Come on, Baxter. We need to go to the wine cellar. Mrs. Chubb, please ring for Inspector Cranshaw. Tell him it's a matter of murder and we need him here at once."

Baxter followed her down the hallway as she almost ran

for the lobby. Once outside he called after her. "You don't really think Westhaven means to hurt Gertie?"

"I'm very much afraid she may be in danger." She spared him a quick look over her shoulder. "I only hope we're not too late."

Gertie stared into Jeremy Westhaven's eyes and wondered why on earth she had ever thought him handsome. Struggling to appear unconcerned, only a faint quiver betrayed her fear when she spoke. "I was just about to bring you your bottle of wine, sir. I'm sorry if I kept you waiting."

Jeremy smiled. The most evil smile she'd ever seen. "Never mind the wine. I don't think I'll be needing it now."

"Oh, very well, sir. I'll put it back." She made herself smile at him, making no effort to return the bottle to its rack. To do so meant turning her back on him, and she wasn't about to do something that stupid. In any case, the bottle would make a good weapon, should she need one. And something told her she was going to need one.

"You worked it all out, my pretty, didn't you." Jeremy took a step toward her and she backed away.

"Worked what out, sir?"

"Three poor souls on a dead man's chest." He shook his head. "Stupid of me. It was the wine loosening my tongue. The minute I said it I knew it was a mistake."

Gertie took a firm hold on the neck of the bottle. "I don't know what you're talking about, sir. Honest I don't."

"Oh, I think you do. In any case, I can't take any chances.

No loose ends. That's what makes a perfect crime. Leave no loose ends." He took another step forward. "And you, my dear, are unfortunately another loose end."

Again she backed away. "You must not be feeling well, sir. Why don't you go and lie down and I'll fetch you a pot of hot tea. You'll feel better in no time."

"No, I won't." He'd raised his voice, making her jump. "I'm never going to feel better. You don't understand, do you. No one understands. I was going to be married. Yesterday was my wedding day."

"Your . . . your wedding day, sir?" The flame in Gertie's gas lamp flickered with the shaking of her hand. Shadows stretched and danced along the wall, making her think of the ghost in the balcony. She could use a ghost right now.

"Yes," Jeremy said firmly. "My wedding day. A month ago the beautiful young woman who was supposed to become my wife walked into the ocean and drowned herself."

Gertie swallowed. He'd slurred his words, but his gaze was steady on her face. Still, he had to be a bit unsteady on his feet. Maybe she could dodge by him and run up the steps. "I'm sorry, sir." Memory stirred, and she added, "I remember someone talking about that. That's so sad." She shifted a little to her left.

"That balloon bastard had to die. You understand?" He was shouting now, his face contorting into an ugly mask of hatred. "He deserved to die for what he did."

"Yes, sir. I'm sure he did." One more step to her left and she might have enough space to get by him.

"Too bad about the boy." Jeremy swayed, then righted himself. "Too bad. He saw, you see. He had to go." He shook his head, as if trying to clear it. "Then that damn black-mailer. He thought he could bleed me dry. Well, I made him bleed instead."

Gertie eased sideways again. "Yes, sir."

"Such a shame." Jeremy peered at her, his eyes now looking glazed in the light from her lamp. "A shame you found out. Now you have to go, too. Can't have the police finding out. The family name and all that. You have to understand."

"Oh, I do, sir. Yes, indeed I do." Gertie took a deep breath, then deliberately dropped the lamp. It crashed to the floor, and the flame went out, plunging the cellar into darkness.

She leapt forward, hope and fear giving her strength. She'd taken two steps when a hand grabbed her arm, then closed over her wrist. With a cry of despair, she whirled around and struck out as hard as she could with the bottle. She hit nothing but air, yet her grip remained fast.

Fighting for her life, Gertie swung the bottle left and right like a sword, putting all her weight into each swing. Twice, three times she swung, and finally, the bottle found its mark. It smacked against bone with a loud crack and a splintering of glass. The fragrant wine poured all over her arm and shoes as the cruel fingers fell away from her wrist, and she heard him thud to the floor.

She didn't wait to see if her assailant got up again. She tore toward the steps and bounded up them. The door stood open and she hurtled through it, taking in deep gulps of the cold night air. Heart pounding, she slammed the door shut, and leaned against it while she clicked the padlock closed. Then she sank onto the ground and burst into tears.

*   *   *

Later that evening, after Gertie had washed the last of the wine from her arms and changed into a clean skirt and blouse, she joined Mrs. Chubb and Pansy in the kitchen for a nice, comforting cup of cocoa.

"I never did like wine," she declared, as she sipped the steaming liquid, "but now I swear I'll never touch another drop of it for as long as I live."

"I don't blame you." Pansy dropped onto a chair next to her and leaned her elbows on the table. "I wouldn't want wine either, after all you went through. Though I just can't believe a nice gentleman like Mr. Westhaven could turn out to be a murderer."

"Well, I hope he's safely locked up by now. When they carried him out of the cellar I thought I'd killed him with that bottle. Lucky for me he were only out cold. Mr. Baxter said they were taking him to the hospital but that he'd be well enough to stand trial for the murders."

"As he jolly well deserves," Mrs. Chubb declared.

Gertie sighed. "If it weren't for Roland, I'd be feeling a bit sorry for Mr. Westhaven. I know what it's like to lose someone you love, and he didn't even have a chance to be married, poor bloke."

"That doesn't give him the right to go around killing all those people." Mrs. Chubb placed a cup of cocoa in front of Pansy.

The maid smiled her thanks. "Well, you're not the only one who had a lucky escape, Gertie. That Miss Boulanger was trying her best to get Mr. Westhaven's attention. Good job he didn't notice, or she might have been the next one to be murdered."

Gertie nearly spit out a mouthful of cocoa.

Mrs. Chubb stared at Pansy. "What on earth are you talking about, child?"

"It's true!" Pansy folded her hands around her cup to warm her fingers. "I saw Miss Boulanger waiting in the hallway for him to come out of his room, then she dropped a glove. He went right by without even noticing it. She had to pick it up again herself." Pansy giggled. "And every mealtime she stopped at his table to speak to him, and when we were at the concert, she was going around asking everyone if they'd seen him."

"So that's who she was secretly admiring," Gertie murmured. "I wasn't the only one daft enough to be taken in by him."

Mrs. Chubb shook her head. "I don't know what you young people are coming to nowadays, really I don't."

"I'm just happy there's no ghost in the hotel," Pansy declared. "Scared me to death, that did. I still haven't taken the carpet sweeper back upstairs."

Mrs. Chubb looked annoyed. "So where did you leave it, then?"

Pansy gave her a sheepish grin. "I hid it behind the aspidistra in the lobby."

Mrs. Chubb clicked her tongue, but before she could say anything, Gertie jumped in.

"I'll go with you when you take it back tonight." She glanced up at the housekeeper. "Don't yell at her, Chubby. It's Christmas, and we've all been in enough trouble as it is. Let's just be glad it's all over and done with now."

Pansy sent her a grateful look. "I keep shuddering when I

think of Ned lying dead in that laundry chute. I'll remember that every time I go there now."

"What you need to remember," Mrs. Chubb said, "is to stay away from the likes of him. You could have ended up dead like him."

Pansy's shoulders quivered, and she drank some of her cocoa. Putting down the cup she said quietly, "I think the next time Samuel asks me out, I'll go."

Gertie grinned. "You'll be surprised how much fun Samuel can be." She got up from the table. "Anyway, I can tell you, I'm bloody glad to be alive. Now let's get the washing up done so we can get to bed. My twins will be up at the crack of flipping dawn tomorrow."

Throwing her arms around Mrs. Chubb, she gave her a hug. "Thank you for worrying about me."

Mrs. Chubb gave her a gentle push. "You won't get the washing up done standing there, now will you." She turned away, but not before Gertie saw the gleam of tears in her eyes.

Made her feel good, it did, to know that someone cared that much about her. Helped to make up for Ross not being there. Smiling, she made her way to the stove and reached for the cauldron of hot water. "It's going to be a good Christmas after all," she said.

"As usual, my dear, you were right about everything." Baxter yawned, and stretched his arms above his head. "I must say, that was a brilliant piece of deduction. Even the inspector seemed impressed."

Seated at her dressing table in the boudoir, Cecily snorted.

"Piffle. Anyone with an ounce of sense could have worked it all out. I'm just surprised it took me so long. I must be losing my powers of reasoning. A sign of age creeping up on me, I'm afraid."

Baxter walked over to her and wrapped his arms around her shoulders. "You lose your powers? Never. That is like saying Madeline is losing her peculiar abilities."

Cecily smiled at the mirror image of their two heads together. "Madeline will never lose her powers. Nor her youth. She continues to look younger every time I see her."

"Yes, well, I suppose if you're a witch you can arrange these things."

Looking at his face, she could tell he was only half joking. "Madeline knew Ned Barlow would be killed before we found the body. She told me as much when we were in Dolly's tea shop. Of course, she simply said the clown would be gone forever. I didn't know she meant Ned Barlow at the time."

Baxter shook his head. "Sometimes that woman gives me the shivers."

Cecily laughed. "She's quite harmless, you know. I've never known her to hurt anyone, despite her sometimes gruesome threats."

"Speaking of threats, poor Gertie had quite a fright tonight." Baxter straightened and crossed to the wardrobe. "She was extremely fortunate she wasn't hurt, or even killed." He slipped out of his coat and reached for a coat hanger.

"Yes, she was." Cecily picked up a brush and began drawing it through her hair. "Thank heavens she had the presence of mind to drop the lamp. Goodness knows what might have happened to her if that dreadful man had managed to get his hands on her."

"Seemed such a nice fellow, too. It just goes to show, you can never tell by looking at someone just how evil they are inside."

"I don't think Jeremy Westhaven is evil." She paused in her brushing. "I think he was driven to distraction by grief. After all, he intended only to avenge the violation of his young, innocent bride."

"Yes, well, there are better ways to handle the situation. Still, I can understand him wanting revenge. I should feel the same should something like that happen to you."

She smiled at him. "Thank you, darling. Knowing you, however, I'm quite sure you'd have more control over your emotions, and would deal with the matter in a far less violent manner."

"Indubitably. I sincerely hope, however, that my level of malevolence is not tested in that way."

"Actually, Mr. Porter was the evil man. What he did to that young girl was despicable. As for the other two victims, they were unfortunate enough to be witnesses to the deed and had to be eliminated." She began brushing again. "That's the problem with committing a crime. Very often it leads to more and more crimes in the effort to avoid being apprehended for the first one."

"It does, indeed." Baxter pulled on his smoking jacket and returned to his wife's side. "Look at all the skullduggery I had to go through in order to keep those dratted tickets a secret from you."

"And how foolish I was to think you were pursuing Miss Boulanger."

"Rather flattering, though." He leaned down and kissed her on the cheek. "I'm so thankful everything has been sorted out and the inspector has our villain safely under lock and key. Now we can enjoy our Christmas Day."

"So we can." She lay down the brush and smiled up at her husband. "Happy Christmas, darling. Let us wish for a peaceful end to the year."

"And a peaceful New Year to follow. No more ghosts or dead bodies to contend with, I hope."

Cecily was inclined to agree, though she had to admit to a tiny hope that there might still be just a little more excitement in her future.

Cozy up with Berkley Prime Crime

SUSAN WITTIG ALBERT
Don't miss the nationally bestselling
series featuring herbalist China Bayles.

LAURA CHILDS
The Tea Shop Mysteries are the
toast of Charleston, South Carolina.

KATE KINGSBURY
The Pennyfoot Hotel Mystery
series is a tea-time delight.

For the armchair
detective in you.